COMING HOME

Teresa Keefer

To Lynn –
I hope book
reading opens
up new worlds
for you!
Teresa Keefer

ISBN: 148262706X

ISBN-13: 9781482627060

CHAPTER ONE

The soft cool air flowing gently from the air conditioning vent ruffled the pages in her hand and she lifted her head to glance across the desk. Mr. Gibson, her grandparents' attorney, peered across the top of his wire-rimmed glasses and dabbed at his sweaty red face with a handkerchief. Maggie Stanford pushed a lock of dark hair behind her ear as she read over the documents in front of her. Everything appeared to be in order as far as she could tell and what she didn't understand, the balding, old attorney patiently explained to her.

She was the sole heiress to one hundred acres of land, the farmhouse, outbuildings and all the contents of her grandparents' farm. In her mind, she pictured the pleasant, peaceful area in the Smoky Mountain foothills just outside of a little town called Possum Creek. The last time she had been there was three years ago when her grandmother passed away and she hadn't been able to stay long because her ex-husband, Philip, had been eager to get back to Chicago.

The summers she had spent on the farm when she was growing up with the last one being the summer before her senior year in high school. Her grandparents' farm had been a welcome respite away from the massive brick estate outside of Chicago where she lived with her mother and step-father who were seldom home. A peaceful haven full of warmth and love where you could be comfortable and feel welcome. Not to mention the memories of her father which had been displayed proudly around the farmhouse. Paul Coulter, killed in a car accident on the toll road outside of Chicago on his way home from the office he hated being confined to but did out of the love he held for her mother. She had been twelve at the time and remembered the grim look on the face of the two police officers who came to the door that icy winter night.

The attorney cleared his throat to get her attention. "Missus Stanford, are you sure that you are ready to undertake this large of a project by yourself?" He was referring to her idea of turning the farm into a bed and breakfast inn. "You do realize that it's doubtful that the trust money that is left will be enough to cover the repairs that need to be done to the property, let alone ready it for guests?"

Maggie lifted her chin proudly. “Mr. Gibson. Please. Call me Maggie.” She leafed through the documents again and noted the balance of the trust account. He was right, there was probably only enough to make the repairs that the property inspector had estimated it would take to make the home livable again. But she invested some of the money from the settlement and took a job in Chicago after the divorce so hopefully that would hold her over until she could take paying guests.

Standing, she smiled at the attorney, and reached for the set of keys that he had passed over the top of the desk earlier in their meeting. "I will do just fine. I'll do what work that I can by myself and find someone local to do the things that I can't." She and her friend Dixie had researched the area and knew there were local contractors who willing to do odd jobs at a rate she could afford. To show the man her confidence, she straightened her spine as she stood up and reached across the desk to shake his hand.

He gave her a grim look as he came around the desk to walk with her to the door. "I did like you asked and arranged for the power to be turned on yesterday. The phone company won't be able to get out there for a couple of days but I see you have one of those cell phones. Probably not going to get any reception out there at your granny’s place, but you might be able to find a phone if you need one down the road in town." He opened the door and put a hand on her shoulder. "Good luck with everything and if you need anything from me, just call. You have the spunk of your granny so if I were a betting man, my wager would sure be on you." He patted her on the back as she exited his office and motioned for his next client to follow him.

Maggie took the elevator down to the parking garage and hit the button to unlock the door to the imposing, black, Lincoln Continental filled with all the possessions she had could stuff inside. Every available space, including the passenger seat, was tightly packed. Slipping behind the wheel, she started the car and maneuvered out of the garage and directly into downtown Knoxville traffic. Even after living in Chicago, she hated city traffic with a passion and she cursed as a small yellow Volkswagen with a scraped side cut in front of her. “No wonder you have a dent in your damned car you maniac!”

She drew a sigh of relief once she had taken the exit ramp onto the interstate that would take her in the direction of Gatlinburg and turned the radio to a local country music station. She rolled down the windows and let the unseasonably warm spring air blow through her hair and fill the car with the scent that she had always associated with the mountains. Pine trees and earth. Her spirits lifted as she began this last neck of the journey to her new life.

Taking the first Gatlinburg/Pigeon Forge exit she watched for her turnoff and discovered so much had changed over the years. Where there used to be open expanses of rolling hills there were now billboards touting helicopter rides, flea markets, and outlet malls. She slowed behind cars waiting at a newly installed traffic light and glanced up at the road sign. Her turn. She signaled and pulled to the right of the waiting traffic to turn onto the winding road that would eventually take her to the country road leading to the small lane at the farm.

As she took the curves and hills, she enjoyed the scenery. It was comforting and familiar with the red bud trees just starting to bloom and the mountain laurel filling the landscape. The Smoky Mountains were a glorious sight to her, with the mist that gave them their name hovering over the mountain tops. Some people might enjoy the sights of big buildings and civilization, the Chicago lakefront, the busy streets but for Maggie it was like having a piece of heaven to be back in eastern Tennessee.

A lot of resort areas had sprung up since her last visit with log cabins and chalets tucked in wooded areas that had signs in front of them like Laurel Ridge Resort and Smoky Chalet Village. When she saw the sign notifying her that Possum Creek was three miles ahead, she slowed the car even more and watched for Lower Foothill Road. She almost didn't recognize it. A convenience store stood at the corner and was named appropriately for the town just around the next bend. Possum Creek General Store.

Taking the turn, Maggie began to see familiar sights as the road narrowed as it climbed up the hill. There was the gate closing off the entrance to the lane that led to the farm. She pulled the car off the road as much as she could and found the key that went to the padlock. The gate was rusted and the fence in disrepair. She took a deep breath and got out of the car stepping over a mud puddle to reach the gate. The padlock was rusted but she got it open with ease, most likely because it had been opened recently after she contacted the attorney to let him know she was sending an inspector to look at the house. She struggled a little with the gate when it got hung up on some dead weeds that had grown up around it but eventually it swung back and she fastened it open with the chain and padlock. She made a mental note that the gate would need removed and replaced with some sort of arch. When she had the extra money.

Maggie returned to the car drove slowly through the mud puddle. The car bumped and thudded down the lane to the barnyard where she drove through more of the same, splattering mud and muck all over the windshield. She laughed out loud as she pictured what Philip's face would look like if he saw the shiny car all covered with mud and grime. Laughter was going to be her best policy over the next few weeks as she worked to make her dream come to fruition. She braked to a stop in front of the farmhouse and shut the car off.

She sat in the car for a few minutes and studied the sagging porch roof and broken window to the right of the front door, the window to the living room. She noticed that the tin roof was rusted and surmised that it probably leaked. Part of the porch railing was laying in the lawn and two of the shutters were missing from the upstairs windows while several of the others hung haphazardly from the frames.

The main yard needed mowed and the area where her grandmother had lovingly tended masses of colorful perennials was grown over and covered with dead leaves from autumns of years gone by. Maggie sighed deeply and reached for the ring of keys lying next to the manila envelope next to her in the seat which contained the legal documents to the property and the bank account information for the small trust fund. She glanced at the tightly packed back seat and made a mental note to contact Dixie and have the remainder of the things she had stored in Dixie's garage shipped as soon as possible. Keys in hand, she got out of the car and walked determinedly up the cracked and overgrown sidewalk to the front porch.

She sidestepped a couple of boards that had rotted and given way to reach the heavy, oak door that thankfully still had its oval, beveled glass intact. Maggie discovered that the door hadn't been locked, so she hesitantly stepped inside, listening for any sound that might indicate that an intruder had found refuge in the old house. "For crying out loud, silly. This isn't Chicago where a homeless person might break into an abandoned building to find refuge." She laughed at herself and the sound of her laughter echoed throughout the abandoned rooms that had very few furnishings remaining. "A homeless bum out here in the middle of nowhere. What were you thinking?"

Her heels clicked against the wood planks of the floor as she walked through each room. The dining room on the left of the entry way was empty except for a couple of ladder back chairs that appeared to be in fairly good shape. In the living room, the old piano still stood against one of the walls where the paper was peeling. Her grandmother's cane rocker and her grandfather's wing chair, with springs poking out of the upholstered seat were all that remained with the piano. The yellowed, sheer curtains were tattered and blowing in the breeze that was coming through the broken window.

She backed out of the living room and ventured down the hall where there was a den on the left and a bathroom on the right. At the end of the hallway was her grandmother's enormous kitchen with a screened across the entire rear of the house. The stove and refrigerator were gone and the black and white, vinyl tiles had come up in places, leaving the wood floor exposed. Two cabinet doors were propped up against the wall where the stove used to be. Everything was covered with years of dust and grime from not being used.

Maggie put the ring of keys on the counter and walked back up the hall while she tried to decide whether to inspect the upstairs next or start carrying in her things from the car. A sudden fit of sneezing overcame her so she decided that it was time to get outside away from the dusty, musty smelling interior of the house. Once outside, she glanced toward the old barn and smoke house then over to the path that led to the small pond formed by a freshwater spring on the property. She felt the urge to take the path and sit by the water to relax and reflect for a while. To ease her tired back from the long drive from Chicago and the uncomfortable hotel bed she had slept in when she stopped in Louisville the previous night. To overcome the sadness of seeing her grandparents' property in such disrepair.

While she stood by the hood of the car, her thoughts were interrupted by a muffled barking and she listened to try to hear where the barking was coming from. She walked toward the barn and heard the barking become more distinct. She slid the large, main door open on its track with some effort and heard a growl come from the darkness of one of the old stalls. Maggie stood still for a moment wondering whether she should venture any farther into the barn or retreat to the house and try to use her cell phone to call the local animal control authorities.

Before she could make the decision, a large black dog with a matted coat came out of the stall. The dog's tail was wagging faintly and she looked at Maggie with wary eyes. A chorus of muffled, puppy sounds came from the stall. "Hey there, girl." Maggie slowly knelt and talked to the dog in a soft tone. "It sounds as if you have some babies in there." She held out her hand and called to the dog. "Come here, girl. I won't hurt you." The dog hesitantly came toward her, the tail beginning to wag more energetically. She stopped in front of Maggie and sniffed the outstretched hand then bumped a cold nose against her fingertips, finally holding up a big paw in invitation. When Maggie started stroking the dark matted fur, the animal's whole body started wagging along with her tail.

"I'll bet you are hungry and thirsty, aren't you?" The dog let out a large bark and went back into the stall. Maggie followed her to the entrance but did not go inside, fearing that the dog would feel threatened. From where she stood, she saw four little balls of fur sniffing and seeking out their mother. The stall was littered with what looked like remains of someone's garbage. Her eyes welled up at the thought of this poor dog rooting in someone's garbage to feed herself so that she could feed her babies. "I'll be back with some food and water for you." The dog barked and wagged her tail again. "I promise."

Maggie walked out into the spring sunshine and across the yard to her car. She reached in the cooler and removed what was left of the sliced ham she bought the previous night before she checked into the cheap motel in Louisville. She then went into the house in search of something to put water in for the dog. She found an old plastic bowl in one of the cabinets and went to the sink to fill it with water. The pipes groaned before expelling a stream of rusty water into the sink and she flinched and hoped the well wasn't going dry or something. Eventually, the stream cleared and she breathed a sigh of relief that the water situation may not be that bad at all. Armed with the ham and the bowl of water, she walked across the yard to the barn, stepping carefully around some hills of dirt that appeared to be the work of a busy mole.

The dog greeted her in the entrance of the stall and she put the water down first and tore the ham up in pieces. The dog sniffed the meat then looked at Maggie with hopeful, brown eyes. "Go ahead, girl. Eat it up. This should hold you over until I can figure out something else." The puppies were curled up and sleeping together in a pile of old straw. The dog started eating then walked over to where Maggie was sitting and gave her a thankful lick full in the face. Maggie laughed and rubbed the dog's fur with both hands. "We'll be alright, won't we?" When the dog resumed eating, left the barn and headed for the car.

She picked up her cell phone and tried to dial information but the old attorney had been right, only one bar was registering and it soon disappeared as soon as she punched in the number. Might as well go into Possum Creek and see if she could find a veterinarian that might be willing to come out and look at the dogs. She remembered from her summers here, her grandfather always had a vet come out and check the horses. He had been younger than her grandfather but counting back the years, she would bet he was retired by now. She turned the big boat of a car around in the yard and bumped back down the overgrown lane adding a whole new coat of mud to the black finish on the car.

When Maggie pulled into the gravel lot of the convenience store, a group of motorcyclists stood by their bikes at the gas pumps and a small, rusty pick-up truck was parked next to the building. She turned off the engine of the car and grabbed the keys out of the ignition before she got out of the driver's door and walked determinedly to the entrance of the store. A bell chimed above her head and she noticed the clerk at the counter talking to a teenaged girl with red hair pulled up into a pony tail and a smattering of freckles across her nose.

"Excuse me, but is there a phone here that I could use?" The clerk smiled at her and put a telephone on the counter. "Sure is. Are ya havin' some trouble?"

Maggie approached the pair and smiled. "I'm moving into the Coulter farm down the lane and there is no landline installed yet." She reached for the phone. "And it seems I have no cell service either."

The woman's blue eyes lit up and she came around the corner of the counter. "Oh my word! I remember you! You've done went and grown up." The woman grinned at what Maggie was sure a total blank look on her face then found an arm around her shoulders companionably. "I'm Tammy Sue Weaver; I used to come buy eggs off your granny when I first got married."

Recognition dawned on Maggie and she smiled back. "Sure, I remember you now. You were the lady with the three little boys that used to raise havoc and chase the chickens around the yard." She covered her mouth in shock that she said that out loud and felt her face heat up. "I'm sorry, that wasn't kind."

The woman burst out laughing. "Yep, that would be the three terrors. Only they are bigger now. They go to the high school. They are still a handful but I don't think they chase chickens anymore."

The girl with the red hair stepped forward. "Hi there, I'm Ellie Miller. Pleased to meet you." She reached out a small hand to shake Maggie's. "Are you *really* going to live at the old farmhouse?" Maggie couldn't avoid the wandering glance over her dress clothes and she wished she had taken time to change into jeans and a sweatshirt.

"Yes, I just got here today. I found a mother dog with four puppies in the barn and I think that someone abandoned her. I was hoping to find a vet that might make a house call." Maggie started to reach for the phone and Tammy Sue stopped her. "No need for a phone call. This here would be the vet's niece. Honey, why don't you radio your uncle?"

Ellie had already removed the radio from the holder on her belt. "Why don't you go on back home and we'll meet you out there?"

Maggie nodded gratefully and went back out to the car. Glancing down at her soiled dress slacks and muddy pumps, she made a move to glance in the rearview mirror then thought better of it. No sense in embarrassing herself twice in one day. She headed back toward the farm and Ellie pulled in the driveway about five minutes behind her. The young girl jumped out of the old, rusted truck and shouted a greeting at Maggie. "My uncle will be out here in about thirty minutes or so. He is just up the road a piece tending to old Mrs. Davenport's spoiled poodle." Maggie smiled at the girl and invited her to follow her out to the barn where she had found the dog and her puppies.

CHAPTER TWO

Sean McDonald maneuvered the diesel truck down the familiar lane which was now rutted lane and full of puddles from the rain that lasted all last week. He hadn't driven down this lane for twelve years. He fondly recalled the last summer he spent working for Douglas Coulter, helping with the horses and the cows that once grazed these fields that were framed in the horizon by the Smoky Mountains. The Coulters were good people and the elderly couple came to be like a second pair of grandparents to him. He learned so much from Doug in that brief summer. The old gate was pulled to the side and anchored with a piece of old chain, the mailbox lying over on its side next to it. Up ahead, he noticed that the farmhouse needed more than just a coat of paint to make it look nice again. It would take a crew of construction workers and thousands of dollars to make it livable. The barn, once a bright red, was now faded and the metal roof rusted. The chicken coop was almost blocked from view by the weeds that grew up around it. It was a shame that someone in the family hadn't taken better care of the property.

In town there were rumors that someone from the Coulter family was coming down to get things in order to sell the old farm and land. He would have bought the house and land himself if there were time to work a farm full-time along with his veterinarian practice.

However, he knew it would take hours of work and a lot of money to restore the farm and get it to the point of being a profitable venture. Besides, it was a house built to hold a family, and Sean didn't see that in his near future.

He remembered walking the paths that led to the woods and the creek that meandered lazily through the property. It was like a piece of heaven right here on earth. It was unfortunate the farm was let go for so long or even permitted to get this rundown and he hoped that whoever bought the property would be able to restore it to the home it been before. He doubted it would be fixed up if rumors held true and more likely it would be bought by one of the developers and turned into a fancy resort. That's what was happening to most of the land around here over the last couple of years.

A late model Lincoln Continental was parked in front of the sagging porch, the back seat packed full with boxes containing everything from kitchen-ware to clothes. He smirked at the mud-spattered finish on the big fancy car that seemed so out of place in lawn. Must be one of the in-laws because from what he knew of the Coulters, they were proud yet simple people that would never allow themselves the ridiculous luxury of this kind of car. Other things were much more important to them.

Sean grabbed his pack out of the seat beside him as he swung his long, blue-jean clad legs easily out of the high sitting truck. All his niece told him when she radioed him was someone apparently found a stray dog with puppies in the barn and they appeared to be in distress. His scuffed western boots crossed the lawn to the barn in a few, long strides while his hat shielded his blue eyes from the sun overhead. He walked into the barn and Ellie greeted him. "Uncle Sean, these puppies are so adorable. I think they are healthy but the mama sure is possessive and won't let us anywhere near them." As his eyes adjusted to the darkness of the barn his heart went to his throat when he recognized the petite woman sitting a safe distance away from the female dog which was growling in warning.

Recovering as best he could from the sudden bittersweet twist in his gut, Sean took in the black slacks that were now covered with dust and old straw and the lime colored silk blouse that draped over narrow shoulders that wore nothing but old tee shirts and tank tops. The dark curtain of hair was cut in a chin length bob now. He remembered how it used to hang almost to her waist twelve summers ago. He braced himself as the familiar face turned toward him. For a bittersweet moment, he thought he saw a glimmer of the girl he used to know then remembered how time had a way of changing everything.

"You might want to get up before you ruin those fancy, city girl clothes." He spoke in a harsh tone that his niece's eyebrows rising in shock. He knelt opposite of Maggie and started talking to the animal in hushed tones until she finally reached out a nose tentatively to sniff his palm which held a dog biscuit. Finally, she snatched the biscuit out of his hand then turned to eat it while four puppies were searching for their own dinner. He petted the dog on top of her head and talked to her some more before he started to stroke her gently, partly to soothe and partly to examine just how malnourished she was.

The air in the barn was thick, not from the years of dust and dirt gathered there over the last few years, but from the two people sitting opposite of the dog. It was silent except for the sound of the puppies nursing noisily and the panting of the dog as she finally befriended Sean and laid her head on his lap. Outside the barn a flock of birds flew over, calling to each other noisily. He was not going to allow himself to think about how difficult it was to see Maggie dressed up in her expensive clothes after all these years. They were both adults now, and had obviously chosen to go different ways in their lives. Yet, his heart still jumped seeing her here, in this place, where they had once thought that they were foolishly in love with each other.

Sean took a deep breath and counted to ten, then twenty, before he composed himself enough to speak. "I suppose that you want me to take them into town and see if I can get rid of them for you, right?" He didn't notice Ellie back toward the stall door to make her exit. Maggie lifted her head and looked straight at him, her brown eyes flashing with anger.

"No, I don't want you to take them into town and get rid of them." She snapped the words out and motioned for him to leave.

He stood up, easing the dog's huge head off his lap gently. "Well, what are you going to do, give them to the people who take this farm off your hands? I doubt the resort developers would do more than dump them down the road somewhere." He brushed the dirt off his jeans and waited for her response. She just sat and glared at him with those hard, brown eyes that at one time he thought were as soft as the fur on a newborn calf. "I hardly see it appropriate to stuff a bunch of animals into that fancy thing out there that you rich folks call a car and haul them back to the big city with you." He threw his pack over one shoulder. "Dogs like that need a place to roam and be cared for by someone who won't tire of them and take them to a pound somewhere."

Sean started to walk past her but she stood as he passed the spot where she had been kneeling. "I don't know where the hell you get off judging me like that! You don't even know me anymore!" She came to stand toe to toe with him in the small space of the stall and poked a finger into his chest. "For your information, I own this farm and I won't have you standing here insulting me on my own property!"

He watched her turn on her fancy heeled shoes and storm out the barn door and across the yard, not stopping until she reached the front door of the farmhouse. Sean's instinct made him move toward her as she tripped over a loose board. Then he heard her curse as she grabbed the rotted railing. Nope. No way was he going over to her. It was just best if he left well enough alone for now.

Ellie was standing by the driver's side drawer of his truck when Sean walked across the yard. Hands on her hips, eyes narrowed, and her toe tapping rapidly against what was left of the gravel in the drive. He motioned her away. "Go on up to the office and get a bag of the good food and bring it back out here for her." She put her hands on her hips and tossed her pony tail. "You were downright rude to that lady. Mamaw would have your hide if she heard you talk to a lady like that!" Sean kicked a piece of broken tree limb out of his path as he stalked toward his truck. "Mind your own business and just go do what I asked you to do." Sean swung up in the truck and took another glance up toward the house, hoping to get one more glimpse of Maggie before he left. He cursed at himself. To see her again only brought back the warm feelings that he remembered having that summer twelve years ago. As a girl, she was refreshing and a joy to be around. As a woman, she would be dangerous with those liquid brown eyes and firm, petite body. He started the truck and turned it around in the yard. He looked around the property at all the work that needed done and wondered how Maggie thought she was going to turn this dilapidated piece of property back into a farm. That's when it dawned on him; she probably had a husband around to help her. He gave the truck a bit of gas and it shot down the pitted lane toward the main road.

CHAPTER THREE

Maggie unpacked the car in a lot less time than it had taken her to stuff it full to begin with. She was angry. Furious. "The nerve of that man! How dare he!" She slammed the boxes of kitchen supplies on the counter alongside the box of cleaning products and paper towels. ""What an arrogant asshole!" Two suitcases of clothes slid across the living room floor when she gave them a heave. The box of books—cookbooks, decorating books, how-to books, and a few unread novels——hit the wood floor in the dining room with an echoing thud. She was just carrying in an armload of bedding when she heard tires on the gravel speeding up the lane and looked up to see the old pick-up truck with Ellie behind the wheel pulling in behind her car.

The girl bounced out of the truck and went around to the rear to pull out a big bag of dog food. "Hi there again! Uncle Sean asked me to bring you some supplies for the dog." A bright smile filled her face as she approached.

Maggie dropped the armload of bedding on the porch crossed the scraggly bit of yard to meet her. "Hello, you didn't have to do this." She examined the girl"s expression and body language for any sign that Sean had said anything to her about their past.

Ellie looked at her shyly. "I'm sorry Uncle Sean was such a jerk earlier. He's usually a pretty nice guy." She handed the bag of dog food over to her and turned to head back to the truck. "I have all kinds of stuff. A dog bed, food and water bowls, flea shampoo and a brush."

Maggie exhaled a sigh of relief that the young girl didn't seem to have the same low opinion of her that her uncle did. "Don't worry about it, Ellie. It wasn't you that was rude so there's no need for you to apologize for him. He's a grown man and can do his own apologizing when he sees fit." She had no idea what she had done to provoke his reaction to seeing her again. *After all, he's the one that dumped me not the other way around.* She shook her head and sighed. They had only been kids.

When Ellie offered to stay and help get the dog bathed and settled in, Maggie was grateful for the distraction the young woman offered so she agreed to let her help. As they worked, Maggie discovered that Ellie was a student studying veterinary science at Purdue University in Indiana. Her parents had divorced when she was a baby so when her mother passed away from cancer when she was nine, she had gone to stay with Sean.

Maggie ticked off the years in her mind and concluded he would have probably been in his last year of vet school at the time. Taking responsibility for a young child would have been a big responsibility on him but she wasn't surprised that he had stepped in. But what did she *really* know about Sean? Years had passed and it seemed a hardness emanated from him. Or at least where she was concerned it did.

The mother dog was agreeable to being bathed in the old claw foot tub, brushed and dried off with the blow dryer. Both Ellie and Maggie were drenched by the time they were done. As their eyes met across the top of the dog they laughed at the mess they were in.

"Should we try to set the bed up on the back porch and bring the puppies in from the barn for her?" Maggie raised an eyebrow and deferred to the more knowledgeable of the two of them.

Ellie nodded and plucked at some wet dog hair clinging to her shirt. "I think that would be a good idea. Let's see how the mama acts. I'll go get them and you stay here with her. Fill her bowl up with food and see if she will take one of the vitamins in the bottle I left on the kitchen counter." She got off the floor and smiled as she patted the dog's head. "I'll be back, girl. We'll get you and your babies settled in no time."

By the time Ellie returned to the house with four wriggling puppies, Maggie had filled the dog bowls with food and water and set the dog bed by the back door. As Ellie lay each of them on the soft surface, Maggie noticed that they were just starting to get their eyes open. That meant they were probably only a couple of weeks old.

"Wonder how she got here? You think she ventured away from home and got lost?" Maggie asked Ellie as they sat on the floor of the back porch and watched the mother dog greedily devour the dog food filling one of the big, stainless steel bowls.

Ellie shrugged her narrow shoulders. "I don't know. More likely somebody dumped her. It happens all the time around here." She reached out and stroked the dog's ears. "Uncle Sean has had his share of strays up at the animal hospital. Nurses them along, cleans them up, then he tries to find a home for them."

Maggie remembered the time Sean found an old cat with one eye outside the fairgrounds. He bundled the old thing into a blanket and took it back to the farm. Hissing, biting and clawing at him the entire time. His arms and hands were bleeding from numerous scratches and bites when he got back to the farm. They both tried to tame the cat all summer with no success but it did remain on the farm for the next couple years, happily chasing mice in the barn. Her grandmother wrote and told her the old cat wandered off late one fall and she hadn't seen it since.

Ellie interrupted her thoughts. "Did you and Uncle Sean know each other before now?"

Maggie considered the girl's questioning eyes and nodded. "I stayed at the farm every summer. One of those summers he was worked for my grandpa."

Ellie frowned. "Did you dislike each other then?"

Maggie was taken aback by the blunt question. They had liked each other that summer. A lot. And she had no idea what happened between them once she returned to Chicago for school in the fall. "No, but I guess we've both changed a lot since that summer."

Ellie shook her head. "I don't think so. Uncle Sean's always been the same." She jumped up and brushed off her jeans. "Is there anything that I can help you with before I go back and fix supper?"

Maggie embraced the girl in a companionable hug. "No, but thank you for asking. I've just got to try to find someplace to get a meal myself since I fed my lunch meat to the dog." She put a hand to her growling stomach to try and silence it.

Ellie burst out laughing. "You are just like Uncle Sean, he'd probably feed an animal his last bit of food, too." As they reached the old truck and Ellie grinned mischievously. "I don't suppose you'd be interested in some homemade meatloaf with scalloped taters would you?" The blue eyes danced.

"Not if it means intruding on your uncle's dinner." Maggie stepped away from the truck and lifted a hand. She couldn't imagine sitting and eating a meal with Sean taking pot shots at her. "I'm sure there is someplace in town that has good food."

"It would serve him right after the way he acted." Ellie giggled and started the engine which coughed and sputtered before it roared into life. "You could go to Char's Place which is on the main street through town if you want a good home cooked meal or there"s the restaurant at the resort at the top of Burton's Ridge. They are kinda fancy there."

Maggie thanked her and waved as the girl turned the truck around in the yard and drove down the lane. She stood on the porch and took a deep breath. The air here was so refreshing and was beginning to get chilly with the approaching evening. She hugged her arms around herself to warm them, and then turned to walk into the deserted house. After changing into clean jeans, a sweatshirt and sneakers, Maggie drove into town.

Most of the shops were already closed for the day, but there were several cars parked in front of Char's Place. She could hear country music playing when as a pair of older gentlemen came out and lit their pipes. She walked past their curious stares and opened the door. Inside, there was a smattering of people. A couple of men perched on bar stools nursing mugs of beers and watching a fishing show on the television above the bar. By the door, a young couple sat in a corner booth with two toddlers making a mess of their spaghetti dinners and a foursome of middle aged people that looked like tourists were sitting at a table in front of the window. The fragrance of food wafted out of a doorway where she assumed the kitchen lay beyond and a lone ceiling fan was attempted circulating the air. A juke box blared a Waylon Jennings tune.

Maggie walked over to an empty booth and seated herself and reached for the menu tucked behind a napkin holder. "Hi there. What can I get for you?" A waitress appeared beside the booth, her manicured hand poised above an order pad. The woman had chin length blonde curls and wore a bright red tee shirt emblazoned with the name of the establishment in white retro letters. Her face was wholesome with just a hint of mascara and lip gloss and her smile was enough to light up the room.

Maggie smiled up at her. "What is the special tonight?" She could smell the fragrance of garlic and oregano and it made her mouth water and her stomach growl.

"We have spaghetti and meatballs with garlic bread and a salad tonight." She sat down in the booth across from Maggie and waited with her pencil poised above the pad.

"I guess I will have that, then. With a diet drink." She folded the menu and stuck it back in the napkin holder.

The waitress wrote on the order pad. "You ain't from around here, are ya?" She stood up by the booth and held out a hand in greeting. "I'm Charlotte Grimes, most folks around here call me Char."

Maggie took the Char's hand and found her grip strong and welcoming. "Actually, I just moved here from Chicago. I am going to be starting up a bed and breakfast at my grandparent's farm." When the other woman released her hand, she smiled shyly. ""My name is Maggie Stanford, used to be Coulter."

Char's brow furrowed in thought then she nodded. "I knew granny, she was a real sweetheart. I was sorry to hear about her passing and didn't get the opportunity to come to the funeral. I was down in Florida visiting my parents." She tore Maggie's order off the pad and yelled her order at the cook in the kitchen before retreating to the bar to stick the order on a clip.

Maggie was halfway through eating her salad when a group of young men walked in. They scanned the room until their eyes came to rest on Maggie. The taller of group nudged one of his friends and said something that made him laugh before they approached the booth where Maggie sat.

"Howdy. I'm Tom Grimes and this here's Danny Barnes and Eddie Hallmark. What's a pretty lady like you doin' sittin' here all by herself tonight?"

Maggie wiped her mouth with the paper napkin and took a sip of her drink. "I'm eating my dinner." She replied with a smile. "What are you boys doing here without a date?" She couldn't resist playing along with them.

Tom slid into the booth across from her. "My mama said that a pretty young woman just got to town. Thought maybe we'd come on down and welcome you town properly."

Maggie held out her hand to shake his, only to have it grabbed and kissed sloppily. "I'm Maggie, and who is your mother?"

He smiled, revealing a set of teeth silvery with braces. He pointed over to the waitress that had served Maggie. "Char there is my mama." Maggie removed her hand from his and resumed eating her dinner. Gossip sure did spread quickly in Possum Creek and it appeared that the waitress was the main source of the gossip tonight. "I hope you don't mind if I finish my meal so that I can get back out to the farm before it gets dark."

Tom grinned again and Danny snickered this time. "Not at all, just wanted to say welcome to town and say that if you needed any help working out at your place to just give us a call. We do lots of handyman type stuff for real cheap." He scrawled his name and a phone number on a napkin and slid it across the booth to her.

About that time, the waitress approached with her dinner and admonished the boys. "Get on with you boys and let this lady eat." She swatted at her son with a menu, and Tom jumped up from the booth.

The other men nodded at Maggie before following Char up to the bar. "See ya around Miss Maggie." Tom grinned and waved as they disappeared into the kitchen with his mother.

She ate as much of the spaghetti and meatballs as she could. The serving size was enough for a very large man and she made note when she ate here again to ask if they had a child sized portion. The food was very good, the meatballs were to die for and the bread looked and tasted like homemade.

After Maggie paid her bill at the bar, she turned around and saw a familiar figure come in the front door. She diverted her eyes and put her change back in her purse as Sean took a stool at the opposite end of the bar from where she stood. She ignored him and walked out the door, feeling like his eyes were boring through her back as she retreated. When she reached the sidewalk outside, she took a deep breath and walked across the street to her car, which was now parked directly in front of Sean's truck. *So, he knew I was in here when he parked his damned truck.* She silently wished he'd choke on his beer as she started up the car and pulled away from the curb.

CHAPTER FOUR

Sean didn't usually make time to go out on dates. Tonight was an exception to the rule. Not that he had much of a choice. It was either sit at home and listen to Ellie talk on the phone to her boyfriend who lived in Indiana and get a headache from all the whispers and giggles or listen to Ellie talk about all of Maggie's wonderful traits. Not to mention, Julia Evans hadn't taken no for an answer.

Julia was one of the real estate developers that had descended on the area with the flock of other vulture-like developers to take advantage of the recent boon in resort development. Julia had flitted into Char's earlier in the week right after Maggie had glided past him without so much as a glance in his direction. For the second time since she had arrived. To give her the same treatment, he invited Julia to sit with him just as Maggie had reached the front door of the bar. It had been spiteful and he cursed himself for stooping to that level of behavior. For God's sake, he was a grown man playing games like a jilted teenager.

He had bought Julia a drink and listened to her talk about how much good the resort business was boosting the economy. Somewhere between the fourth and fifth round, he had listened to her sing karaoke. Or rather, he listened to her try to sing a poor imitation of Loretta Lynn's Coal Miner's Daughter, while a group of younger men hooted and hollered like she was some country western music star. When he walked her to her car, he realized that she too much to drink to be safe behind the wheel of a car, so he escorted her to the bed and breakfast inn at the end of Main Street where she had taken up temporary residence. At the door, she had invited him in and he politely refused, asking for a rain check instead. So here he was, sitting at a table in one of Knoxville's most expensive restaurants feeling as out of place as a prostitute in church.

Sure, he had dressed the part of the suave gentleman in a black suit and silk shirt with a tie that was choking him with every sip of beer he took. He had even put his old worn out cowboy boots in the closet and opted to wear his newer, black leather boots that felt like they were going to pinch his feet in half. Sitting in an expensive restaurant with a fancy looking woman wasn't his idea of fun on a Saturday night. He'd rather have been sitting on the sofa with a soft pretty girl watching a movie on the DVD player.

Sean glanced over at Julia Evans just as she pushed a strand of platinum hair behind her ear. A garnet earring dangled in the light of the candle set in the middle of the table in a glass hurricane lamp. She looked at Sean across the table through spidery lashes coated with black mascara. Her lips, painted in a slick red color, left a print on the rim of the glass of wine that she was sipping from. Her expensive cologne was so strong that it would have masked the scent of antiseptic in his animal hospital if she so much as walked through.

"So Sean, what have you been up to this week?" She smiled across the table at him and touched his work roughened hand with her softer one. Her voice was husky with a hint of seduction.

Sean put down the pilsner of beer and picked up the menu to study. He was suspicious of Julia's sudden spark of interest in him. He had taken her out a couple of times before and usually their dates consisted of her chattering about her own success. Bragging about buying up real estate from locals who discovered that their acres of untouched land were worth a lot more than they ever imagined as resorts sprung up through the Smoky Mountains and foothills. Tonight, she appeared to be genuinely interested in him, because she now leaned forward in eager expectation of his answer. He couldn't help but notice the expanse of skin above the low-cut top of her snug dress.

"Well, it was kind of a rough day. Dancer, she's the Morgan's mare, had some trouble birthing her colt last night. Took me most of the night to get that beautiful, little stallion into the world." He didn't get much sleep the night before. He tumbled into bed just before dawn only to be woke up by his alarm at six in the morning so that he could open the clinic for his first appointment.

"How interesting it must be to actually watch one of those long-legged little colts come into the world. I just love the sleekness and power of the horses down here." She took another sip of her wine then toyed with the stem of the glass. She tapped a finger against the rim of the glass as she waited while Sean ordered dinner from the waiter. "I heard that you went on a call out to the old Coulter place. Is one of their kin out there cleaning the place out so that it can be put on the market?"

Sean took another drink of beer before he answered. His mind and heart were still reeling at the prospect of Maggie settling here permanently. He wasn't sure that was such a good idea for a woman used to being pampered by a rich mother and then rich husband. "Matter of fact, I was out there to attend to a stray dog she found in the stable when she arrived. Good looking dog I suspect once she gets cleaned up and fed some. Nice litter of puppies, too."

He tried to picture Julia sitting in the old barn in her fancy clothes, coddling to a bunch of discarded puppies. He smiled at the image of Maggie in black slacks and a lime green shirt with straw in her hair like he found her that day last week. Somehow, he didn't think Julia would dare risk getting her silky clothes all dusty, straw sticking in her hair.

"So, she is cleaning out the old house so that she can market it then?" She raised a perfectly arched eyebrow above her silvery eyes that were dramatized by careful make up tricks. She crossed her slender legs and allowed a calf to rub against Sean's leg.

He shifted and apologized for his leg getting in her way. Last thing he wanted was for her to get the wrong idea. And he still had a suspicious feeling there was more to this dinner date than just a couple of adults enjoying each other's company.

She smiled with a seductive look on her face. "Not a problem, I never mind rubbing legs with a gentleman."

Sean felt the heat of embarrassment start at his cheeks and work all the way to his hairline. Sometimes Julia could be a lot of fun, like when she joined a group of them in Gatlinburg one weekend to go horseback riding through the mountain trails. But in settings like this, with fancy orchestra music playing quietly in the background and patrons around them talking in hushed tones across candlelit tables that made this restaurant more intimate than he preferred, she just plain made him a bit nervous. Like he was the main entrée for the night instead of the steak and lobster he ordered for the two of them.

When he didn't reply, she reached across the table and slid a fingernail along the top of his hand. "I've heard some say that the two of you were an item one summer. Any chance she came back to try to revive that old flame now that her husband divorced her?" She tipped a head to the side and waited for his reply.

"That was a long time ago and you shouldn't listen to the local gossip." Suddenly, the tie around his neck felt tighter, if that was possible. He had wondered how long before people would remember how he and Maggie had been inseparable that summer and started speculating on her return to Possum Creek. He wondered if old Charlie Thomson, the town sheriff back then, had told the story about how he had found the two of them parking down in Mason's Holler. His face flushed as he remembered the old sheriff giving them a talking to. He ended up sending them on their way with a promise not to tell Douglas Coulter if he didn't catch them there again. And that whole summer, he hadn't.

"Sorry, Sean. I forget that the people from town seem to thrive on gossip. I should have known that someone as genuine and caring as you would have very little in common with a spoiled little girl." Her smile didn't quite go to her eyes as she took a jab at Maggie through a compliment to him.

"I'm not sure what she's doing here, Julia, and I don't much care. Sure, I knew her when I worked for her grand pappy when I was in college. But as far as knowing her, I never really did." He picked up his beer and stared thoughtfully into space as he ran through the meeting with Maggie in the barn last week when she first arrived. She was grown up, beautiful, and still had the ability to send his heart to doing somersaults. But there was now a hardness and accusation in her eyes that he couldn't understand. After all, she dumped him all those years ago. Even worse, she hadn't had the nerve to tell him herself. He had to listen to her uptight mother tell him the news as he stood at the front door of their apartment in Chicago on Christmas Eve.

He reached across the table and put his rough hand on top of Julia's. "Sorry, if I snapped at you. It's just that I'm tired from being up all night. I should have asked you for a rain check for tonight. I'm not very good company when I'm tired." The truth of it was, his mood was bleak and had been since he realized that the petite woman sitting in the middle of the old barn was Maggie. It was downright foolishness for a grown man like himself to cry over milk that had spilled twelve years ago. It had been too long since he had any sort of relationship with a woman. Maybe it was time that he did something about that. Julia would be just the woman to take a man's mind off a certain pair of dark eyes that went from twinkling in mischief to smoldering with passion under an August moon. He reached across the table and took Julia's hand. "Would you like to dance?"

They danced a couple of slow songs, with Julia rubbing her slender body against him as seductively as she could. When he started to get uncomfortable, he walked her back to the table and feigned a yawn. "Sorry, but I really am beat tonight. Would you mind calling it a night and try again some other time when I'm not so tired?"

They were both quiet on the drive back to town from Knoxville, with Julia occasionally reaching over and touching his leg to say something insignificant. Quite frankly, he didn't pay attention to what she was saying because his mind kept wandering to a certain pair of brown eyes. However, he wasn't above trying to get his mind off those eyes by climbing into bed with Julia. Just as they reached the edge of Possum Creek, Sean's pager went off. "Dammit." He recognized the number of the Morgan horse farm and knew that they probably had another mare ready to foal. He turned on the cell phone and called the number to verify that was the case. So much for his plans to play under the sheets with Julia tonight. Probably not a good idea anyway.

"What's the matter, Sean?" Julia ran a hand down his thigh and he felt his muscles tighten. "Sorry, I'm going to have to cut it short tonight." He glanced over at her as he pulled the truck up in front of the bed and breakfast. "I'm really sorry, Julia. I had hoped maybe..." He cut his words off, not knowing what to say.

"That's alright, honey. We can pick this up another time." She leaned over and brushed her lips across his and ran her hand up his chest. "Rain check." She opened the door and got out of the truck. Sean watched her walk up the sidewalk to the bed and breakfast, letting herself in with a key. He pulled away and felt a sudden relief that the call to the Morgan farm had come when it did.

Once inside her room at the bed and breakfast, Julia pulled her cell phone out of her purse and dialed a number. An answering machine picked up and she heard the familiar, male voice ask the caller to leave a message. "Hello Phillip, it's Julia. I couldn't get much information out of the vet tonight other than your ex-wife is planning on staying at the farm and turning it into some sort of bed and breakfast. You need to call me right away! this isn't what you promised me was going to happen!" She clicked the phone off and kicked her shoes across the room. "Dammit, I was supposed to own that damn property by now!"

CHAPTER FIVE

Maggie sat on the floor of the dining room, threading a rod through the lacy, curtain panels she found yesterday at a garage sale. The delicate rose pattern would be a nice addition to the burgundy drapes she brought with her from Chicago. The drapes were silk and very expensive and had been a donation from her best friend, Dixie. Outside, on the porch, the puppies frolicked in the sunlight and she smiled as she listened to their little yips and growls. Their mother sat guard over them on the rug in front of the door. She watched them for a few minutes and smiled at their clumsy antics. There was a nice breeze that drifted in the open door and it carried the scent of hyacinth to her nose. She took a deep breath of the fresh air and decided she should probably get back to work.

The sun streamed through the newly cleaned windows in the dining room and the walls were freshly painted creamy white. The built-in china cabinet had been stripped and the first coat of stain was drying. She had hoped to find her grandmother's china in the attic when she had spent an afternoon exploring while a spring rain drenched the green grass outside. However, she hadn't turned up even one box with a few pieces of the old china. She figured that she would just go into Gatlinburg and shop around for a couple of serving platters and bowls and fill the rest of the cabinet up with the crystal glasses that Dixie was shipping to her.

Dressed in an old pair of sweatpants and tee shirt, her hair covered with a ball cap, Maggie climbed the ladder to hang the curtains. After she made the final adjustment to the curtains, she climbed down from the ladder and stood back to survey her work. She was just getting ready to fold the ladder up when the dog, which she simply named Mama, let out a warning bark. She heard tires rolling over the gravel that the quarry delivered yesterday. She went to the screen door and watched as Ellie pulled in behind Maggie's car. Ellie had been a great help to her, not to mention welcome company in the lonely, old house.

Yesterday, Ellie and she had driven from garage sale to garage sale, and had stopped for lunch at a little diner between Possum Creek and Gatlinburg. The girl waved and smiled at Maggie. "Hi there! What are you up to today?" Ellie's red ponytail bobbed as she jogged up to the porch, stopping long enough to pay attention to the dog and her puppies.

Maggie smiled back at the girl and stepped off the porch, which was now repaired and waiting a fresh coat of paint. Maggie couldn't help but notice how much Ellie favored her uncle, Sean. "I just got finished hanging curtains in the dining room and I think I am going to try to tackle painting the living room today." She held open the screen door, inviting Ellie in.

"Do you need any help?" Ellie stood in the dining room and looked around the room. "Uncle Sean is in a bad temper today. Serves him right for going out with that snobby Julia last night. She'd be enough to test a saint's patience."

Maggie felt a tug of disappointment that Sean had gone out with a woman last night. It wasn't her business, she reminded herself. They weren't the same people they were in the past. He was a grown man and she was sure he dated many women over the last twelve years. But she couldn't help but be curious about this Julia woman. Was she local or was she a transplant? Someone he met at college? She shook her head and turned toward where Ellie was watching her closely. She smiled at the younger woman and brushed her dirty hands down the sides of her jeans. "Would you like a glass of iced tea and some banana nut bread or muffins?" Maggie walked back toward the kitchen and Ellie followed.

The kitchen was clean, but needed a lot of work. Maggie didn't want to tackle it until Tom and his buddies were here because all the appliances needed to be moved out and she didn't want to try that herself. There was an old spool in the middle of the room that was serving as a table and Maggie had covered it with a yellow and white checked vinyl cloth and two folding chairs were pulled up on either side.

Ellie sat down on one of the chairs and stretched her long legs out in front of her. "So, will you rescue me from Uncle Sean's bad mood today and let me help you around here?"

Maggie poured them each a glass of iced tea and sat the plate with the banana bread she made this morning between them on the table. "Ellie, I feel guilty letting you help me with stuff and not paying you."

It was true, over the last week Ellie spent at least four or five hours helping Maggie and refused the money that she offered her. Maggie felt like she was taking advantage of the friendly, young girl. But it seemed that there were so many offers of help that she received from the kind people here, which the people were yet another reason Maggie so badly wanted this all to work out.

"Maggie, I'm having fun helping you. Besides, you are nice and easy to talk to." She took a drink of her tea. "And it's quieter out here than it is up at the clinic." Reaching for a slice of banana bread she noticed a shadow in the hall and looked up just as Tom and one of his friends walked in. "Hey guys, are you helping Maggie today?" She sat up in the chair straighter and flicked her ponytail to one side. Her movement was one of unconscious flirtation and she sure drew the attention.

"Hi there, Ellie. Are you living out here these days?" Tom grinned at her and reached for a slice of bread.

Maggie got up and poured two more glasses of iced tea for the boys. "Do you guys feel like helping me tackle the kitchen today? I need to pull out the appliances and then make a trip into the city to buy a new stove and fridge." She handed them their tea and went back to lean against the counter.

Tom laughed. "Sure, but what are you going to use to pick up the new ones?" He drank his tea in one gulp while he gave Ellie the once over.

Maggie shrugged her narrow shoulders. "I have no idea. I doubt if they will deliver clear from Knoxville will they?" She took Tom's empty glass and sat it in the sink. "Never mind, I guess we could do that another day. I need to paint and put new floor down in here anyway before I go moving new appliances. That way, they only have to be moved once."

Ellie jumped up. "I've got an idea! How about I see if we can use Uncle Sean's truck? He can use mine if he gets a call out somewhere?"

"No, Ellie. I need to get the other things done in here first. These old appliances are fine for just my use." Maggie walked over and put a hand on her arm. "Thank you for offering, though." The last thing she wanted was to borrow from Sean or be indebted to him in any way.

The boys set out to work on the screened back porch. They were closing in the area so she could use it for her own bedroom and office. So far, they had managed to remove all the screens and replace some of the boards that had been water damaged. Tom had drawn out the plans for a suite that included a private bath and sitting area. He had suggested a set of electric baseboard heaters to provide warmth in the winter months and thought he could find some at a good price at the local hardware.

Maggie and Ellie went into the living room and opened the cans of paint that were sitting on a tarp in the middle of the room. "Ellie, are you sure you wouldn't rather spend your weekend doing something else?" Maggie stood in the middle of the room holding a roller in one hand and a brush in the other. She blew a lock of hair away from her forehead and shook her head at the work that was still ahead of her. Still, for all the work that was yet to be done, the progress made so far was much to be proud of.

Ellie grinned, her eyes sparkling. "Next weekend you won't have my help. Todd, my boyfriend, is coming down for a whole week." She danced around the room. "I can't wait to see him! It's been almost two months."

Maggie smiled at the Ellie and she was struck with a bittersweet memory of how excited she was to get her a letter from Sean right before Thanksgiving. She danced around her bedroom, just like Ellie was doing right now. He wrote that he was going to visit her over the Christmas holidays. It was the last letter she ever received from him. She pushed the memory out of her mind and bent over to pour paint into the rolling tray.

One of the boys had brought a portable stereo with them and they all worked to the sound of southern rock music until lunch time. Maggie's stomach was growling when she put the roller down and walked over to wipe a smear of paint off Ellie's nose. "Take a break, Ellie. Come in and sit down in the kitchen while I fix us all some lunch." The sun was high in the sky filling the cloudless blue with a bright ball of yellow light.

She fixed them all corned beef sandwiches with chips and dill pickle spears and the boys sat on the counter ribbing each other about girls in town. She was sure some of the mention of other girls was intended to make Ellie jealous, but it was obvious the girl only had eyes for the absent boyfriend back in Indiana. When they were finished, the boys headed back out to the porch and the quiet was once again filled with the sound of hammering and music and a couple curse words peppered in the middle.

By the time she and Ellie finished the first coat of paint in the living room, the sun had begun to set and when she looked out the screen door she could see the first signs of fog gathering on the mountain tops. “Come on, let's stop for the day.””

The boys had left an hour before to go home and eat dinner and get cleaned up for a poker game and after they washed the brushes and rollers in the kitchen sink, Maggie and Ellie sat on the porch steps and watched the puppies playing in the grass. Both were paint spattered and tired. "Thank you so much for helping me get the living room painted today." Maggie leaned against one of the new posts that supported the porch. "Are you sure you won't let me pay you something for helping me?" She asked the question, even though she knew the answer was going to be the same.

"No way, Maggie! You did me a huge favor letting me hang out here instead of at the clinic with the grouch." She pursed her lips and blew a stray lock of red hair away from her face. "I don't know what has gotten into Uncle Sean lately but I think he"s having some kind of problem that he can't talk about with me. Probably, something to do with that clingy fake real estate lady."

They heard tires crunching over gravel and glanced up to see who was coming down the lane. Maggie recognized the diesel truck as it pulled up in front of the barn and her heart fluttered. She focused her mind enough to calm herself as the vehicle came to a stop behind Ellie's truck. She would not let him fluster her or rub her the wrong way today. Part of her wanted to just bolt up from the steps and go inside but that would be cowardly.

"Speak of the devil himself." Ellie muttered. "Wonder what he is doing out here?"

Maggie watched as Sean swung his legs out of the truck and could see that the knees of his jeans were muddy, as were the bottoms of his worn cowboy boots. He looked exhausted by the way he trudged up to the porch with one had rubbing his neck.

"Uncle Sean, you look beat." She moved over on the step and patted the spot beside her. "Sit down before you fall down."

He hesitated for a moment, shooting a questioning glance at Maggie. "Am I interrupting anything?" He diverted his eyes almost as soon as they made contact with hers and focused his attention on Ellie. He made no move to sit down next to either of them.

Maggie took the lead and smiled at him as if nothing had ever passed between them, recently or in the past. "Not at all, we were just sitting here talking a bit before Ellie heads home." She motioned for him to sit down. "You look dead on your feet, Sean."

He sat on the step and put his head in his hands. Maggie noticed shadows under his eyes and it looked as if he hadn't slept in days. Mama lumbered up and sat down in front of him, then swiped his face with a big, pink tongue. When he looked up at the dog, she put a paw in his lap and he grinned. "What are you begging for, ol' girl?" He reached out and rubbed her coat vigorously. He looked over at Maggie. "She sure cleaned up real nice, and she looks like she's put some weight on, too."

"She should have put on weight, the way she eats that dog food you sent out here." Maggie reached down and picked up one of the puppies and held it on her lap and let it bite at her fingers. "She has eaten almost that whole fifty-pound bag you sent out, I need to get into your clinic and buy some more next week." She fell into a fit of giggles as the puppy's tongue tickled her palm.

Sean watched Maggie play with the puppy in her lap, while two others jumped at her for attention. "Don't worry about it, I'll send some out to you. On the house." He glanced from Ellie to Maggie. "Speaking of food, I'm starved. Are you girls hungry? I was thinking about getting some pizza if you are interested."

Maggie sat in stunned silence, was he including her in his invitation? She wondered if his lady friend, Julia was busy or if she was going to be joining them. She decided that the other woman, from Ellie's description, wouldn't be the type to sit and eat take-out pizza.

Ellie jumped up from the step. "Oh yeah! Pizza sounds great!" She grabbed Maggie's arm and tugged. "Come on Maggie, Uncle Sean's buying pizza."

Sean smiled at his niece. "I may be buying, but you are going to do the clean-up." He got up off the step and took the puppy from Maggie, placing it back on the ground with the rest of the puppies. "I'll call ahead for the pizza and you two can go pick it up while I go home and take a shower and put on some clothes that don't smell like Mr. Abernathy's sows."

Maggie found herself in the passenger seat of Ellie's old truck as they drove through the back roads into town. The roads curved and rolled through the foothills that were densely wooded. They slowed as a doe and two of her fawns walked across the road ahead of them; pausing at the edge of the woods to watch the truck drive past before they darted into the darkness of the trees. Two little boys sat atop a stone bridge over Possum Creek with fishing poles, their innocent faces breaking into smiles as Ellie waved and called out the open window to them. The knees of their jeans had gaping holes and one of the boys' smiles sported a gap from two missing front teeth. A plastic pail sat in the grass at the edge of the bridge and a couple of partially full soda pop cans were balanced on the bridge.

The pizza place in town was in the rear of the general store and Ellie pulled the truck into an empty spot. Inside, Maggie could smell the garlic and spices of fresh-baked pizza and she noticed that the parlor doubled as a video rental store. Movie posters were taped in the window alongside pictures of pizzas and sandwiches with the weekly special written in neon green paint. A bell over the door rang out cheerily as the two women entered the shop and Maggie"s mouth watered as the smell of fresh baked pizza drifted to her nose. Her stomach growled and she realized that she hadn't eaten a whole lot that day. Ellie walked up to the counter and told the teenager that she was there to pick up their pizza.

While she waited for him to put it in the box, she turned to Maggie. "Uncle Sean said we should pick up a movie to watch. Why don't you grab that new horror movie over there for us?"

Maggie walked over to the display and picked up the movie case that Ellie was referring to and wondered why Sean was being so nice to her this evening. Maybe he just didn't want to exclude her when he had shown up at the farm. She was having second thoughts about going to his house for pizza and a movie. A sudden, overwhelming charge of apprehension drowned out the growling in her stomach and she turned around to ask Ellie to take her back home. She realized she was just being ridiculous and took a deep breath and approached the counter.

"Hey Maggie, what do you want to drink? We have iced tea and soda at home, but the soda isn't diet." Ellie took the pizza box from the counter and waited for Maggie's answer.

"I think I will go for the gusto and drink regular soda tonight." Maggie walked up to the counter to join her, handing the boy the movie box. She reached into the pocket of her sweat pants and pulled out some money but Ellie stopped her.

"Uncle Sean said to just put everything on his tab." She signed the ticket and handed it back to the boy. "Hey, thanks Gabe. See ya around. Tell your mama that I said hello." She turned and bounced out the door with Maggie hesitantly following her.

They drove down the main street of town and turned right at the last street, which was marked with a dead-end sign. At the end of the street, Maggie could see the animal hospital. It was a sprawling, concrete block building with a group of fenced in runs to one side of it. As they pulled in the parking lot, Ellie drove behind the building and there was a small log cabin nestled in a wooded area. Behind it, the land started rising gradually into a hill where Maggie could see a walking path had been cleared. The cabin had a porch across the entire front and there were two rocking chairs sitting side by side to the left of the door. On the right, there was a charcoal grill and a small table. The mat in front of the door said "All Are Welcome Here". *Bet that doesn't mean me.* Taking a relaxing breath to steel herself for what she was sure could be a difficult evening, she followed Ellie into the cabin.

The main room took up the entire front of the cabin. The wood floors had brightly colored rag rugs scattered in front of the comfortable looking furniture that was covered in a tan, corduroy fabric. A stone fireplace stood at one end of the room and a picnic table sat at the other end. The room was open to the roof, and the rough-hewn beams were exposed. There was a light on in the loft at the top of the open staircase. "I'll be right down!" Sean called from upstairs. "Go ahead and put the pizza on the table and get some glasses and ice out of the kitchen."

Maggie looked down at her paint spattered clothes and hands. "Ellie, where is your bathroom so that I can go wash this paint off my hands?"

"Come on, it's right through here." She led her down a short hall where a door stood open to a small bathroom. "There are clean towels on the shelf and if you want to use soap that doesn't smell like a man, use the liquid soap by the tub."

Maggie closed the bathroom door and looked around. There was a claw-footed tub tucked into a cubbyhole on one side and a shower on the other. She looked at herself in the mirror above the sink and was aghast at how disheveled she looked. Her hair had come loose from its band and stuck out in places and there was a streak of white paint through it. She washed her hands and face with the bar of soap on the sink and realized that it was probably

Sean's. The scent was like some woodsy, aftershave. She left her hands damp and tried to pat her hair back into place. There was nothing she could do about the paint in her hair until she got home later and could slip in the shower. She looked longingly at the tub and wished that the water pipes in the farm house hadn't needed replaced to the tub there. What she wouldn't give to take a leisurely bubble bath right now. A damp towel hung over one of the towel bars and there were still spots on the floor where Sean had walked after leaving the shower.

She went back into the living room of the cabin, where Sean and Ellie were putting pizza on plates at the picnic table. Maggie went over to them and was surprised at the soft smile Sean gave her as she approached. He had changed into clean jeans and a tee shirt, but was barefoot; his hair still damp from his shower. He handed her a plate of pizza and poured a soda into a glass full of ice.

"Here you go, make yourself at home." He took a plate for himself and loaded it down with pizza, topping it with dried red pepper. "I see Ellie got that new horror movie for us to watch, I will put it in the DVD player in a minute."

She went over and selected a spot in the corner of the sofa, putting her glass on a coaster. Not sure what had brought on this sudden change in attitude from Sean, she was a little bit edgy. That was exacerbated even more when Sean chose the opposite end of the sofa after he had put the DVD in the player. He reached for the remote and switched the movie on.

Maggie began to feel more comfortable as the evening wore on and was relieved that the plot of the movie was so intense that there was no need for conversation. At one point, when the villain appeared in a flash of lightening in the female character's bedroom, Ellie jumped and let out a shriek.

Sean burst out laughing. "How about I turn out the lights so you can really be scared?" Sean joked with his niece, who was now curled up on the recliner biting her fingernails.

"How about you just leave them on? Otherwise I might have to come and sit on your lap like I used to when I was little?" She acted like she was going to get up from the chair and started laughing as Sean grabbed a pillow and threw it at her. Ellie threw the pillow back at him and he put up an arm, causing the pillow to glance against Maggie's head.

Sean and Ellie looked at each other and then ducked when Maggie grabbed the pillow and acted like she was going to throw it at one of them. Not being able to resist, she tossed it at Sean's head. She took a moment to be mortified when she did it, but then relaxed as he grinned and tucked the pillow behind his head.

Ellie started clapping. "Good one, Maggie!" She grabbed the remote and sat back in the chair as she rewound the part of the movie they missed during the pillow altercation. "Now stop it, both of you! We are missing the best part of the movie."

By the time the movie credits started rolling, Ellie was sound asleep with her head held up by one slender arm. Maggie nudged Sean and pointed at her. "Her arm is going to get sore if she stays that way." She couldn't help but feel familiar feelings when her hand met up with his bare arm and she pushed away those old thoughts.

Sean nodded and went over to Ellie. "Hey, why don't you get up and go to bed? I'll give Maggie a ride home." He looked over at Maggie, his eyebrow raised as if to ask her permission for him to drive her home.

Ellie murmured something unintelligible and got up from the chair, lifting a hand to wave at Maggie. "I'll see you tomorrow."

Maggie smiled as she noticed her stumble sleepily toward the hallway and curse under her breath when she stubbed her toe on the corner of the wall as she turned. "I bet that hurt. I heard it crack."

Sean stood and headed toward the door. "I'm sure it did. Come on and I'll drive you home."

Maggie sat on the passenger side of the big truck as Sean drove toward the farm. The stars hung high and bright in the black velvet sky. A full moon hung heavy and provided some light as they traveled the back roads. Both windows were open and she leaned back and closed her eyes, inhaling the fresh scent of the mountain spring that touched the air as it blew across her upturned face. Being in the truck with Sean like this was almost how it had been all those years ago, except he had left her and she didn't know why.

His smooth voice broke her thoughts in the quiet truck. "So, are you really planning on sticking around here?" Sean gave Maggie a sidelong glance as he drove. "Ellie said that you were going to turn the farm into a bed and breakfast." His voice had deepened over the years and held a hint of sensuality that had not been there before. Almost like a smooth bourbon, she thought.

Maggie nodded and yawned. Her body ached from all the work she had done over the last few days. "I thought it would be a way that I could keep the farm. With all the tourism, I'm sure there are people out there who would like a peaceful retreat that wasn't a commercialized resort."

"There's a lot of work to do out there before that can happen. I heard that you hired Char's son and his buddies to do some of the carpentry."

"Yes, they are doing a good job for me. I don't have a lot of money to go on, just some trust money and some money from the divorce settlement." Maggie put her head back against the leather of the seat and closed her eyes again. "I need to go get some industrial sized appliances in Knoxville as soon as the boys get the kitchen floor redone with the new flooring. Do you think that I could tie the appliances to the top of the Lincoln?" She murmured as she dozed off.

ꕥꕥꕥꕥꕥꕥꕥꕥꕥꕥꕥ

Sean pulled up in front of the old farmhouse like he had done many years before. Almost like a different lifetime he thought to himself. He allowed himself the luxury of watching Maggie sleep in the passenger seat for a few minutes. He could see the paint streaks in her dark hair and he grinned because it reminded him of the time she offered to help paint the barn with him. They got into a paint fight that day and ended up covered from head to toe with red paint.

Word around town was that she was a determined woman. She had made quite an impression on most of the locals with her willingness to jump in and do what it took to refurbish the old farmhouse. He remembered how the old Maggie had been and she had never been a shrinking violet. *Or a catty sex kitten like Julia.* Like it or not, she was here to stay and for some reason he wasn"t upset anymore that she had come back here.

Maggie's eyes fluttered open and she sat up with a start. "Oh! I must have fallen asleep." She stretched her legs out and reached for the door handle at the same time Sean did. His hand covered hers and it seemed like minutes passed before either of them moved.

He wasn't sure which of them removed their hand first. "Let me walk you up to the door." He got out the driver's door and met her as she climbed down from the truck. They walked up to the porch together, not speaking until they were under the cover of the porch. "Maggie, I'm sorry that I was so short with you the first day you got here." He hung his head and kicked the toe of his boot against one of the new boards. "I guess it was a shock to see you after all this time. My behavior was inexcusable."

Maggie reached out a hand and put it on his arm. "Sean, it's okay. We're adults now and we can't go dwelling on what happened in the past between us." Their hands touched again on the doorknob to the house and she pulled away immediately. "Thank you for dinner and the movie tonight. I had a good time. Ellie is such a sweet girl and I have enjoyed having her company around here."

Sean nodded and looked down where their hands had met. He didn't know what moved him, but the next thing he knew he was leaning down and brushing his lips against hers. "Goodnight, Maggie." He used every bit of strength he had to walk away. Right across the porch and down the steps to the truck. Had he waited a few more minutes he would have seen the glimmer of tears threatening to spill out of her eyes and heard her softly spoken words. "Sean, I've missed you so."

CHAPTER SIX

The morning sun beat down on the Maggie's back, the sweat starting to moisten the dark sleeveless shirt she wore. Kneeling in front of the overgrown flower bed that circled the front porch of the house, Maggie was delicately sorting weeds from flowers. Her ball cap covered her dark hair and the old volleyball knee pads from her high school days covered her knees. She brushed at a drop of moisture that started to trail down her neck and stretched her back. This gardening was hard work and she remembered how her grandmother had meticulously taken care of these flower beds, even when she needed assistance from a cane when she was walking very far.

Tom and two of his buddies were at the back of the house hammering, finishing up the siding on the sun porch. Two other boys joined them today, and they were tearing up the old linoleum in the kitchen. From the sheepish looks they all had this morning when they knocked on her door, she assumed they were paying penance to someone for their late-night poker game. She felt sorry for them, they all looked worse for the wear but refused to take the day off.

Mama and her brood were resting on the porch, joined by a curious cat with thick grey fur that turned up out of nowhere this morning. The cat sat nervously on the rail, being watchful for the dogs to wake up so that she could run hide from their curious noses. Maggie found a can of tuna and the cat gratefully rubbed against her legs in the kitchen while she put it on a paper plate.

Using some pictures that she found in her scrapbook that had been taken on one of her summer visits, Maggie tried to remember what perennials her grandmother had planted. That would help her know more what she was looking for as she weeded. Finding the black-eyed Susans, the Shasta daisies, and the coneflowers was relatively easily because they were larger plants that tended to spread out even when they were unattended. She couldn't find the smaller plants so she made a mental note as she cleared away weeds that the bare spots would need to be filled with something. A trip to the local greenhouse might be in order tomorrow.

The cordless phone on the step beeped, interrupting her work. Taking off her gloves, she reached for it. "Hello." She swatted at a bee that was buzzing around her sweaty face. When it continued to dive for her, she stepped quickly backwards into the lawn to avoid it.

She was surprised at the familiar voice. "Hello Maggie. It's Sean." He hesitated for a moment and Maggie thought she might have lost her signal. However, he went on. "I was going to be out checking on a couple of mares this afternoon, would you like for me to bring some more dog food out?"

Maggie started laughing, this was good timing for her since she didn't want to take the time to run into town and pick up the food for the dogs and her newly acquired cat. "Funny you should ask."

"Why would it be funny? Have you run out of food?" He paused for a moment. "If you have, I can run it out before I go check on the mares."

"No, I have enough for today. But it appears that I have another visitor that might want something fishy for her lunch." She stood up and patted the cat on the head and was rewarded with a lot of purring.

"Something fishy? Do you have a pet raccoon now?" Sean chuckled and she could hear him start his vehicle. "I take it you have adopted a stray cat today?"

"Yes, she showed up on my doorstep this morning. I fed her my last can of tuna and she is sunning herself on the porch railing and watching to make sure the dogs don't get too curious." As if to prove her point, Mama got up and took one look at the cat and started barking. The cat screeched and jumped from her perch on the rail up onto a tree limb by the porch.

"Okay, I will be out sometime this afternoon. Are you going to be home or should I just leave it somewhere?"

"I'll be here. I've decided to weed the flower beds today and do some work outside instead of staying cooped up in the house again." After he told her good-bye and hung up, she picked up her empty glass and went into the house. She was terribly thirsty and she figured the boys might like something cold to drink as well. It was an unseasonably warm day, even for this part of Tennessee. Maggie busied herself preparing some fresh lemonade from the last of the lemons in the old fridge. She wanted to use up everything so that she could empty out the fridge and try to figure out a way to go get the new one. She knew that she would need an industrial sized one and the only place to get that would be in Knoxville.

She stepped over a pile of old tile that the boys ripped up and went onto the back porch where all five of them were deep in discussion about some girl in town being "wild". All sets of eyes looked up in embarrassment not sure whether she heard any of their conversation.

Tom recovered first; he seemed to be the boldest and smoother of the group. "Ummmm...hi Miss Maggie."

"Hey guys, I thought you might like something cold to drink other than beer." Her eyes danced as she teased them, knowing full well what the signs of a hangover were. Her comment got a chorus of self-conscious laughter.

"That would be great. We sure do appreciate it." Tom looked at the rest of the boys. "Don't we guys?" They all nodded in agreement.

"Well, come on in. I put out some cold cuts and cheese for sandwiches too. I've got chips and dip as well. You have to eat sometime." She turned and went back inside and took out the last of her paper plates, setting them on the makeshift table. The old cat had managed to slip in the open back door and was rubbing against her ankles begging for scraps. "You can just wait till Sean gets here with your own food. I should think that can of tuna would have held you over for now." She was answered with a meow.

Maggie was back in front of the flower beds right after they finished the sandwiches and chips for lunch. Reaching over and picking up a towel, she mopped her face. Sweat was dripping into her eyes and the band of her cap was drenched. Her goal was to get them all weeded and the ground ready for the new plants that she was going to go get tomorrow. Deciding to take a short break, Maggie was sitting back, admiring her progress, when a shadow fell across her. Assuming it was Sean; she turned around and smiled only to be disappointed in who her visitor was.

"Philip." Maggie had never expected to see her ex-husband again. She assumed he was too busy tearing up the bed sheets with his new secretary. "What the hell are you doing here?" She stood up and put the towel around her neck.

"Now Margo, honey, don't be that way." He took a step toward her and she backed up. "I've driven all this way to see you." His voice was smooth and refined and his face held a look of disdain, one that Maggie recognized well and knew it was permanent and went along with his condescending attitude toward others.

Stepping around him, she turned her back to him. It couldn't be good that he was down here in Tennessee. "Well, you can turn around and drive all the way back to your girlfriend. Whoever she is this week."

Before she could get to the porch, Philip took hold of her arm. "Stop. I came down here to apologize and try to make things right."

"Make things right." Maggie echoed. "Things were never right. Not until I divorced you and got the hell away from Chicago." Jerking free of his grasp, Maggie walked quickly up on the porch. She felt fury boiling inside of her, not the kind that bred the despair she felt when she discovered his indiscretions but full blown fury that had her wanting to pummel a wall. Philip Stanford was a fit, handsome, and well-groomed man. Today he was dressed in a pair of khaki pants and golf shirt with a designer logo on the breast. His feet were clad in a pair of loafers, and Maggie about laughed at the picture he made. How out of place and silly he looked in the foothills of Tennessee in his fancy, city clothes. "Tell you what, Philip. Why don't you just turn around and go back the way you came?" Opening the screen door and going inside, it slammed behind her as she went. Hoping that he would go away, Maggie realized that wasn't Philip's way. He would try to cajole her into staying around until she heard him out.

Turning around, she looked at him, standing inside the door. "Margo, I know that I did wrong by having an affair with Beatrice." He looked around the dining room and made a face. "I made a mistake. Now I want to fix things and be with my wife again." He started toward her.

"Philip, it wasn't one mistake, it wasn't one affair. You were screwing anything and everything that you could get your hands on!" Putting her hands on her narrow hips, she shouted again. "And I'm not your wife anymore!" She turned and walked out of the room toward the kitchen.

Philip followed her. "Awww, Margo. I miss you. You were such a good hostess and my business associates miss you too." He reached for her again and she slapped his hand away.

"Don't you dare touch me! And don't call me Margo! I have no interest in having anything to do with you! Our marriage was a farce, it always was. You wanted a little trophy wife who would occupy herself with entertaining your business associates and attending to charity functions to make you look good." Grabbing a dish towel, she started cleaning up from lunch.

"Margo, you belong in Chicago with me. Look at this place." He motioned around the room. "It's a dump." He smirked at the torn-up floor and the makeshift table in the middle of the room. "You are wasting your time trying to fix this place up into a bed and breakfast.

It would be better if you sold it, made yourself a nice profit from one of the developers around here. I could put you in touch with one."

Unable to hold her anger any longer, she threw the towel at him, smacking him squarely in the face. "Get out! This is my home. It was my grandparents' home before that! I will never sell it to some developer so that they can tear it down to build one of their overpriced resorts!" She started to walk past him and saw a familiar figure coming down the hall toward the kitchen.

Sean's long strides quickly brought him to stand in front of Philip, who was just reaching for Maggie again. "Excuse me, but I think the lady told you to get out." Sean spoke calmly, but Maggie could see the anger simmering below the surface as his face reddened and his eyes bored through Philip. Sean's fists were clenched at his sides and his jaw was twitching.

Philip looked up at Sean and smiled, holding out his hand for Sean to shake. "Hello there, I'm Philip Stanford. I'm Margo's husband."

Sean ignored the hand that was extended to him. Behind her, Maggie could sense the group of boys standing in the doorway to the back porch. "Philip, leave now. I don't want you here. Nor do I ever want to have to see you here, or anywhere else again."

Philip looked beyond her to the boys assembled in the doorway; he then turned and looked up at Sean again. "Gentlemen, it appears there is a misunderstanding here. I simply want to have a discussion with my wife." He looked at Maggie, his eyes now cold and flat.

Sean broke the silence. "Maggie, are you ready to go for that ride we talked about last night?" His eyes urged her to go along with his story.

Maggie recovered and stepped toward Sean. "I sure am, if you could give me a moment to take a shower and change my clothes. I hadn't realized it was so late." She started to walk around Philip, pausing for a moment. "If you will excuse us Philip, I have plans for this afternoon. You have wasted a trip. It's a long drive back to Chicago so you might want to get started." Maggie walked toward the staircase and started up the steps, glancing back to see Philip going out the front door with Sean following him.

She went into the bedroom that she was currently using and flopped down on the bed. Immediately, three questions went through her mind. *How did he know where I was? Where did he learn about me turning the farm into a bed and breakfast? Did Dixie inadvertently say something to the wrong person?* Maggie lay on the bed until she heard tires spinning out on the gravel driveway. Getting up from the bed, she pushed the old curtains away from the window and saw the only cars remaining in the driveway were hers and Sean's truck. Maggie watched as he unloaded a bag of dog food from the back of the truck and carry it up to the porch. The front door slammed, and the sound of his footsteps told her he was approaching the stairway.

"Maggie, how much longer till you are ready to go?"? Sean called up the steps.

What on earth was he talking about? Go where? Maggie looked at herself in the old mirror above the dresser and grimaced. The only way she'd be ready to go anywhere was if she really took a shower and change clothes. Pulling a clean pair of jeans and cotton shirt in pale yellow out of the dresser, she threw them on the bed. Grabbing a towel, she headed for the bathroom to clean up. "Give me about fifteen minutes and I'll be back down!"

❧❧❧❧❧❧❧❧❧❧❧

Philip Stanford was angry. He picked up the cell phone beside him on the seat of the rental car and punched in a number. The hand that remained on the steering wheel was clenched so hard that the knuckles were white. He waited as the call connected and the woman's voice answered. "Hello?" The sultry voice murmured through the phone.

"Julia? It's Philip." He pulled over to the side of the road, watching in his side mirror for approaching vehicles. "I guess we have to come up with another plan, she kicked me out with the help of some hayseed in a pick-up truck."

Julia's voice changed from sultry to dripping with venom. "I don't give a shit what plan you come up with. Just get her to sell that property to me. We had a deal, Philip. If you could have kept your pants zipped for a few weeks longer, everything would have been fine." She abruptly hung up.

Philip slammed the phone against the dash. If only he could have convinced her to agree to sign the papers before she caught him with Beatrice, he wouldn't be in this awful hick town in the middle of nowhere. He picked up the phone and dialed another number and waited for the voice mail. "It's Philip. I want Margo to come back to me, I love her. I need your help." He left his cell number and the number of the hotel in Knoxville, and then pushed the button to end the call. Lying came easily to Philip Stanford.

CHAPTER SEVEN

Sean was perched on the edge of an unpacked crate when Maggie came downstairs. Because of his height, well over six foot, his knees were bent at an uncomfortable looking angle. Beneath his well-worn jeans, his boots were scuffed and dirty. He looked up as Maggie walked into the living room; his blue eyes bright and aware. "You really didn't mean to take me somewhere, did you?" It was nice of him to rescue her, but with Philip gone, he didn't have to stay. She paused on the foot of the stairs and smiled at him thankfully. "I really appreciate you coming up with something to get him to go."

Standing up, he walked toward the door. "Come on, you need a break. Ellie said that you've been working from dawn to dusk for days now." Reaching out for the door handle, he looked to make sure Maggie was coming. "I thought maybe we could drive out to the riding stables and go for a ride."

Maggie hadn't been on a horse in years. When her grandfather kept horses here at the farm, she rode all the time. If Maggie wanted solace and peace in the days that she stayed at the farm, she would ride. Over the rolling fields, alongside the creek, wherever she felt like going. Usually, those times were when she had been in an argument with her mother. *I'm not going to think about her right now.* Her mother had a way of making Maggie feel inadequate by way of comparing her to her father and the simple way he had preferred to live. Paul Coulter was a born and raised east Tennessee man, meeting her mother while he was away at college. Brenda Coulter-Davisson was a refined woman from the city, who preferred the finer things in life. When Maggie's father had been killed in the car accident, Brenda had immediately found a man who could give her those finer things. Maggie had been twelve and devastated at the loss of her father. Had it not been for spending summers at the farm with her grandparents, she would have been miserable all the time.

Sean opened the passenger door of the truck and she climbed up, using the running board and the side of the door frame to help her. He stopped to pat Mama on the head as he walked around the front of the truck to the driver's side and then told her to go up in the yard with her babies.

"I'm sorry you had to come in on that scene earlier." The anger was gone and had been replaced with embarrassment at the scene that Sean had come in on. She cringed at what he must think about her.

"Nothing to be sorry for. The guy was an ass." Turning the key in the ignition, he glanced over at her. "I can't believe you were married to that uppity jerk."

"I guess I didn't have much choice. My mother just pushed us together and that's how it ended up." She gripped the armrest as the truck hit a hole in the lane, causing her to bounce in her seat. "I never saw him a whole lot after we were married anyway." Philip worked long hours, or so she had been led to believe. They were married before she started work on her graduate degree, and she hadn't noticed how much time she spent alone until her studies were done. Remembering a fight the night she told Philip she was going to take a job at a hotel chain, he stayed gone on a business trip for several days. *On business my ass.* Her mother had visited during those days and insisted that working was not what she should be doing. Maggie was the wife of a prominent businessman and there was no need to work. She should use her talents advancing his career through charity work and being his hostess.

"Where did you meet this guy at?" He pulled the truck onto the interstate and merged with the Sunday traffic.

"He worked with my stepfather and came to dinner one night while I was in my senior year of college. We just got thrown together and when he asked me to marry him, my mother was thrilled."

"I'll bet she was." Sean murmured in a tight voice.

"What did you say?" Maggie couldn't remember her mother ever being at the farm while Sean was there. Maybe she was mistaken, it had been a long time ago and her mother's trips to the farm were never pleasant.

"I said, I'll bet your mother was pleased that her daughter had found such a gem of a man. He sure can pour it on thick; it would be hard to see through him."

"He definitely can put on a good show when he wants to. Otherwise, I would have been able to recognize him for the philandering jerk he was from the beginning." Sex with Philip had been rushed and unsatisfying. Maggie had always blamed herself, thinking it was her fault that he hurried through the act. *Probably because I kept remembering what that first time was like, the time that Sean and I made love by the creek.* That had been special to her and she always measured other relationships against that one brief, summer love.

"Well, hopefully he got the message not to come back." Sean grinned suddenly. "I loved it when you threw that towel in his face!" He started laughing, his eyes dancing as he glanced across the seat at her.

"Oh my God! How much of that scene did you see and hear?" How mortifying that he saw that part!

"I think I came in right before the towel flew. But I heard most of it from the porch. It wasn't like you were trying to be quiet." He continued to chuckle until Maggie reached across the seat and poked him in the side.

"Stop laughing. It wasn't funny, it was pathetic. The nerve of him coming down here trying to get me to come back to Chicago with him." The divorce had been final for over a year and he hadn't once tried to see her while she was still in Chicago. "My God! The boys were all out back!" If Char at the diner got the story, it would be all over town by the next day.

As if reading her thoughts, Sean grinned again. "You will be the talk of the town by nightfall."

"I know. That's all I need is for everyone in town talking about me. I am not going to be able to show my face at the diner for a while. *I've already been the talk of the town, rumors flying around about me coming back because of Sean living here.* More than one person remembered and commented to her about what a nice little couple they made.

"I doubt it will be bad. Folks around here don't take too kindly to outsiders like him pushing a lady around in her own house." He turned the wheel of the truck to take an exit toward Gatlinburg. "Do you remember Alex Miles? He has the stable at the edge of Gatlinburg. I have a couple of mares boarded there myself."

"Sure I do. He used to board a couple horses at Papaw's. They used to sneak in the barn and drink that rotgut whiskey that Alex used to bring with him from Kentucky." Laughing at the image of the time her grandmother had caught the two of them, like two drunken sailors playing poker on a bale of hay and swearing up a blue streak. "Mamaw took the broom to them and old Alex ran the wrong way out of the barn and fell in a pile of horse manure."

"Now I know why Doug told me to hide that bottle of wine from your grandma. He didn't want the same fate for me I guess."

Mentioning the bottle of wine that he had hid in the creek bed brought back memories for Maggie. He kept fidgeting at dinner that evening, trying to get her attention by nudging her leg with his boot. Unfortunately, it was her grandfather's leg that he kicked one too many times. "Damn boy, you got a twitch in that leg?" Her grandfather got a kick from her grandmother for his language. Later that night, Sean climbed up the tree by the porch and told her what he had hidden in the creek. They sat on a blanket that July night and drank wine out of paper cups. *Stop it. Don't even start thinking about that night. It's over and done with.*

You can't bring it back.

The sun wasn't as high in the sky when they arrived at the stables. There were only a few tourists preparing to follow the guide up the mountain trail. One woman sat stiffly on the back of her horse while the guide gave them instructions on what they should watch for as they rode up the mountain. Alex hobbled out, his short legs bowed from years of riding horses. He extended a hand that was twisted and gnarled from age. "Howdy Doc. I see you brought a pretty lady with you today. Want me to saddle up both mares or do you wanna ride my new stallion?"

Sean clapped a hand on the old man's back. "Just saddle up the mares. I'm thinking that we just want a nice quiet ride this afternoon."

About halfway up the trail, Maggie was beginning to be comfortable on the mellow chestnut that Sean called Doe Eyes when Sean stopped and held up a hand.

"Shhh...look over there to the right. Between those trees."

An enormous buck stood in the clearing, his ears twitching as he listened for intruders to his world. There was some rustling in the brush, and a doe appeared next to him. Both looked at the two riders then dashed into the darkness of the trees. Except for the sound of the new leaves rustling in the trees, it was perfectly still and quiet.

"They were magnificent!" Maggie trotted her horse until she was even with Sean. "I forgot how beautiful it was up here." She lifted her face to the sky and felt exhilarated. Even though it was overcast, it was an otherwise beautiful day. They wound through the trails until Maggie felt a sudden, chilly dampness in the air. "Are we close to the top? I'm starting to feel chilly." She shivered and took her hands off the reins to hug herself.

Sean looked up through the leaves and branches of the overhanging trees. The sky had become even more overcast. "I think we better head back to the stables. Looks like we are going to get a spring rain. These trails are hard to manage when the rain starts flowing down from the top of the mountain." He nudged his horse in the side and started down a trail that would take them back to the stables.

The rain started before they made it back and they were both drenched when they met Alex in the barn with the horses. "Alex, I can dry these ladies off. You go on in the house and get warmed up so your arthritis doesn't bother you."

The old man had donned a yellow slicker and his cap was collecting rain. "Naw. Ain't gonna let a little bit of ache get in the way of taking care of the horses. 'Sides, I got me this boy from town workin' in the barn. He can earn his wage this way." The old man grinned, showing tobacco stained teeth. "You take this little gal home. You both smell like them damn horses."

Inside the truck, Maggie sniffed her damp clothes. Alex was right, she smelled like wet horse flesh. When Sean flicked on the truck's heater, the smell was even more pungent. Her thighs and backside ached from being in the saddle for the first time in years. Burrs had attached themselves to her wet jeans and her hair hung limply around her face. She shivered from a sudden chill.

"Are you cold? I have the heater on." He reached over and pushed another button on the dash. "Here, I turned on the heated seats, which should help some."

There were goose bumps on her arms and her hair hanging around her face in wet clumps. "Just a little chilly. And Alex was right, we both smell like wet horses." She watched him drive and let the warmth from the heated seat sooth her aching, cold frame. There were laugh lines in the corners of his eyes that had not been there years ago and she noticed a scar that ran from right below his ear and under his chin. "Where did you get that scar?"

He reached up and unconsciously rubbed the scar. "I got kicked by a colt that I was helping to deliver my first year up here. Knocked me for a loop and bled like a stuck pig."

That scar wasn't as big as the scar on her heart, though. She didn't realize the direction they were going but he ended up driving the vehicle in the opposite direction of her house and wound it through the back roads until they arrived at his cabin. He should have just taken her home, but the day had gone well and she wanted to spend more time with him. She felt like she was treading on dangerous footing, only an idiot would go back to where she had been before, but her heart took over where her mind should have made her mouth tell him to take her home.

"How about we go in and get you dried off and warmed up? This rain is going to go on for a while and we could wait it out, maybe watch a movie, until it passes." He looked at her, waiting for her response.

As she reached for the door, she realized she was making a big decision. One that could get her hurt all over again. But she took the chance and got out of the truck. She followed him up the walk and onto the porch, both of them sprinting to avoid getting any wetter than they already were. Sean opened the door and stood back to let her go in first and she immediately was met with the warmth of the cabin's interior. She stood on the small rug by the door and slipped her shoes off, they were wet and muddy and she wasn't about to track in dirt on the clean floor that Ellie would probably have to clean up.

"Where's Ellie today?" She noticed the quiet of the cabin and came to the realization that the two of them were alone.

"She drove down to my mom and dad's in North Carolina this morning. I think she was going to stay until the middle of the week." Having slipped his boots off, they were standing next to her shoes on the rug, and he was walking past her toward the hall. "I'll be right back and we will see about getting you warmed up."

When he returned, he carried a one-piece bathing suit and was wearing a pair of swim trunks. "Here you go, my cousin left this here last time she and her husband visited. I think she is about the same size as you are." He handed the black suit to her and nodded toward the bathroom. "I have a hot tub out back and we can get warmed up in that.""

Maggie went into the bathroom and stood for a moment. *I'm not sure this is a good idea. Ellie being gone and me and Sean in the hot tub. Well, at least I know he doesn't have the same interest in me as he did before. And damned if I wouldn't like a nice dip in the hot tub.* She stripped out of the wet clothes and wrinkled her nose at the smell of wet horse and then stood in front of the mirror and looked at her reflection and wondered if Sean still found her attractive. She hadn't felt attractive in such a very long time. Philip had ruined her confidence in herself, and she so wanted to feel like a woman again. She reached for the bathing suit and put it on, then used Ellie's hairbrush to brush the tangles out of her hair. When she came out of the bathroom carrying her clothes, he reached for them.

"Here, let me toss these smelly things in the washer for you." He handed her a terry cloth robe. "You're shivering, put this on and we'll go back and get in the hot tub."

The hot tub was sitting on a screened in porch off the kitchen, it faced the hill and woods to the back of the house and someone planted evergreens on either side to give the space more privacy. *I wonder how many women have been back here with him. Someone as attractive as Sean, surely there has been women here. Like that Julia woman Ellie talked about.* The steam rolled off the hot tub and it was so inviting, bubbling and churning water that she knew would make her aching muscles relax. She took off the robe and climbed up the steps into the tub, letting her body sink into the relaxing water. Sean joined her, choosing a spot across from where she sat, careful not to touch her. She was grateful, because at that very moment, had he touched her she would have given herself to him even knowing that there were no romantic feelings involved.

They sat quietly for a few minutes before he spoke. "What made you decide to come back down here?" Other than the fact that you wanted to get away from that jerk.

She sat across from him, her eyes closed, the dark lashes fanned out beneath her closed eyes. "I would have come back a couple of years ago, but..." Maggie looked out toward the mountains and continued. "Initially, Philip wanted me to sell the property and the more he pushed, the more I realized that I wasn't where I wanted to be."

"This is a big undertaking, turning the house into a bed and breakfast." Ellie tells me how you work so hard trying to get things done. It's a shame that you must do so much of this work yourself." He paused and spread his hands expressively. "I think it's a great idea, though. Tourism down here is booming as you can see by all the resorts that have been built since you were a teenager."

"I know. I worked as a travel agent the last year and a half. A lot of the clients I worked with made this their summer vacation destination." She had done well selling trips to this area because of her first- hand knowledge and her clients always were pleased with their experience.

"When were you planning to be ready to take guests in? Ellie said you intend to be ready in time for the fall foliage."

The autumn months were some of the busiest tourism months in the area but she was beginning to have her doubts she would be able to get that farm ready in time for the fall season. "I hoped to be ready by July, but realistically, I won't be ready until September. I have a friend at the travel agency in Chicago that has some clients that she is going to send my way for fall. I can't let her down." She knew that Dixie had all her rooms tentatively booked for every week in October and she had to have the interior ready by September to send the promotional photographs. "This was a nice thought, Sean." Already, her muscles were feeling loose and limber. She leaned back and closed her eyes. "I so wish that the bathrooms at home were finished. There have been evenings I would have killed for a nice bubble bath before bed." She was so focused on getting the guest rooms ready first that she couldn't think about her own quarters and comfort.

"Are the boys working out alright for you? They seem to have accomplished quite a bit."

For all the mischief that crew got into, she knew they were good kids and she trusted that they would do a good job for her. And it sure helped him to know that they wouldn't try to take advantage of her or harm her in any way. Not like some of the workers that were brought in by the resort developers, they were one motley crew and there were rumors that some of them were parolees and drug users.

"Yes, they have been a godsend. I was lucky that they heard that I needed help. They are a lot less expensive than a licensed contractor." As much as some of the gossip in this town got on her nerves, she was grateful for Char telling her son about the new woman in town. "I was fortunate to meet up with Char the first night I was back.""

"You will still have to hire a contractor to do the plumbing, if you are going to have the place pass inspection."

Her expression tightened and realized that she probably hadn't planned on the expense of getting someone to do that. Her finances were starting to get tight. "I know. I'm hoping that with the trust fund I can manage to afford it. I need to have a bathroom added to the other three bedrooms upstairs." The fourth bedroom was larger and connected to the bath that she was currently using. The downstairs bathroom shared a wall with the family room; she was just going to have the door switched so that it opened to that room. And there was the newly framed back porch she would be using for her own quarters. She thought about having a gas fireplace added to the room to make it homier for her. But that was down the road.

"Well, I have a buddy from back home that helped me build this cabin. I bet he'd be willing to do the work pretty reasonable."

"You built this cabin yourself?" You always talked about building your own cabin back then, I'm not surprised." *You certainly fulfilled your dreams, didn't you? I guess you must have changed your mind about me being part of them.* She almost wished she hadn"t brought up the memories of how they talked about the home they were going to have together.

"Yep, I bought one of those kits and made some modifications. Before it was done, I had a bed and couple of chairs in the clinic. I got to sleep with the sound of dogs barking in the kennel since that room was right next to it." He laughed and let himself sink deeper into the tub so that he could rest his head on the edge.

They sat in silence for quite some time. Overhead, the rain picked up and was now beating against the tin roof of the screened in porch. Once, they heard a rustle outside and Maggie saw the flash of red eyes glowing. Sean assured her that it was just the pesky raccoon that recently settled in his garage, out foraging for trash.

"Would you like something to drink?"

Maggie opened her eyes. She must have dozed off for a moment. Wetting her lips with her tongue, she realized that she was thirsty. "Yes, that would be nice." It was certainly different sitting here with Sean as an adult. He hadn't changed all that much. His rich, auburn hair sported a couple of tell-tale strands of gray and there were laugh lines crinkling from the corners of his eyes that hadn't been there before. A moustache extended past the corners of his mouth to join a goatee. But the blue eyes still twinkled like pieces of sapphire when he smiled. There was a little more muscle than he had years ago; but overall, he was still the same Sean that held her against him that hot, July night on the blanket by the creek. Her thoughts were interrupted when Sean returned.

"How about we go in the living room and sit in front of the fire?" He picked up the terry cloth robe and held it up as she stepped out of the bubbling water. "I made us some snacks and poured some wine."

She followed him into the living room and sat down in the same place on the sofa where she sat a few nights earlier. There was a plate of summer sausage, cheese, and vegetables with dip sitting on a tray on the cocktail table along with two stemmed glasses and a bottle of white wine. She waited while he poured them each a glass and picked his own up.

"A lot better than that cheap, strawberry wine we used to drink." He grinned and reached for the remote. Instead of the television coming on, a stereo started playing a Faith Hill CD. He leaned back on the sofa, stretching his legs out in front of him. Maggie's legs were curled up under her and she could feel the warmth of the fire as it crackled in the grate. When a storm came through these parts, even in the summer, it got chilly quickly. They talked about his job as the local veterinarian, how glad he was that people trusted him to take care of their animals when old Dr. Ogle retired. He returned here as the old doctor's assistant for the first few years, then as the only veterinarian in town when the doctor retired five years before. After he bought the clinic building from Dr. Ogle, he started work on the cabin.

Maggie didn't want to talk about the past years of her life. They weren't much to be proud of. Four years of college, then married to a man that just wanted a wife for the sake of having a wife. Two years of graduate school where her studies kept her too busy to wonder where her husband was most nights. Then three years of misery wondering why her husband was only attentive to her when he needed her to entertain his business associates over cocktails and dinner parties. From the outside, they looked like the perfect couple, but Maggie grew depressed and restless until the evening she appeared in his office unexpectedly. There, she found him with his secretary's legs wrapped around his naked body.

Sean set down his glass and reached over to touch her on the shoulder. "Penny for your thoughts." His face was close to his and the blue eyes were watchful and searching.

Maggie smiled wistfully. "I was thinking how peaceful I've felt since I got back down here." *How I wish things would have turned out differently between us. I wish that you hadn't grown up and lost interest in me. I never would have met Philip, let alone married him.*

Sean reached out and pushed a lock of hair behind her ear. His knuckles rubbed the side of her face gently, and then he rested his hand on her shoulder. Their eyes met and locked, his a dark sapphire and hers like melted chocolate. His hand went behind her neck and pulled her to him, his lips just barely grazing hers. When he pulled away, she put both hands on his chest, feeling his heart beat under the terry cloth robe. His head dipped again, his lips still softly caressing hers until she started kissing him back.

When Maggie responded to his kiss with a moan, he moved closer, drawing her against him as he urged her lips open. Their tongues met and danced together, the kiss deepening with each passing moment. Maggie felt liquid warmth spread through her entire body and Sean drew her onto his lap. He pulled away from her lips and held her face in his hands, caressing her temples with his thumbs. Her eyes fluttered open and she ran her hands from his chest to his shoulders, then back down again. She was lying against the arm of the sofa and he leaned into her again, taking her lips with unrestrained passion.

Her hands tangled in his hair as she moved against him, wanting to feel the hard length of his body against hers. She sighed as his moved to kiss her neck and the sensitive area behind her ears. Just as suddenly, he stopped kissing and pulled away from her. Opening her eyes again she watched as he sat up.

"Damn it. Who could that be?" He gently moved her from his lap and got up, pulling his robe around him and tightening the belt before he started for the door. He turned and smiled gently. "You might want to fasten your robe too."

She could see the evidence of his arousal straining against his underwear before he pulled the robe closed and it made her even more conscious of her own desire. That's when she heard the insistent knocking on the front door. Making sure the robe was around her body and tucking her legs up under her, she watched as he walked toward the door. A female voice, sultry and seductive, floated into the room.

"Sean, darling. I thought you might want a little company. What better night for that rain check, than a rainy one." The woman walked into the room, oblivious to Maggie sitting on the sofa. She removed her rain jacket and handed it to Sean, who was just standing by the door, a blush creeping up from his neck. He made no move to take the jacket, even as the woman continued to push it toward him.

"Julia, I didn't expect you this evening..." He stammered and looked toward the sofa where Maggie just rose from her seat. "It's not really a good time tonight."

The woman followed his gaze and smirked when she saw the woman standing there in a robe. "Ahhh. You already have company, I see." Walking over to stand behind the sofa Julia looked down her nose and took in Maggie's mussed, brown hair. "Sorry to interrupt you, my name is Julia Evans."

Maggie nodded, unable to say anything in return. She gazed at the woman's short, blonde hair and perfect make-up. Her slacks were a deep blue, silk fabric that clung to her hips. The woman wore an expensive lace camisole underneath a blouse that matched her pants. A princess cut diamond hung from a gold chain, she wore earrings to match. The scent of expensive perfume permeated the air in the cabin.

"Julia, this is Maggie Coulter...I mean Stanford." Sean stood by the open door, one hand on the knob. His face was unreadable and he seemed very awkward in this situation. He glanced between Maggie and the blonde then looked at the floor.

Maggie finally recovered and got up from her place on the sofa. "I was just getting ready to go." Her attention went from the woman to Sean. "Sean, do you think that my clothes are dry yet?" She started toward the bathroom, not glancing over her shoulder despite her urge to do so. Inside the bathroom she waited until Sean knocked and she cracked the door enough to reach for the clothes he had in his hand before pulling it firmly shut once she had them. She heard him outside the door for a long few moments before his bare feet walked away. *Dear God, what might have we done if she hadn't shown up? I would have gone willingly into his bed even though he obviously has a relationship with this woman. This is not what I need right now.* She leaned her head against the door and felt a hot tear roll down her cheek.

CHAPTER EIGHT

Outside the house, Maggie could hear the puppies growling and playing on the lawn in the bright sunshine. Looking around the living room and dining room, she was pleased with what she had accomplished over the last week. Working from dawn till dusk every day had paid off and served two purposes. A lot of work was finished on the downstairs rooms and there had been little time to reflect on the evening she spent with Sean. The wood floors had been stripped by Tom and his friends, the stain applied, and a top coat reflected the sun that was streaming through the drapes. Her grandmother's old piano, the only piece of furniture in the living room, now sat in the corner; cleaned and polished. Glassware was now lined up neatly in the china cupboard in the dining room. Walking down the hall to the kitchen, she stood in the middle of the room and admired the new laminate flooring. The cabinets shone with the fresh coat of white, glossy paint and new brass handles; the walls were a sunny yellow. The boys had built an island in the middle of the kitchen where they installed a six-burner stove top on one side and a built-up part that was going to serve as an eating area on the other. "Maggie! Are you back there?" A voice called from the front of the house. "Ellie!" Maggie smiled as the younger woman entered the kitchen. "It's good to see you! I just got back from my grandparents' last night. I'm amazed how much has been done since I left last week." Red hair fell across her shoulders, instead of being in the usual ponytail; her blue eyes danced. "My boyfriend will be here tomorrow, I'm so excited."

"I'm sure you are excited; do you have a lot of things planned?" Maggie was caught up in Ellie's excitement and she laughed as the girl flitted around the kitchen.

"Well, for starters, I'm going shopping in Knoxville. I came out here to see if you'd go with me. I thought about doing the mall then a salon for an added treat. Are you up for it?" She reached out and grabbed Maggie's hand and tugged on it. "Please? You need to treat yourself to a day of fun."

Maybe this is just what she needed, a shopping trip and some pampering. *I have felt like a total sloth after Julia Evans' visit at Sean's the other night. She was so polished and groomed.* "What the heck. I've worked hard all week and I think I need a shopping trip and salon visit. Wait while I go change into some clean clothes."

Once the Lincoln had reached the interstate, Maggie set the cruise control and headed to the west. Beside her, Ellie was going through her billfold to see how much money she had to spend. Maggie reminded herself to stop at the bank and transfer some of the trust fund money into her own account. She didn't want to be frivolous, but she needed the distraction of spending some money on herself.

"I heard that you and Uncle Sean went riding the other day up at old Alex's stables." Ellie grinned and looked at Maggie expectantly.

"Yes, we did. I hadn't ridden a horse in years and I forgot how enjoyable it could be." *And I about fell in bed with your uncle.*

"I'll bet that nasty old Julia about shit herself when she found you in a robe in our living room." Ellie giggled and poked Maggie in the ribs. "So, do tell."

Where did that piece of information come from? Did Sean tell her or was this the topic of gossip at the café this week? Maggie felt her face color thinking that it was all over town. "I don't know. She left while I was putting my clothes back on." *Oh hell, Maggie, that sounded just great.* She stammered out a quick response. "We got caught in a rainstorm and your uncle washed and dried my clothes."

Ellie giggled. "You didn't have to explain. Uncle Sean already did when I teased him last night about it. Char, at the café, heard Julia on her cell phone complaining about it to someone." She had a smug smile on her face. "I had hoped that someone would come along that would get that dreadful woman away from my Uncle Sean before she sunk her claws in him. You might just be the person to do it."

"Well, I hope that Char is being selective who she is telling about this." *All I need is a bunch of rumors circulating all over town about Sean and I.*

"She only told me. Uncle Sean would be mad if she said anything to make either of you look bad."

More likely he doesn't want anyone to think that anything is going on between us. Good thing Julia came when she did, otherwise it's hard telling how far that things might have gone. "That's good that he has some influence over Char."

"Oh, him and Char are really good friends. Char would never do anything to hurt Sean...or you."

"Well, I don't know about that. She doesn't know me all that well." She steered the car off the exit that would lead them to the mall and watched the approaching traffic through the rear-view mirror as she merged.

"Sure she does, she told me that Uncle Sean talks about you all the time." Ellie stopped abruptly and covered her mouth. "Oops, I wasn't supposed to know that."

I wonder how much Char knows about Sean and me. "Don't worry about it Ellie. Sometimes people tell stuff that they aren't supposed to tell. It's not your fault that Char told you things that your uncle talked about."

"Maggie, did you love Uncle Sean when you stayed here before?" She reached over and put her hand on Maggie's arm as if to offer comfort.

"Yes, I loved your uncle very much. But we were just kids having a summer romance. I shouldn't have ever expected it to last." She reached across the seat and patted Ellie's leg.

"Don't worry about it." *I'm not going to think about how hurt I was when he stopped writing me and never showed up for Christmas like he promised. I was only seventeen that summer and he was already on his way to being a man. I'm going to put this out of my mind and just have fun with Ellie today.*

At the mall, they went from store to store, Ellie buying everything from jeans to lingerie. By the time they reached the salon, Maggie was ready to sit down in the chair and have the attendant put her feet in the whirlpool bath in front of her. Leaning back, she pushed the button on the chair and sighed as rollers started going up and down her back. "This is awesome. I haven't felt this relaxed since..." Since the hot tub.

Both had manicures and pedicures, their hair washed and styled. Maggie cringed as she signed the charge card receipt. *I shouldn't have spent this much money on myself when there is so much left to buy for the house.*

As if Ellie had read her mind, the young girl put a hand on her arm. "A woman deserves a little pampering occasionally." She gave Maggie and exaggerated wink; which sent both into a stream of giggles. After the salon, they had a late lunch at one of the restaurants in the mall. Beating the dinner crowd, the restaurant was almost deserted and they took their time over steaks then ordered a dessert to split. Ellie managed to steer the conversation away from Sean, and for this, Maggie was grateful.

Venturing through the discount department store at the end of the mall, Maggie decided to spend some money on dishes. Selecting a set of bone china with mauve roses trimmed with gold for the dining room, she also found a set of cobalt blue stoneware to put in the kitchen for more casual dining. "I need to find some stuff to decorate with. What do you suggest, Ellie?"

They were standing in the center of the house-wares department, surrounded by nick knacks and artwork. Ellie picked up a brass container that looked like a miniature wash tub. "I like this for the center of the dining room table. You could have Char put an arrangement of roses in it to match the dishes. She is awesome with flower arrangements." Just as quickly, she dropped the container in the cart and ran over to a display of faux watercolor paintings.

"Look at these." She held up a pair of delicate roses painted on a cream background with burgundy matting and brass looking frames. She dropped those in the cart as well. By the time they left the store, Maggie had added four barstools in boxes for the kitchen along with a cobalt blue pitcher and canisters to match. They loaded the trunk and back seat of the car with their purchases and headed back toward Possum Creek. The drive home was a little more tedious as they had managed to stay at the mall just long enough to get hung up in the five o"clock rush hour traffic. Maggie was used to traffic congestion after living in Chicago but that didn't mean that she had to like it. By the time they hit the interstate outside of the city limits, she was looking forward to just getting back to the farm.

??????????

Sean sat on the porch of Maggie's house, absently petting Mama on the head while he watched the sun go down over the trees. *Where are those women?* Tom said that they left hours ago talking about shopping. *Stop it, you are worrying for nothing.* Women and shopping could take all night. *I just don't like the idea that Char served a strange man fitting the description of Philip Stanford.* Or that Julia Evans was sitting with him.

He stood up as he saw headlights coming down the lane. Relieved to see the Lincoln pull up by Ellie's truck, he casually strode out to meet them. "Hey, you two. Did you buy out the mall or something?" By the look of the back seat, loaded down with boxes and shopping bags, they had certainly come close to it.

"Hi Uncle Sean! It's a good thing you are here. You can help us carry all this stuff in the house." Ellie handed him one of the boxes containing a bar stool and stacked another box with dishes on top.

Grumbling, he carried the boxes into the house behind Maggie. *She won't even look at me. I knew I shouldn't have lost my control the other night and started kissing her. She didn't speak to me all the way back out here that night. Christ, what would have happened if Julia hadn't shown up?*

"Thank you for helping carry all this stuff in. Looks like I'm going to be putting together bar stools and hanging pictures the rest of the night." She stood with her hands on her slender waist and surveyed the stuff piled in the dining room.

"I could stay and put the bar stools together for you while you hang the pictures." *You idiot! What are you doing volunteering to stick around when you know you want to do more with her than help her put together bar stools?*

"That's nice of you to offer. You would probably get them put together a lot better than I would." She smiled brightly and touched his arm. "I so appreciate your help."

Looking down at the hand that had touched his arm, he noticed that her fingernails had been painted. They hadn't been painted when she put her hands on his chest Sunday night. He felt himself start to grow hard beneath the zipper of his jeans at the memory of what they had done the other night. "No problem. I'll grab my tool box from the truck and be right back."

In the yard, Ellie was loading packages in her truck. His Mom and Dad must have given her some money while she was down there. Typical teenager, spending it all in one place. Grinning, he recalled the battles they used to have over her allowance not lasting her until the end of the week. *God, how she nickel and dimed me when she was in high school.*

"Did you spend it all in one place?" He helped her put some more things in her truck and thought about asking her to stick around so that he and Maggie wouldn't be alone. A smile came across his niece's face and her eyes danced, that smile brought back memories of his sister, Kate. *Kate, your daughter has turned into a beautiful young woman, I hope you are up there watching over her.* Up in the night sky, stars twinkled and an errant cloud floated by.

"You always ask me that!" Wrapping her arms around her uncle, she hugged him tightly. "And my answer is always no."

"Are you going to come in the house?" He couldn't help asking Ellie to stay behind. He just knew that as much as he wanted to be alone with Maggie, he was not built to take on what it might lead to if they were to continue where they left of the other night. And that's what he wanted to do, take her in his arms and kiss her senseless until she gave herself to him. After all these years and all the hurt, he still wanted her.

"Nope. I think I'll go back home and go to bed early since Todd is coming tomorrow." As she walked away, she stopped and turned. "Maybe Julia won't show up to ruin things for you tonight." Giggling, she *made a dash for the truck. That left Sean standing in the lawn, alone with his thoughts.*

Well, you might as well go in and help her like you offered. If those brown eyes don't go all soft on me I should be alright. Who are you kidding? All it takes is for you to hear her voice to remember how it felt to hold her in your arms while she murmured your name. Sighing, he reached in the back of the truck for his tool box and walked back to the house.

??????????

The man and woman sat at a table in the hotel restaurant. The woman held her back straight, her motions graceful and practiced. The man leaned across the table and gripped her hand. "Please Brie; I know that I made mistakes with the marriage. But I love your daughter and want her back." Philip forced himself to allow tears to well up in his eyes. "Talk to her for me. She has always tended to do what you wanted, regardless of what she thought she wanted." He squeezed Brenda Davisson's hand.

"Oh Philip. I understand that men occasionally stray. It's their nature to do so. A good wife would have looked the other way. God knows that I do." A woman like Brenda Davisson knew that to live the way that she did, with all the privileges of wealth, she had to turn her head and pretend her husband wasn't screwing the neighbor. "I'm afraid that Margaret has never been smart about what was good for her. That's why I have intervened in her life frequently."

"So you will talk to her?" Philip was beginning to feel a relief in his gut that perhaps his part of the deal with Julia might happen. "I so appreciate it. I fear that she already has a romantic interest though. The local veterinarian, Dr. McDonald I believe his name is."

Brenda's face became tight and her eyes glittered with anger. "Sean McDonald?"

"You know of him?" Philip was amazed at the anger shooting from the woman's eyes. "I got him out of my daughter's life once. Damned if I won't do it again!"

CHAPTER NINE

Upstairs, in one of the bedrooms where Maggie was applying wallpaper, the afternoon sun was making the room like an oven. The furnace company was outside installing the new central air conditioning unit and their promise was to have it completed by the end of the day. Her back and arms ached from the exertion of putting the paper on the wall and she just wished that the chore was finished. Working alone for most of the week, since Ellie was busy with her boyfriend being in town, Maggie was worn out. The heat inside the upstairs was miserable and her arms were sticky from the paste she used to hang the pretty paper, embossed with tiny violets and sprigs of green. When she swiped an arm across her face to remove the perspiration that was beading on her lip, she could taste the paste and she made a face."Arrrgghh, this stuff is terrible."

"Well, you aren't supposed to eat it!" Sean startled her from where he stood in the doorway. His eyes danced with mirth.

Laughing, she stood back and surveyed the room. "I wasn't eating the paste. I was trying to wipe the sweat off my face!" She looked at him leaning against the door frame, one of his forearms resting on the wood and his long legs placed apart. He was probably the most attractive and sexy man she had ever met. His boyish grin melted her heart and she put a hand to her stomach to still the butterflies.

"Why don't you take a break this evening? Ellie and Todd suggested a barbecue and thought you might want to join us." Sean's jeans and boots were dusty, his cap having a piece of straw sticking to it. He had obviously been out visiting some farm or stable.

"Can we sit in the air conditioning? Please?" She climbed up the ladder again to smooth a wrinkle out of the last piece of paper she had put up. "I am so hot, thirsty, sweaty and miserable that if I don't get some relief soon, I feel like I"m going to melt into a puddle of muck on the floor."

"Well, I think we were planning on sitting out on the porch. There's a storm coming across the mountains so it should cool down some tonight. But if you insist upon air conditioning, we could go up to the bar and listen to the locals sing karaoke." He crossed over to where she was standing halfway up the ladder and grinning, he reached out and tucked a stray piece of hair behind Maggie's ear.

"Well, I think barbecue sounds good and so does sitting on the porch. Would you like for me to bring something?" Mentally, she tried to think of something that she could fix that wouldn't require using the stove.

"How about you just bring yourself? I'm making the ribs and Ellie is doing the rest. That is, if I can pull her away from Todd long enough." He made a face that was bordering on a scowl and then shook his head. "Those two. That's all I can say.""

"What time would you like me to come by?" Glancing at her watch, she could see that it was already close to four. It would take at least an hour to clean up the wallpaper mess as well as cleaning herself up.

"I could come back and get you in an hour." Sean bent down and helped pick up some of the pieces of wallpaper that she had tossed on the floor.

"No, that's alright. I will drive in to your place. It's too inconvenient for you to drive me back home later." She stood and admired the view as he was bending over to pick up the wallpaper and then mentally slapped herself. *Stop it! You don't want to go there.*

Agreeing that she would drive in to town as soon as she cleaned up, Sean retreated down the stairs leaving Maggie to finish the cleanup. Sometime later after she had showered and her hair was wrapped in a towel, she heard a knock at the door. *Damn, who could that be? I am already running behind here!* The furnace man had already spoken to her about the air conditioner not being operational until morning and Sean should be at home cooking.

Descending the steps, she heard Mama barking and a female voice telling the dog to go away. Recognizing the nasal tone, her heart sank. *Oh brother, this is just what I need!* Standing on the porch outside the screen door was a familiar figure dressed in a designer, linen suit. Approaching the doorway with dread, she came to stand just inside the door and gazed out at the woman standing there. "Mother, what are you doing here?"

"Margaret, is that any way to greet your mother?" Brenda reached for the door handle and pulled the screen open with two fingers as if she were afraid she would dirty her hand. "I have driven all this way to try to talk some sense into you." Pushing into the room she gazed with disdain at the simple furnishings. "Whatever has gotten into you? I didn't raise you to live like this." Dramatically, she swept around the room, using her arms to make her point.

"Mother, I don't have time for your dramatic scenes this evening. I am running late for an appointment." She didn't have the patience to deal with her mother this evening. For the fact that she loved her mother because of who she was to her, she didn't love the person that her mother was on a personal level. It was all about money and prestige to her, nothing about love or caring or loyalty. She shook her head and walked over to take a piece of mail out of her mother's hand that she felt she had the right to pick up and look at.

"Margaret, why did you come back down here to this dirty, old farm when you could be up in Chicago living in the condo?" She shook her head and feigned a cough. "My goodness, what is that smell?"

"If you remember correctly, Philip got the condo in the divorce." Tugging the towel from her hair, she reached in her purse and took out her hair brush. "Just where was I supposed to live?" Not that she would have lived in the condo if she had gotten in the divorce. It was too impersonal and cold.

"Philip called me. He said that he wants a reconciliation. How could you turn him down? You could have everything that a woman wants if you would just swallow that silly pride of yours and take the man back." She reached for another piece of mail on the table and Maggie grabbed it before her mother could pick it up.

"Oh please! Like I would have that cheating pig back in my life! The audacity of him to call you after I told him to get out of here and never come back." She was getting angry and she just wanted her mother to leave.

"Margaret, sometimes a woman has to overlook certain indiscretions to have what she wants from life. He says he loves you and I believe him. He's waiting in Knoxville for you to come to your senses..." In a move designed to feign caring for her daughter, she reached out to touch Maggie's arm. "Maggie, I know it hurts the first time it happens but eventually you are able to see past it because of all the wonderful things that a good husband is able to offer you."

"Mother, you go to Knoxville and tell him that I'm not interested. I came to my senses a long time ago when I quit pretending that we ever had a marriage. Now, if you don't mind, I need to get dressed for my appointment." By this time, she had reached the screen door and held it open, motioning with her hand for her mother to leave.

"Margaret, I will not leave here until I have talked some sense into you. What do you have here but a dumpy old house in the middle of nowhere with a mangy dog to keep you company?"

"This is my home now, so you and Philip might as well get used to it. I certainly hope that you don't mind waiting in your car. I have to get ready and I really don't need you following me around while I get dressed." Maggie left her mother standing in the middle of the dining room while she went back upstairs to get dressed. Taking her time, she selected a pair of jean shorts and tank top and slipped into a pair of sandals. To kill more time, she applied a touch of mascara and lip gloss. Finally, she went back downstairs only to find her mother still standing in the middle of the dining room where she left her. "Excuse me, but I need to lock up before I leave." Even though she didn't normally lock the house, she went through the motions just to avoid her mother's interference. Brenda followed her around as she did so, making snide comments about the house and sniffing here and there making remarks about some odor she detected.

"Margaret, don't be silly. Grab your bags and come back to Knoxville with me. We have a suite in a very nice hotel and Philip is waiting patiently for us there. Such a sweet man to wait for you to get over your little lapse in judgment."

"Mother! You haven't heard me! I am not going back to Knoxville with you!" Taking a deep breath, she continued. "I am not going to go back to Philip and I'm not going to go back to Chicago!" Briskly, she walked over to the door and held it open again. "Go home to your husband and stay out of my business."

"I'll give you a few days, dear. Then I'll be back and we can talk some more." Brenda held her head up as she walked out the front door with Maggie behind her. "Don't bother. There's nothing else to talk about."

Driving to Sean's cabin, Maggie muttered to herself. "The nerve of her coming here trying to tell me what to do." Thunder rumbled in the distance and lightening split through the clouds that were moving over the mountains. The incoming storm matched her mood. "How dare he call my mother and ask her to intervene for him." The rain started pelting the windshield and she switched on the wipers. "I'm a grown woman and I don't need either of them trying to convince me to leave here. Coming here was like coming home from a long, miserable trip with people that I don't even like to be around." Suddenly, the car veered toward the ditch and she felt the front tire bumping against the pavement. Easing the car off the road, she sat for a moment before venturing out into the rain. The right, front tire was flat. "Damn it all to hell!" Kicking the tire for good measure, she walked back around the car and got back in. Picking up her cell phone from the seat, she dialed Sean's number and told him what had happened. Securing a promise from him that he would call a tow truck and be there in a few minutes to get her, she hung up and laid her head back against the seat to wait.

CHAPTER TEN

Maggie sat on the porch, holding a paper plate full of ribs, potato salad and baked beans. She had all but forgotten the confrontation with her mother. Todd had finished cooking the ribs while Sean went to pick her up, and his tee shirt was stained with barbecue sauce. Ellie sat on the rail, her feet propped on Todd's chair. Sean uncapped two bottles of beer and handed one to Maggie. She had calmed considerably from the confrontation with her mother then the flat tire fiasco.

"Thank you. These are the best ribs that I've ever eaten." She tipped the bottle and took a long drink of the ice-cold brew. The last time she had drank a beer was when she was in college at a party. Philip never would have beer in the house, he was convinced that beer was for rednecks.

"Secret family recipe." Sean grinned as he took a drink of his own beer. "Best ribs this side of the Mississippi." He smugly wiped some sauce off his fingers and shrugged his shoulders.

Ellie burst out laughing. "Don't let him fool you. He grabbed a bottle barbecue sauce at the store and added some Tabasco sauce to it."

Her comment was answered with a grunt from Sean. The rain fell steadily, with an occasional flash of lightening and rumble of thunder. The air was considerably cooler since they had been sitting on the porch. Country music drifted through the open door into the night. Todd entertained them with stories about his roommates in Indiana, a group of die-hard jokesters that were continually getting into trouble at school for playing practical jokes. Sean joined in with tales about how he and his classmates used to terrorize the sorority sisters with jars of dissected animals placed strategically around their house. One of the sisters was a veterinary student in his class and helped the guys sneak the jars in when the other girls were out.

When they were finished eating, Maggie helped Ellie clear away the paper plates, napkins, and empty beer bottles from the porch while Sean and Todd were searching for a deck of cards in the house. Maggie felt the effects from the two beers she drank before and during dinner, and when she tripped over her own feet, both women sat down and laughed until they cried.

"What's so funny?" Todd came out on the porch and handed Maggie another beer. He raised an eyebrow at the two women laughing hysterically and then shook his head. "Women."

"I think we need to cut Maggie off, she can't even stand on her own two feet without tripping." Ellie wiped the tears from her eyes.

"Is that so? Maggie, do you want that other beer?" Sean joined them on the porch, holding a deck of cards in his hand.

Maggie took another drink from her beer. *After the day that I've had, so what if I get a little bit drunk tonight?* "I'm just fine and I think a little more beer will make me even better. Are you guys ready to lose at euchre?"

Sitting around the picnic table, the foursome bickered over who was cheating and who wasn't. Outside, the storm increased in intensity and the lights flickered before finally going out altogether. Sean retrieved a camping lantern and lit it, immersing the room into a yellow glow. When he turned around he caught Ellie mouthing something to Maggie.

"That's it! I caught you talking across the table to Maggie! That's cheating." Sean towered over his niece and attempted to look at the cards in her hand.

"Oh, aren't you sneaky! Trying to look over the top of Ellie's head to see what was in her hand! That's cheating, too!" She climbed on the bench, grabbed the hat off Sean's head and put it on top of her own, with the bill facing backwards. In response, Sean grabbed Maggie around the waist and deposited her back in her seat.

"Ok, enough of this cheating. Todd! Hurry with those beers and we will proceed to beat these girls at a game of cards!"

"Don't you mean that you will get beat by us girls?" Maggie leaned across the table and gave Ellie a high five. Sometime later, they were tied at six points each and Ellie dealt Maggie a loner which made the girls the winners of the game. Three more empty beer bottles sat in front of Maggie and she was having trouble focusing.

Todd got up from the table and smirked. "Well Sean, I guess that it's you and me cleaning the kitchen."

"Sure you don't want to play the best two out of three?" Sean took the last swig from his bottle of beer as he remained seated at the table and looked around at the rest of them with a crooked smile on his face.

Ellie yawned and looked across the table at Maggie, who was having trouble keeping her eyes open. "I think that we won and you guys can clean the kitchen while we go and sit in front of the television and pretend that the electricity is on." Nodding, Maggie got up from the bench and stumbled a little.

Sean reached over to steady her. "Whoa there, think maybe you might have had a little too much beer to drink little lady. Come on. Let me help you into the living room."

Maggie let herself be led over to the sofa and sank down into the cushions. Closing her eyes and tucking her legs under her in the corner, she felt the room lurch along with her stomach.

Ellie carried the camping lantern over and put it on the coffee table and removed a book from the chair. "We'll be here waiting for you guys to get the kitchen cleaned."

ꕥꕥꕥꕥꕥꕥꕥꕥꕥꕥꕥ

When Sean came back in the room later, Maggie was asleep. "Ellie, why don't you go to my bedroom and pull back the covers. I will carry her up and settle her in and then sleep down here on the sofa. Todd, you get the recliner."

He lifted her petite frame easily into his arms and she rested her head against his chest. He about came undone when she nuzzled his neck and he laughed nervously. “Stop that or you may find company in that bed.” He whispered into her ear as he ascended the staircase.

"Mmmm...In that case..." She nuzzled his neck again and wrapped a slender arm around his shoulders.

"Maggie..." Walking across the bedroom, he lay her down on the sheets and pulled the quilt to her chin. "Please, don't test my control. I don't want to feel guilty for taking advantage of you while you are drunk." He removed his cap from her head and leaned down, brushing his lips across her forehead.

"Don't you want to just lay down here with me for a minute?" Maggie murmured through lips that were full and beckoning then lifted a heavy arm to touch his chest.

"Oh Maggie...I don't want to just lay here with you for a minute." He lowered his head again and brushed his lips across her mouth. "I could lay here with you forever. But not tonight." A smile split his face as she started snoring; he kissed her forehead again and tucked the quilt around her sleeping form. Next in line was going to be a cold shower. Instead, he took a moment to sit on the bed and watch her sleep. How had things gone so wrong between them? He had wanted a future with her and she had pushed him away. That’s what had gone wrong. He shook his head then stood and headed for the stairs.

CHAPTER ELEVEN

The morning sun danced across the quilt and Maggie opened one eye, uncertain at first where she was. Her head was pounding and her mouth was dry. Turning her head into the pillow, she inhaled and smelled the masculine scent of cologne. *Oh my God! I got drunk and passed out last night.* Reaching across the bed, she patted the empty space. Poor Sean, he must have slept on the sofa last night.

Groaning, her eyes opened again and the sun coming in from the skylight above the bed assaulted her. The sound of voices came from below, and she thought that she recognized a female voice. She pushed the quilt back and slid out of bed as quietly as possible, then walked over to the rail where she could see who was downstairs talking to Sean. Brenda stood in the middle of the living room holding her check book. "How much is it going to take to get you to leave my daughter alone?" Sean ran his fingers through his damp hair. "Mrs. Davisson, I don't know what makes you think that money is the answer to everything. Not everyone can be bought off." He glanced toward the loft railing and Maggie ducked out of sight.

"Dr. McDonald, my daughter is too good to live down here like a hillbilly. I'm sure if it weren't for you, Margaret would go back to Chicago. I am prepared to offer you twenty thousand dollars..." Brenda trailed off and Maggie watched wide eyed as her mother started writing out a check.

"Mrs. Davisson, Maggie came down here without even knowing that I was here. What makes you think that I'm the reason she is staying here?"

"Margaret is accustomed to having the best of everything. She would never settle for living down here in this Podunk hole of a town surrounded by a bunch of inbreeds." Brenda tore the check from the checkbook and held it out to him. "Here, a check for twenty thousand dollars."

Sean glared at the woman standing in front of him. "Maggie's life is worth a lot more than your money could ever buy. She's happy with her plans; I have nothing to do with her being here."

"Come now, doctor. The girl was infatuated with you as a teenager that summer. She found other interests when she returned to Chicago in the fall. If I hadn't run interference when you appeared in Chicago that day..."

Neither Sean nor Brenda heard Maggie come down the stairs and she now stood directly behind them. "Mother, what the hell are you talking about? What do you mean that you ran interference when Sean came to Chicago?" Her brown eyes glittered with unshed tears of anger.

Brenda tried to shove the check into Sean's hand and was unsuccessful, the check fluttering to the floor. "Margaret, what are you doing here?"

Stalking up to stand in front of her mother, she straightened her back and glared. "I asked you a question. What did you mean about running interference when he came to Chicago. Tell me the truth, Mother!"

"Now Margaret, you know that it was for your own good. Everything that I did was for your own good. What kind of life would you have had with a small-town veterinarian compared to the life Philip gave you?" Brenda's eyes flitted back and forth between Maggie and Sean. "You had the best of everything in Chicago."

"No Mother, I didn't have the best of everything. I was miserable. I cried myself to sleep every night during that Christmas season. Then I cried myself to sleep on the nights that my perfect husband was busy screwing everything that wore a skirt. How dare you!"

Brenda reached out and tried to grab her daughter's arm. "Margaret, listen to me. You don't belong here..."

"Shut up! I want you to pick up your damn check and get in your car and never come back! I don't want to see you again until you realize that you cannot play games with my life. Twenty thousand dollars! Is that all I'm worth to you? Get out!" Fighting back tears of fury and despair, Maggie ran out of the room and locked herself in the bathroom. Once alone behind the closed door, the tears came fast and furious while her shoulders heaved from her sobs.

All these years I thought that Sean deserted me, that he broke his promise to me. I accepted it and went on with my miserable life and didn't look back. How could my own mother do this to me? And why didn't Sean try harder to reach me? Finally, coming out of the bathroom, she found Sean leaning against the rail on the porch. Her bare feet were soundless when she crossed over to stand next to him. "Sean, would you mind taking me home now?" Looking down at her tear stained face, he started to put a comforting hand on her shoulder but she drew away.

"Please Maggie, don't shut me out. I didn't know, I *really* didn"t. How could I have been so damned stupid not to believe in what we had together, believe in you?" His blue eyes pleaded with her.

"Please Sean, I just want to go home and be alone for a while." The throbbing in her head was intensified from crying and from the brief glance in the bathroom mirror, was aware that her eyes were puffy and red. "I need to pull myself together."

~~~~~~~~~~~~

The path along the creek was lined with wildflowers, ferns, and rhododendron plants.
~~~~~~~~~~~~

Maggie walked slowly along the path, reflecting on the events of the morning. Sean was silent during the drive back to farm, and he didn't try to follow her up to the house when she climbed out of the truck. She imagined that they both had a lot of things on their minds today. Mama and her puppies were trailing alongside of Maggie as she walked, they would occasionally stop to sniff at a plant or chase a butterfly. The puppies were getting old enough now that she should start trying to find homes for them. Her plan was to keep Mama, the big dog was a great watch dog and living out here alone, the company of a pet would be welcome.

Overhead, a hawk glided through the cloudless sky on a hunting expedition. Finally, sitting down on a fallen log by the creek, she closed her eyes and let the peacefulness of her surroundings ease her worried thoughts. The big dog sat down and laid her head on Maggie's lap. She absently stroked the dog's fur. "You've got it easy, old girl. Someone feeds you, bathes you, and makes sure you have shelter. A dog's life is so uncomplicated." A big, wet tongue licked her hand in response. "Nobody meddling in your life. No broken hearts to mend. How nice would that be?"

Going over finances had been her outlet upon returning home from Sean's. It helped to take her mind off her raw feelings for a short period, but added to her distress when she realized how rapidly her funds were depleting. Determined more than ever to make this venture a success, decided it was best to sell the car and buy an older model truck. If she could transport her own supplies and furniture, it would save her delivery expenses. Besides, she hated the Lincoln anyway. Then she went into the bedroom and opened her jewelry box. The platinum wedding ring set as well as a couple of other pieces of expensive jewelry, gifts from Philip, twinkled at her. She'd just sell those, too. Perhaps, even check to see if Char needed help down at the bar and grill.

With the finance issue partially solved, her mind replayed the events of the morning. Anger was replaced by a sense of betrayal as she thought of her mother's admission to meddling in her life. Hate was not an emotion that Maggie was familiar with, and she didn't hate her mother. Brenda had always been a woman of appearances. If she had a nice home and expensive things as well as a place in society, she could put on the appearance of being happy. Happiness to her was measured in dollar signs. That's why Brenda hadn't been happy in her marriage to Maggie's father. He was a man who enjoyed the simple things in life, his happiness coming from family and genuine friendships. Her mother would never have been permitted to interfere in Maggie's life had he still been alive.

Mama's ears pricked up and she looked watched down the path. A low growl emanated from her throat before she got up from her resting place and started barking. Maggie then heard a female voice calling her name. Rising from the log, she retraced her steps on the path toward the house. Mama darted off in front and Maggie called her back. Uncertain who was calling her; they may not be too keen on the massive mutt running up to them. The car in the drive was a late model compact with a rental company tag on the front. A tall, slender form came out of the barn and Maggie recognized the mass of blonde curls.

"Dixie!" She ran across the lawn and hugged the other woman, while Mama ran circles around the two women. "What are you doing here?"

The lanky woman tossed her thick curls and grinned. "I've decided to spend my vacation helping you out down here." Dixie motioned toward the car that was loaded down with cartons. "I stopped at every yard sale I could find. Let's go unload this junk and catch up on things."

The animal hospital waiting room was full of four legged patients when Sean arrived an hour late. Ellie volunteered Todd to help her with some of the simple things such as flea dips and dispensing of heart worm tablets. Both sighed with relief as Sean entered through the back door and went through to the waiting area to call back the first furry patient. He busied himself with attending to the animals, making it easy to keep his mind off Maggie as he talked with their owners and dispensed vaccinations or soothed pets that tended to get nervous as soon as they smelled the antiseptic clinic. When he went into his private office, he riffled through the stack of pink message slips Ellie had left on his desk and put them in order of how he would attend to them later.

By the end of the day, he was determined to finish up in the clinic and go out to talk to Maggie. He went to get his last patient from the waiting room. Bonnie was a fifteen-year-old beagle that was having difficulty with her hips. The dog was well past her hunting days, as was her owner who now stood with the glimmer of tears in his watery blue eyes. This was still one of the hardest parts of Sean's profession, to have to give the advice to the old man that he was about to give.

"Max, Bonnie here is having a lot of pain. I can't do anything to help her anymore." He crossed over to the old man and lay a hand on his shoulder. "We've talked about this a couple of times and I know this is a hard decision to have to make, but we're to the point that the best choice for her is to let her go." He felt the man tremble under his hand and he squeezed gently.

Max Fisher looked up at Sean as he leaned on his cane. "Doc, I know it's the best thing to do." He nodded his head and hobbled over to the examining table where the dog lay. His hand touched the old dog's back and her aged brown eyes reached out to him. "It's gonna be lonely around that ol' house without you little lady. You've been my partner for a long time." A tear rolled down the man's weathered face and he brushed it away with his sleeve. A gnarled hand stroked the dog's fur and her trusting, brown eyes gazed at her owner. "I'm gonna miss you, Bonnie." He gripped the table and bowed his head.

After Sean administered the shot and Bonnie closed her eyes for the last time, he led Max into his office and helped him into a chair. Crossing over to the small refrigerator, he took out a bottle of water and handed it to the man. Already, his mind was on a solution to the old man's pain. "Max, I have an idea." Sean propped his lean frame against the desk. "A friend of mine has a litter of puppies that are ready to find homes. What do you say we drive out there and look?" He knew that one of the puppies wouldn't replace Bonnie, but it might help ease Max's loneliness for companionship.

"Aw, Doc. I don't know 'bout that. I'm an old man and probably won't be around a long time..." He bowed his head again before continuing. "Guess it won't hurt to go and look, would it?" Sean grinned and stood up. "Hang on a second while I go get my keys. We'll take a ride out there."

CHAPTER TWELVE

Both women sat in the middle of the living room floor among boxes of treasures. Maggie picked up a pair of white throw pillows with tiny violets embroidered on them. "These are absolutely perfect for one of the guest bedrooms upstairs." Dixie sat Indian-style on a large floor cushion and grinned, her blue eyes dancing. "Not bad for fifty cents, huh?"

"You've got to be kidding? You only paid fifty cents for these?" Maggie laid them aside and reached into another box, pulling out a full-sized Texas star quilt. "This is awesome!" She was already picturing it in one of the other bedrooms atop of the old iron bed frame she found out in the barn. It was sanded down, painted black, and waiting for a mattress set.

"I think I stopped at every garage sale between here and Chicago. If I liked something, I bought it!" Stretching out her long legs in front of her, she looked around the room. "Looks like I should have rented a truck and brought you some furniture for this living room so I wouldn't have to sit on the floor."

Maggie laid the quilt down and wrinkled up her forehead. "I just haven't had time to go look for furniture. Besides, the delivery charges for bringing furniture from Knoxville are outrageous."

"Well, you and I are going shopping first thing tomorrow. We'll tie the stuff on top of old

Philip's Lincoln and drive down the highway like the Beverly Hillbillies!"

"Actually, I'm thinking of selling the Lincoln and buying a truck. Use the extra money for the furniture and load it in the truck to save delivery charges." Maggie grinned and jumped up. "Can't you just imagine the look on his face when he finds out that I sold his precious car to buy a truck and some furniture?"

"How would he know that you did that?" Dixie frowned at her friend, her disgust for the man who had hurt her friend obvious on her face.

"You mean you didn't know he came down here?" She set down a set of candle holders that she was admiring and frowned at her friend.

"I haven't seen that philandering pig since the day that he came by while you were staying with me last year." Dixie's eyes widened. "You mean that he came down here?"

Nodding her head and picking up a vase that she had plucked from one of the boxes, she chided herself for thinking that Dixie had told Philip where she was. "Yes, he showed up last week begging me to take him back. He was awful." She remembered the derisive way he looked around her home.

Leaning over, Dixie put a hand on her friend's arm. "What did he say?"

"It doesn't matter. Sean came in and made him leave." She shrugged her shoulders and moved her position since her legs were starting to go to sleep.

Astonished, Dixie grabbed Maggie's arm and squeezed. "Are you talking about the same Sean that dumped you when you were a senior in high school? The one that you cried over for weeks?" Her forehead wrinkled in a frown. "What was he doing here? Looks like I'm just in time to save you from doing something dumb."

Sighing, Maggie pushed her hair back from her face. "It's not like I thought it was. It seems that my mother chased him off when he showed up in Chicago for Christmas break that winter. I found out this morning when she showed up at Sean's..."

"Wait, what the hell was she doing at Sean's? Never mind, what were you doing at Sean's this morning? Did you spend the night there?" Dixie tossed her curls and narrowed her eyes. "This is certainly getting to be an interesting conversation and I can't wait to hear more. Never mind I was worried a minute ago about my bestie running back into the arms of a man who had broken her heart years ago."

"Apparently, Philip called and asked Mother to try to convince me to come back to Chicago with him." She fingered a lacy doily and shook her head. "And the rest isn't like it sounds. I had dinner there last night and drank too much beer after my car had a flat. It made sense at the time."

"Girl, you are going to have to tell me the whole sordid story later. I hear a car outside." She jumped up from her spot on the floor and held out a hand to help Maggie up. "We're going to have to open a bottle of wine and you are going to tell all. I love a good story and it sounded like this was a major one."

When they went outside on the porch, Sean had pulled his truck in the drive with an elderly man seated next to him. They watched while he got out of the truck and went around to help the old man down from the cab. The old man was clutching his cane in front of him as he stared at the big dog with her litter of pups trailing after her.

Dixie put a hand on Maggie's shoulder. "Look, he's trembling and looks so sad."

Sean waved at them with one hand as he helped the old man up the lawn toward them. "Hey Maggie, this here's Max Fisher and he wanted to come look at your puppies."

"She sure is a nice lookin' gal." Max smiled as two of the puppies started fighting and their mother nosed them apart. "Nice lookin' little pups, too." He leaned toward Sean. "Which one of these pretty girls belongs to you?" The old man chuckled as Sean's face colored at the comment. Max socked him in the arm. "Come on doc, which one are you takin' a fancy to?"

"Come on, Max. I'll introduce you to Maggie Coulter; she was Doug Coulter's granddaughter. You remember him, don't you?" Sean led him up to the porch and introduced him to Maggie. "I'm not sure who your friend is."

Maggie felt her heart flutter as Sean kept a protective arm on the old man. All she could think of was how much time she had wasted. Years. Years that she could have been by Sean's side. She felt Dixie elbow her in the ribs. "Oh, I"m sorry. This is Dixie Thomas. We've been friends since middle school. Dixie, this is Sean McDonald."

Sean gestured toward the old man, who was now bending down letting the puppies nip at his fingers, he continued. "Max here is looking for a puppy. He lost his dog today and I thought maybe one of these critters might fill the gap she left."

Her face heart ached with sympathy. "I'm sorry, Mr. Fisher. You are certainly welcome to take one of the puppies if you like." She walked over and extended a hand to him and he gripped it tightly. "You take your time and pick the one that you like the most."

Dixie stepped forward and held out a hand. "Hello there Sean McDonald. I'm pleased to meet you. I think. I'll reserve my opinion for now."

Taking the hand that was extended, Sean nodded at Dixie. "Well, take your time forming an opinion."

Max picked up the runt of the litter, a female that was solid black except for a white streak on the top of her head. Even though she was the smallest of the puppies, she was the most aggressive of the bunch. She would often instigate a fight by running up to one of her brothers or sisters, barking and nipping at them while they tried to sleep. Now, she was wriggling in the old man's hands and trying to lick at his face as he held her against his chest. "You sure are a feisty one." Max laughed as the puppy was finally successful in her quest to lick his face.

Maggie walked up to Max and put a hand on his arm. "It looks like she likes you. You ought to take her home with you." Nodding, he glanced over to where Sean stood watching Maggie. "Doc, you think it'd be alright if we took her now in your truck?"

"Sure thing, Max. I can even get you some puppy food when we get back to the clinic. On the house." He watched as Maggie kissed the puppy's soft, furry head. "They are pretty much weaned and you did say you wanted to find good homes for them. Max will give this one a good home."

She nodded and smiled. "I have no doubts. Please, Mr. Fisher, let me carry her to the truck for you." Maggie walked with them back to Sean's truck and she held the puppy while Sean helped Max up into the cab. He watched while she placed the puppy in Max's lap and gave it one last pat on the head. "You be good for Mr. Fisher, you little scamp."

Sean smiled across the cab at her. "Do you need a ride to pick up your car later? Dave, down at the garage said that it's ready anytime."

Smiling, she shook her head. "Thanks for offering, Sean. But Dixie's here and she can run me into town in a little bit. Maybe I can show her Char's bar and grill on karaoke night, huh?"

He grinned and nodded. "Should be a real treat for a city gal. See you later, Maggie."

She went back on the porch to stand with Dixie as the truck rolled down the lane to the road. Her emotions were a mess but there was one thing she knew. Her heart still fluttered at the sight of Sean McDonald. But what she was going to do with that, she didn't know.

"He sure is a hot one. No wonder you're all flushed." Dixie snickered at her side. "Does he have a twin brother by any chance?"

"Stop it. You are incorrigible." She laughed at the look on her friend's face.

"You aren't getting by this easy. You are going to have to tell all." Dixie put an arm around her shoulders. "Come on, let's go finish unpacking these boxes of things while you tell me the whole story. Did you have sex with him last night?"

"No. I did not have sex with him last night. I was drunk and passed out at his house." She pulled open the screen door. "Now, quit trying to get a story that isn"t there."

CHAPTER THIRTEEN

The Thursday evening crowd was already filling up the booths at Char's Place. Thursday was karaoke night, and for some reason, it was always the busiest night of the week unless Char invited a budding band to entertain her patrons. She was bustling around the room delivering orders and greeting new customers when Maggie and Dixie walked in.

"Hey there, Maggie girl." She grinned and walked over to them. "I've got those flower arrangements ready for you at the house. Do you want me to have Tom bring 'em out tomorrow?" She lifted a hand as another couple came in the door.

"That would be fine, Char. I don't really have any furniture to set them on right now, but I'll be working on it." She smiled at her new friend who had been excited to do the flower arrangements for her. "Can we get a booth? This is my friend, Dixie. She came down from Chicago to help me out over her vacation."

Char surveyed the tall woman cautiously. "Pleased to meet you. I hope you aren't like the other snobby witch from Chicago. Why don't you both grab a booth before they are all taken and I'll grab you something to drink."

Seated in a corner booth, Dixie leaned over so that Maggie could hear her above the din of the busy bar and grill. "She reminds me of a young Dolly Parton. The accent and the blonde hair, not to mention the boobs."

"Oh Dixie, behave yourself. People down here are super nice and friendly. It's not like being up in Chicago where everyone is too busy keeping to themselves." She couldn't help but smile at Dixie's analogy, though.

Char approached the table with two drinks on her tray. "I hope you both wanted iced tea. I guess I should have asked." She placed the drinks on the table and set down two sets of silverware wrapped in napkins. "Is iced tea alright with you, Dixie? I knew that was what Maggie here wanted."

Dixie grinned and nodded. "Iced tea is fine with me. I will just need some real sugar to put in it instead of this powdery fake stuff."

Tipping back her head, Char burst out laughing. "Honey, if you want real southern iced tea with plenty of sugar, I'll bring you some. This unsweetened stuff I only make for Maggie here, she's the only one who will drink it." Picking up one of the glasses she bustled off to the kitchen.

"So, what is good to eat here?" Dixie looked over the top of her menu and raised an eyebrow. "And I sure as hell hope they've got some good beer on tap for later."

"I haven't eaten anything that wasn't good in the few times I've been here." Maggie understood it wasn't Chicago cuisine, but it sure was good hearty food. If it weren't for all the work she was doing out at the farm, she would have surely packed on pounds from the meals she ate here.

"Do they have big, greasy cheeseburgers? The kind with all the fixings and fries on the side?" Dixie ran her tongue over her lips making a ridiculously outrageous smacking sound.

Grinning, Maggie wondered how Dixie managed to stay so slender with all the fattening food she liked to eat. "Yes, they have them. And they grill them on a char-broiler so they taste like they came off an outside grill."

Char set down Dixie's drink in front of her. "What are you girls gonna have? I've got fried chicken on special tonight, if you're interested." She held a pad poised in her hand, even though Maggie discovered that she never needed to write down what someone wanted to order because she had a fantastic memory.

"Give us both a cheeseburger and fries. Maggie here needs some meat on her bones." Folding her menu then snatching Maggie's, she handed them both back to Char. "Make sure to put everything on them, too." She flashed a smile at the woman. "And give me the bill."

When Char had gone, Dixie leaned across toward Maggie again. "Don't even think about arguing with me. You're gonna eat that cheeseburger and like it."

"I wasn't going to argue about the cheeseburger, I had planned on getting one anyways. But you aren't going to pay the bill, I am." Maggie gave her friend a stubborn look but she knew that Dixie would win out in the end anyway.

"Bullshit." Dixie crossed her arms in front of her. "I'd have had to spend more if I took vacation somewhere else than what it's going to cost me to stay with you and eat at this place." Her eyes followed a tall, dark haired man in a cowboy hat as he walked up to the bar. "And the scenery is better." She winked an eye and motioned toward the man at the bar.

Giggling, Maggie chastised her friend. "Shame on you, what would poor Roger do if he knew you were down here checking out cowboys?"

The smile on Dixie's face faded. "Roger and I aren't together anymore. He decided that marriage wasn't for him so he broke off the engagement. That's part of why I came down here on vacation."

Maggie reached across the table and put her hand on top of Dixie's. "I'm sorry, Dixie. You didn't say anything when we've talked on the phone."

Sniffing back tears, Dixie attempted to smile. "It happened two weeks ago. He said that he felt stifled, that he needed space. I think he just wanted to hang out with his college buddies watching sports and going to Hooters." She dabbed at her eyes with a napkin. "Let's change the subject. Why don't you tell me about you and the animal doctor?"

Over their cheeseburgers, Maggie related the events of the past couple of weeks. She told Dixie about Philip's visit, then her mother's. Finally, she told her that it appeared that instead of Sean dumping her; it was her mother who had made it look as if Maggie didn't want anything to do with Sean.

"So, what are you going to do? Make a play for the handsome hunk?" Dixie grinned and winked at her friend. "He sure is good on the eyes. That tall, lean body sure looked pretty good to me."

"Will you get your mind out of the gutter?" Maggie laughed at her friend. "I don't have time for making a play for anyone. And I seriously doubt if he would be interested in me when he has this smooth realtor chasing after him."

As if on cue, Julia Evans walked into the bar and grill. Tonight, she wore a red silk shirt with designer jeans and a pair of high heeled sandals. She looked around the room as if searching for someone, then walked over to the bar and said something to the bartender. When he shook his head then shrugged his shoulders, she said something else and shortly, the bartender was placing a foamy glass of beer in front of her. She turned around on her stool and searched the room again. Her eyes came to rest on Maggie and Dixie, before she got up and started to walk their way.

"Oh God, speak of the devil and here she comes." Maggie rolled her eyes and Dixie looked up to see the woman approach.

"Hello there. We didn't get to chat the other night at Sean's." She extended a manicured hand. "Remember me? I'm Julia Evans. Do you mind if I join you girls until my companion arrives?" Not waiting for permission, she slid into the booth forcing Maggie to make room for her.

Dixie spoke up and gave the woman a pointed look. "I'm Dixie Thomas, Maggie's friend from Chicago. We were kind of talking business here, if you don't mind." Her blue eyes shot an icy stare at the woman.

"Oh no, not at all. I love to talk business. I'm into real estate. In fact, I've been meaning to get out your way to see if maybe we could come to an arrangement that would suit both of us." Her attention was on Maggie.

"What kind of arrangement could possibly suit both of us?" Maggie's tone was suspicious as she questioned the woman.

"Why, I thought maybe you might want to sell that property out there to a developer and make yourself a tidy profit."

"My property is not for sale. I have other plans for it." Silently, she wished the woman would just go away. She wanted Sean and she wanted her property? There was no way that was going to happen, at least on the property. What Sean did was his own business.

Julia put a hand on top of Maggie's. "I heard that you were going to open a bed and breakfast. Surely you understand that your location out there in the middle of nowhere doesn't make it feasible?" Her tone was condescending and filled with venom.

With a sarcastic tone, Dixie interjected. "Surely, without the experience of being in travel and tourism, you don't know squat about what people want when they plan a peaceful vacation."

Choosing to ignore Dixie, Julia went on. "Mrs. Stanford, I'm prepared to make you a really generous offer for the property. Then you could use the money to go back to Chicago and live the way you are accustomed to living."

"Miss Evans, I have no intention of selling my home to you or anyone else. Now, if you will excuse us..." She broke off her sentence as she saw Philip come into the bar. Both Dixie and Julia followed Maggie's gaze. Dixie's reaction was one of surprise; however, Julia smiled and motioned for him. "Philip, over here."

He approached the three women seated in the booth. Maggie was uncomfortable and would have left had her way not been blocked by Julia sitting next to her. "Good evening, ladies."

"Philip, this is Maggie Stanford and I'm not sure who her friend here is." She raised her eyebrows. "Oh my...are you any relation to Maggie? I just realized that you both have the same last name and you are both from Chicago. How silly of me!"

Philip nodded to the women. "Margo...Dixie...how are you this evening?"

Recovering first, Dixie spoke up. "Why Philip, we were doing fine until your sorry ass walked up. Why don't you take your little friend here and go find a table of your own?" The look she gave him was one of disdain. "Better yet, why don't you find another place to go have dinner?"

"Now Dixie, no need to be so rude to me. Is that any way to speak to an old friend?" Philip leaned down and kissed Julia on the temple. "You look lovely tonight, Julia."

"Why, thank you, Philip. I have been looking forward to this evening." She got up from the booth. "If you will excuse us, Philip and I have some business to talk about."

After they were out of hearing distance, Dixie hissed at Maggie. "I thought you said that he went back to Chicago?" Maggie raised a slender shoulder, her brown eyes troubled. "I thought he had until my mother told me yesterday that they were both staying in Knoxville in hopes that I would come to my senses and come back with them." Her stomach was in knots and she pushed her plate away, the cheeseburger and fries no longer appealing to her.

"Well, if you ask me, there's trouble brewing between those two." She motioned with her head toward Julia and Philip, who were now sitting with their heads close together in earnest conversation.

"Philip, we had a deal. You told me that you would get her to sell that property if I were to make a couple of calls to ensure that you got the Carter account. I kept up my end of the bargain and you got a really profitable account and promotion from it."

"Julia, I have tried to make her believe that I wanted her back. I've even convinced her mother that I wanted her back." He ran his fingers through his hair in exasperation. "Even her mother couldn't reason with her. It appears she's mixed up with some veterinarian here in town that she used to have a crush on when she was in high school. Her mother found her there this morning."

Julia straightened up in the chair. "Really? I assume that would be the good doctor McDonald?"

Nodding and taking a drink from his beer, Philip went on. "Yes, she was at his house this morning and her mother said it looked as if she'd spent the night there."

"Hmmm...this could be interesting. Perhaps if I worked on the good doctor myself. It wouldn't be a hardship in my opinion, as I *really* would like the distraction of a man while I'm stuck down here in the middle of nowhere. Besides, the good doctor owes me a rain check and by God, I'm going to get it." She gazed over at Maggie and Dixie who engaging in what looked to be a pretty serious conversation. "But the fact remains, Philip that you were supposed to make sure this happened."

"Well, I have another plan in mind that just might do it." He leaned across the table and started telling Julia about his plan.

CHAPTER FOURTEEN

Sean glanced out the truck window as he drove down Main Street. Across the street from Char's was the black Lincoln parked in front of a BMW with dealer plates. He drove up the street to the next available spot and parked the truck. By the look of the number of vehicles parked along the street, the diner was probably going to have a full house for karaoke. He grinned to himself as he imagined the various people who would get drunk tonight and sing in front of the whole bar. It was quite entertaining, and some of the people who got up to sing were pretty good. His legs carried him with long strides up the sidewalk toward the bar and grill in the warm, evening air and he could hear the din from inside Char's Place as he approached.

Just as he reached the entrance, he was about ploughed over by two women as they barged out the door onto the sidewalk. He reached out and put a hand on each of their shoulders to steady them. "Whoa, where are you two going so fast?"

The lanky blonde with the wild hair spoke up first. "The company in there leaves much to be desired. Maggie wanted to get out of there but I told her she should stay. I'll tell you what; those two are up to no good." She talked rapidly while her hands worked like she was signing.

Confused, Sean looked from Dixie to Maggie, taking in their frustrated expressions. "Wait a minute. You aren't making any sense. Who's up to no good?" Sean was confused and he stood blocking their way. "Tell me what's going on."

Maggie looked up at Sean, her dark eyes troubled. "Philip is in there having drinks with *your* friend the realtor." Her mouth was pressed into a thin line and her eyes occasionally darted to the door beside them.

Dixie's blue eyes were flashing. "Yeah, and I tell you, those two are up to no good. In there with their heads together like they are conspirators." She looked at her friend and continued. "I told Maggie she shouldn't let them run her off like this."

Pulling his cap off his head, he held it in his hands and shook his head in bewilderment. "Are you telling me that your ex-husband and Julia Evans are together?" He ran his fingers through his hair. "In Char's?" He couldn't picture the preppy Philip in their small bar and grill and as far as he knew, the only times Julia was ever in there was with him. Earlier today, Char called him to tell him that Maggie's mother was there earlier in the day asking questions about him. Leave it to Char to fill him in; she was probably on the phone before the woman ever got her lunch.

Dixie stomped her foot on the sidewalk and put her hands on her hips. "Yes, after she tried to convince Maggie to sell her the farm." Indignantly, she continued rambling. "She sat right down at our booth and tried to tell Maggie that a bed and breakfast would never make it out there in the middle of nowhere. She said she was waiting for her companion then the pig showed up."

Sean grinned at Dixie's description of Philip. He had other words to describe the prissy city boy in his fancy duds. "Is that right? Julia wanted to buy Maggie's farm?" He looked over at Maggie who was nervously watching the door as if she was afraid the city boy would come out any time. "Maggie, don't let that one bully you into doing anything. She's been steamrolling folks around here for months."

Dixie reached out and took hold of Sean's arm. "That's what I tried to tell her. I wanted to stay and see what this karaoke was all about." She smiled up at him with a determined look in her eyes. "Make her stay."

Sean shrugged his shoulders. To him it was quite simple. "Come on, girls. We're gonna go inside and listen to people make fools of themselves." He started to lead the way with Dixie right behind him, only turning around long enough to see Maggie backing away.

"Sean, I don't think it's a good idea. I'm really not up for dealing with Philip or that uppity bitch." Her feet remained unmoving on the sidewalk. "Why don't you and Dixie go ahead and I'll just go on home?"

"Nonsense, it's ridiculous for you to avoid having a little fun because of them." He took her hand and pulled her toward the door. She finally gave in and followed them into the bar. Inside, over the noise of the juke box, customers and pool balls being hit around the table Char called to them.

"Over here! Quick, before someone else comes in and grabs it." She motioned them over to the table she had just finished clearing.

Sean scanned the room for Julia and Philip and spotted them at the same time that Julia saw him. She smiled her sultry smile and motioned for him to come over to the table where she and Philip were seated, going so far as to take a chair from the table next to her and putting it up to their table. He merely lifted his hand in a wave and joined Dixie and Maggie at the table where they were now sitting.

Dixie was sitting comfortably with her long legs stretched out in front of her and Maggie was sitting as if she were ready to dart out the door at any time. Sean thought it would be a good choice if he were to sit blocking Maggie's view of Julia and Philip, so he slid his chair around to do just that. He was pleased to see that his gesture seemed to help Maggie relax a little, and he leaned toward her. "Let me know if you want me to toss him out on his ass." Winking, he nudged her with his shoulder and grinned across the table at Dixie. "What are we having to drink tonight?"

Sean was halfway through his first beer when the karaoke lists started circulating through the bar. As he started to pass the one that he was handed on to the next table, Dixie grabbed for it.

"Hang on there, big guy. I may want to try this out." She grinned and tossed her mane of hair as Sean handed her the booklet. "You aren't seriously going to get up there and sing, are you?" He watched as Maggie stared at her friend in dismay.

Writing her name and song down on one of the cards at the table, she handed it to Char as she walked by with a tray of drinks. "Why not? I sang in our high school choir once upon a time." She laughed at Maggie's stunned expression. "Besides, these people won't ever see me again once I go back to Chicago so what's the big deal?"

Maggie shook her head and sighed. "Ok, have it your way. Just don't come crying to me when they heckle you." The three of them sat through a pitiful rendition of Crystal Gayle's Blue Bayou, sung by a middle-aged woman in a pair of too-tight jeans and western shirt, her brown roots showing through her black, dyed hair. As the intoxicated woman crooned through the song, she staggered across the small stage in her cowboy boots while a group of people that were sitting at her table cheered her along.

Sometime through the third or fourth song, Sean noticed Philip get up from the table and head toward the exit shaking his head in disgust. *One down, one to go.* He avoided looking toward Julia, now sitting alone at her table. The last thing Maggie needed was for her to come over and park herself at their table. As if on cue, a young man in a cowboy hat came over and asked if they were using the one empty chair at their table. Relieved, Sean relinquished the chair to the kid.

The next couple singers weren't as bad as the first lady had been. In fact, Sean had to admit to himself, they were better than most he'd heard sing karaoke in Char's. The next person up was Dixie and she walked up to take the microphone among wolf whistles and hoots from some of the men in the bar. She had chosen to sing a Martina McBride song and as her voice rang out with the first few lines, the crowd cheered.

Maggie leaned over to Sean. "I had no idea she could still sing like that!"

Grinning, he nodded. "She sure is good." He was glad that Maggie finally appeared to be enjoying herself. However, that was short lived as her eyes narrowed and he turned to see Julia approaching the them.

"Hello Sean...how are you tonight?" She leaned over and kissed him on the cheek and draped an arm around his shoulders. "Does it have to be raining to take that rain check you offered the other night?" She murmured just loud enough for Maggie to hear, and then watched for a reaction.

Sean was pleased that Maggie just pretended to ignore the remark and watched as she turned toward the stage to continue watching Dixie perform even though he noticed that her posture stiffened a little bit. Sean leaned away from Julia, hoping that she would take the hint. *God, what was I thinking the other night when I asked for a rain check? This woman would eat me alive and spit me out in the morning.* He looked pointedly from her face to her arm draped around him hoping his body language would be enough of a hint.

"Come on, honey...I'd like to take you up on that rain check." She ran her hand across his shoulders and brushed her lips against his ear. He felt her breasts press against his shoulder as she leaned closer, her breath smelled of whiskey.

Sean scooted his chair away from her. "Julia, why don't you go back to your table before someone takes your seat? It's pretty crowded in here."

She glanced across at the chair that Dixie had vacated. "Why, I think there's an empty chair right here. How about I just sit with you?" She started to walk around the table and was immediately stopped by Maggie.

"Someone already is sitting in that chair. Why don't you go back to your own table and quit making a fool of yourself by hanging all over someone who obviously isn't interested in what you have to offer."

Sean sat back and watched the expression on Julia's face change from confidence to anger. This could get interesting. He took a drink of his beer and glanced around to see if anyone else was watching the exchange and was relieved to see almost everyone still had their attention on the stage where Dixie was singing. He had to admit that he was proud of Maggie for speaking up like that. This was another one of the differences in Maggie from when they were younger. He liked it.

"Grow up little girl and see what's right in front of your face." Julie spoke venomously and jerked her head toward Sean. "The good doctor and I have unfinished business from the other night if you understand what I mean."

Oh God, here we go. Sean felt his face redden at Julia's insinuation, even though it was true that he had started something the other night. He hesitated to consider whether he should intervene at this point and was surprised before he had a chance to do so, Maggie took over.

Maggie stood and drew herself up to her full height and poked a finger in the woman's face. "Well, it appears that the good doctor isn't interested in what you are selling tonight."

Sean was relieved when Dixie sang the final words of the song and almost everyone in the bar stood up and applauded. As she maneuvered her way between tables, the tall cowboy that she had admired earlier stepped in front of her. As Julia stood by their table, obviously seething, Sean and Maggie watched Dixie and the cowboy exchange a few words, and then he followed her to the table.

Dixie shoved past Julia, dismissing her. "Excuse me, you're in my way." She looked down at the other woman. "Better go back to your own table, there's no room for you here."

Julia glared at Dixie, then Maggie. "I'll be seeing you soon, honey." She touched Sean on the shoulder as she retreated from the table and made her way through the packed bar toward the door.

Not missing a beat, Dixie turned back to her companion and introduced him. "Maggie and Sean, this is Dane. He's in town visiting just like me." She laughed and pulled up an empty chair to the table. "Only he's from Nashville instead of Chicago."

Sean stood up and shook Dane's hand. "Sean McDonald, please to meet you." He nodded toward Maggie. "And this is Maggie Coulter...ummm...Stanford." Maggie extended a hand toward the man and smiled, quickly recovering from her exchange with Julia.

"I'm Dane Marks, pleased to meet you both. Hope y'all don't care if I sit down here." He slid a chair up to the table and sat down, his lean legs clad in faded, well-worn jeans and a pair of what appeared to be rather expensive boots on his feet.

Maggie smiled at him. "Not at all. Please sit down and join us." She appeared to be relieved to have seen Julia depart but there was still a simmering flame in her dark eyes.

He secretly gloated over her appearance of what he hoped was jealousy and he guessed he was going to eventually need to explain to Maggie what had transpired between the catty real estate developer and him. Which in his opinion wasn't a whole lot. Sure, they had flirted and he had indicated an interest in the woman but now it was different. He might have an opportunity to date the woman Maggie had become. Because he kind of liked her. A lot.

CHAPTER FIFTEEN

Dixie's bare foot was propped up on the dashboard of the used truck that Maggie just purchased. "Yep, ol' Phillip the pig would just have a shit fit if he knew that his precious car was now sitting in the lot of Earl's Car Lot next to a dump truck." She snickered as she wriggled her toes and brushed her hair back as the wind drifted through the open window.

Maggie drove down the interstate from Knoxville and watched for the exit to Pigeon Forge. They were going shopping for furniture today, a wad of cash stashed in her purse as part of the vehicle trade. Secretly, she hoped what she had from the transaction would be enough to buy the furniture she needed so she wouldn't have to take any more from the trust account for the time being.

"You know, I see why you like it down here so much." Dixie was on the second week of her vacation and appeared to be having a good time. "It's peaceful and laid back. Not to mention some of the hunky guys with southern drawls that hang around town."

Maggie laughed. She knew that Dixie was referring to Dane Marks, the rising country music star that showed up at Char's Place last week. "You don't kid me; you are all hot and bothered over Dane. It has nothing to do with being peaceful and laid back down here." She shot a sidelong glance at Dixie, and laughed when she caught her friend sticking her tongue out. "Check you out! You are so immature!"

"So what? I haven't been so relaxed and without responsibility in such a long time. What's wrong with throwing caution to the wind?" She tossed her mane of hair and laughed. "What happens in Tennessee stays in Tennessee." She mimicked the lady in the commercial for Las Vegas, causing both women to burst out laughing.

Maggie wheeled the big truck into the parking lot of a flea market where a semi-trailer driver was unloading furniture from his rig. Her eyes landed on a sofa and loveseat upholstered in a taupe-colored corduroy fabric. "Look, Dixie! That would be perfect for the living room." She started to get out of the truck and a hand gripped her arm.

"Whoa there, innocent friend of mine. Let me do the talking to this handsome truck driver."

Maggie's eyes widened as she looked at the man standing next to the rig. The flannel shirt he wore had the sleeves ripped out and a hairy stomach peeked out from under it. A cigar was clamped in his teeth and his dark hair was slicked back. Worried about her friend's eyesight and taste, she looked back over to see Dixie winking outrageously, which provided a great sense of relief that her friend hadn't totally lost it.

Dixie hopped down from the truck and unfastened a couple buttons on her shirt before she sauntered over to the truck driver, while Maggie followed behind her. She couldn't help but blush at the forward manner that Dixie approached the truck driver and she glanced around to make sure nobody was watching them.

"Hey darlin'." Dixie sidled up next to the guy and touched his sweaty arm. "Sure is hot out here today, ain't it?"

The guy took the cigar out of his mouth and grinned, revealing a set of teeth that were desperately in need of a dentist. "Not as hot as you are, sugar." He took a step toward Dixie, who expertly dodged him with some quick foot work and went over to admire a garish sofa that was upholstered in some animal print fur.

"I sure do like this here furniture." Dixie ran her hand along the back of the ugly sofa.

"Puts me in mind of being in a jungle somewhere." She kicked off her sandals and lay down on the sofa, running her bare foot along the surface.

Maggie thought the truck driver's eyes were going to bug out of his head, and she turned away from the scene to gather her wits. Otherwise, she would have burst out laughing out loud. As it was, her side ached from holding her laughter in.

"My name is Bud. What is your name, little lady?" He hiked up the waistband of his trousers and then lifted a hand to brush at his slick hair.

Maggie about choked when she heard Dixie's response. "I'm Lola Pallooza from Mississippi." She practically purred the words out in that outrageous drawl.

"I hail from Mississippi myself. Just drove up here with this load of furniture to sell for my boss." The truck driver mopped his forehead with a dirty rag he pulled from his back pocket.

"Well now, Bud. I guess that means that you feel a kinship for a couple of girls from down there, then?" Dixie was up off the sofa now and admiring a chair that was shaped like a high-heeled shoe. "This here chair is sure a sexy piece of furniture. I think it would look good in the bedroom." She turned and looked at Maggie. "What do you think sugar plum? Maybe we oughta get two of them. Hers and hers."

Maggie's heart lost a couple beats as she realized the picture that Dixie was painting for old Bud. She gulped and walked over to the furniture that she preferred and tried to play along with her friend. "I think that if we get those two chairs for our bedroom to suit you, then I should be able to pick out the living room furniture." She stuck out a lip in a mock pout.

Flustered, Bud mopped his forehead again and looked from one girl to the other. "Now girls, I can cut you a deal on both chairs if you buy a living room set." He tugged a pen and notepad from his pants pocket and started writing on it. A few minutes later, he showed the figures to Dixie and Maggie, and it was all she could do to not jump for joy at the deal he was making them. She reached in her purse and discreetly dug out the crisp bills to pay for the furniture and in short order, the furniture was loaded into the back of the truck and she was pulling out of the lot.

When they were out of view of Bud and his helpers, both women burst out laughing. "My God Dixie! My conscience will never be the same!" She shook her head and peered at the ugly, shoe shaped chairs in the back of the truck through the rear-view mirror. "And what in the world am I going to do with those stupid chairs?"

Blue eyes sparkled with humor and Dixie's cheeks dimpled as she grinned at her friend. "How about we ship them to your mother and Philip? Wouldn't they just spice up the starkness of their condos?" She doubled over with laughter as she saw the shock on Maggie's face. "Come on, wouldn't it be funny?"

By the time they returned to the farmhouse, the sun was setting in the west over the tops of the trees. An owl hooted from his roost in the barn as the girls tugged and pulled the furniture out of the truck and into the lawn. A stop in town at Char's had relieved them of the ugly chairs. Char thought they would be perfect to put in the women's restroom in the bar so in exchange for a few dollars and two cheeseburgers with fries, Maggie relinquished them to Char more than willingly.

A note on the door told them that Sean had been by earlier and picked up the last of the puppies to give to a new owner. Mama laid on the porch, seemingly relieved that her brood was gone and she could finally rest without having one of the puppies try to nurse at her shrinking teats. The women sat down on the porch swing and ripped into the greasy brown paper bags to get at the cheeseburgers and fries.

Dixie stopped devouring hers long enough to go into the house and pull a couple cans of soda from the refrigerator. "We sure got a lot accomplished today. We got rid of that ugly car and found you a more suitable piece of transportation. We bought furniture and had some laughs. I'm satisfied." Dixie sighed and leaned back against the cushions on the porch swing.

"Yeah, now all we have to do is get this stuff inside. I don't even think that the sofa and loveseat will fit through the front door." Maggie pushed her hair back from her face and stuffed another French fry in her mouth.

"That's where the men come in." Dixie grinned and motioned down the lane at the approaching headlights. "Voila...big, strong men who are more than willing to help a couple of women." She feigned helplessness by putting the back of her hand against her forehead and falling against the cushions. "Nothing like a quick cell phone call while you were in the restroom at the restaurant.""

Sean's truck pulled in front of the house with Dane in the passenger seat and Tom and his friends in the back. Dane jumped out of the vehicle and grinned. "How can we help you pretty ladies?" He stood with his long legs planted apart and his jeans snug against his masculine frame.

CHAPTER SIXTEEN

Maggie vowed she wasn't going to cry as she helped Dixie load the trunk of the rental car. Dixie's vacation was ending and she was going to have to drive all day and night to be ready to go back to work on Monday morning. She walked around to the passenger side of the car and tossed the overnight bag she was carrying in the back seat. Over the top of the car, she watched Dixie carry the last suitcase out of the house, stopping long enough to pat Mama on the head as she passed. The car bounced as Dixie tossed the suitcase in the trunk then shut the lid.

"Well, I think that's it. Come on around here and give me a big hug." Dixie held out her arms and grinned through her tears. """I understand now why you love it here so much. The people were friendly, the air fresh, not to mention that the men were rugged and sexy."

Maggie walked around to the back of the car and the two women hugged. "I wish you had more time to spend with me. It's going to be awfully lonely when you leave." She choked back her tears and squeezed Dixie extra hard.

As they pulled apart, Dixie grinned and waved a hand at her. "Not if you make a play for that hunky vet of yours."

"He's not my hunky vet." Maggie felt her face get warm and she was sure that a deep blush had spread across her cheeks. Dixie had relentlessly teased Maggie for days about what she swore was lust brewing between Sean and her friend.

Dixie just grinned and folded her long slender body behind the wheel of the rental car and pulled the door shut. "You take care and let me know if you will still be able to open up over Labor Day weekend. And don't forget to email me those pictures so that I can get to work on your brochures." With a last wave of her hand, she pulled the car out of the yard and headed down the lane.

Maggie busied herself making up the beds and putting the finishing touches on the two upstairs guest rooms that she and Dixie had managed to finish painting and moving furniture into. Tom and his crew had the bathrooms roughed in and that remained to do was add the fixtures and flooring, which they promised to have done before the upcoming week was over.

She stood back and admired the room she just finished. This was the room with the pretty paper that was covered with sprigs of violets and green. The white, four poster bed was covered with a lavender chenille bedspread and the throw pillows Dixie found at the garage sale added a welcoming touch. A wooden rocking chair sat in the corner with a comfortable cushion in a purple, floral print in its seat. The dresser that they rescued from a trash pile behind an apartment complex in Knoxville sat between the two windows. With a coat of shiny, white paint and new hardware, it looked like a quaint antique with an arrangement of silk irises and baby's breath sitting in front of the mirror. The newly finished, wood floor was bare except for the braided throw rugs by the bed.

As she started into the next room, she heard Mama barking at the foot of the stairs. She went to the landing and saw the big dog looking toward the door and went down to investigate. With the door open, she could see a uniformed officer standing on the porch with a packet of papers in his hand. Maggie opened the door and stepped outside.

"May I help you?"

The officer removed his hat. "Ma'am, are you Margaret Coulter-Stanford?" He glanced at the papers he was holding.

"Yes, officer. I'm Margaret Stanford. How can I help you?" She frowned at the young officer. "Is there a problem?" The officer handed her the papers he was holding.

"I need to serve these documents to you. I think you will see that there is an order to appear in Cook County Civil Court in Chicago, Illinois next month." He nodded his head. "Have a nice day, ma'am." Maggie sank down on the porch swing as the officer walked away and unfolded the papers in her lap. Concern turned to fury as she read the documents. "That dirty, son-of-a-bitch!" Tears of anger filled her eyes. Philip was suing her for fraud in their divorce for failing to disclose assets that would have impacted the divorce settlement. He was alleging that the property in Tennessee was worth more than she originally disclosed and he was suing for a share of it.

The night was dark, there was no moon out tonight, and any stars that would have normally been twinkling in the midnight sky were hidden beneath a heavy cloud cover that rolled in earlier in the evening. Sean drove the truck down the lane to Maggie's farm and automatically steered around the few ruts left in the gravel. When a fawn darted out of nowhere, he slammed on the brakes and waited for the other two that soon followed.

There were no lights on in the farmhouse, but the old truck she bought was parked in front. He glanced at the clock in his dash. It was too early for her to be asleep. He hopped out of his vehicle and walked with long strides across the lawn to the front porch. He decided to make the trip out here tonight because Ellie said that she saw her in the store earlier today and said that she looked pale and distracted. When he went to the diner for lunch, Char said the same thing. Tom told them that she said that she was going to hold off on doing any more work on the farm for a bit when he and his friends showed up earlier in the day. Something was wrong and he was going to find out what it was.

In his mind, he thought the worst and was hoping that she hadn't changed her mind about renovating the farm. Secretly, he feared that she was missing her life in Chicago and was going to go back before he could decide what place she had in his life.

As he jumped down from the cab and shut the door, he heard Mama bark in the distance. He thought that to be odd, usually the dog remained wherever Maggie was. He listened again, and heard the bark coming from the direction of the pond and pasture. He took the porch steps with one jump and stood on the mat in front of the door, rapping with his knuckles on the freshly stained wood of the screen door. When he didn't get an answer, he headed in the direction of the barking.

He remembered the path well, even after all these years. The sounds were even familiar. An owl hooted from its perch in the barn and the croaking of bullfrogs in the grass by the creek filled the night with sound. He listened as the grass rustled on the path ahead of him and was met by the low growl of a dog.

"Ssshhh…Mama…it's me."" He stopped and waited as the dog came up and sniffed him, and then jumped up with her paws landing on his stomach begging for him to pet her. "Where's Maggie? Where's your master?" The dog barked and started back through the brush in the same direction that she had come from.

When they reached the clearing, he could make out a lone figure sitting on a log from the glow of a lantern that was sitting next to her. Her head was buried in her hands and her shoulders were slumped. She raised her head as he neared.

"You shouldn't have come out here." Her voice was soft and smooth as the night air and tinged with a bit of melancholy.

He walked over and sat down next to her on the log. "Why shouldn't I have come out here? Everyone in town is worried about you."

"Why is everyone worried about me?" She sniffled a little bit with her question and was toying with a wildflower that she held between her fingers.

Putting both hands on her shoulders, he turned her toward him. "Have you been crying?" He could see the tear stains on her cheeks and the threat of fresh tears welling up in her eyes. "Maggie, what's wrong?" She pulled away from him and stood up, walking toward the edge of the creek.

"Just go away, Sean. I don't want to talk about it." Her shoulders were slumped and her head was bowed.

Shaking his head, he got up and followed her. Standing behind her, he put his hands comfortingly on her shoulders. "Are you homesick? Do you want to go home to Chicago?" Deep inside, he hoped that was not the case.

"I may not have a choice!" She burst out crying, her sobs wracking her whole body beneath Sean's hands. He turned her around and pulled her against him he held her against his chest as she sobbed out the story about the lawsuit that Philip had filed against her. Sean led her over to the log and pulled her down next to him and continued to hold her, stroking her hair until her tears subsided. "Have you talked to an attorney yet?" His mouth was against the top of her head and he was tempted to kiss her. Her hair held the fragrance of fresh air and sunshine and was smooth and silky on his lips. She shook her head.

"I can't afford an attorney. I've spent almost everything I have on getting the farm ready for guests in the fall. I have just enough to finish the place and pay the bills through the fall." She sighed before she continued. "I was going to see if Char would let me work down at the diner to make a little extra money."

He stiffened, anger flowing through him like a wildfire. "I know an attorney. In fact, he's married to my cousin up in Lexington. We'll go up there tomorrow and talk to him.""

"Sean, you don't understand. I can't afford an attorney." She pulled away from him and stood up, walking further down the path by the creek. He watched as she kicked at a rock along the edge of the creek and heard her swear softly as her toe met the surface of the rock.

"Hey, wait up Maggie! I'm sure we can work something out with him." He picked up the lantern and followed her. "Maybe you can give them a free weekend at your bed and breakfast when you open?"

She stopped in front of him and he nearly ran over her. "Sean, you aren't listening to me! I may not be able to stay here! I may have to sell the property to pay Philip off!"

Frustrated, Sean took Maggie's shoulders and gave her a shake. "Maggie, you aren't listening to me! I'm not going to let that happen without helping you fight him!" He lowered his head and pressed his lips against hers to stop her from saying anything else. Her fists beat against his chest but he continued to kiss her, forcing her mouth open with his tongue. Suddenly, she stopped fighting him and responded to his kiss. All the pent-up frustration and fury was being unleashed in her response. He felt himself straining against the front of his jeans as her hands went around his neck and tangled in his hair. Realizing that she was standing on her toes, he loosened his grip on her and eased her down on the ground. He could feel the dampness of the dew on the grass and could hear the chirp of crickets in the brush. Pulling her into his lap, he kissed her forehead, then her cheeks, then kissed a trail down her neck. When he opened his eyes, he could see fresh tears on her cheeks and he felt ashamed. "Aww, Maggie. I'm sorry. I didn't mean to hurt you." He brushed a tear off her cheek with his thumb. He leaned forward and kissed her nose and pulled her closer to him. "I just want you to let me help you."

"Right now, all I want you to do is kiss me." She pulled his head back down to her and he covered her mouth with his. This time he was gentle, barely rubbing his lips against hers. When she slipped her tongue in his mouth, he felt his heart skip a beat, and he held her tightly against him while the night sounds filled the air around them.

Maggie was soothed by the comforting feel of Sean's arms around her as they lay together on the damp grass under the dark sky. She couldn't remember a time she felt any more safe and secure than she did right at this moment. Sean pulled his mouth away from hers and was just holding her there, by the creek, in the velvet darkness of the night. His hand smoothed through her hair as she leaned into him with her cheek resting against his chest. "Sean, I'm just at wits end. The money is getting low and the house isn't ready for paying guests yet. Now I have to deal with this legal thing." She sighed as he continued to stroke her hair. "I guess I never realized how much needed to be done, how badly the house had run down over the last few years." She pictured the house as it was when she arrived just a little over two months ago with its overgrown lawn and flower beds, the rotted porch, the broken windows. It was certainly not the same, well-kept home that she visited every summer of her youth. Even though she and Dixie, along with Tom's crew had accomplished so much in the past weeks, there was much more that remained to be completed.

"Maggie, I've always lived by the philosophy that if someone wanted something badly enough, they could make it happen. How badly do you want this to happen?" Sean spoke softly against the top of her head.

She remembered the weight that lifted off her shoulders the day she drove here. The farther south she had driven, the more at ease she felt. It was almost like the sun got brighter, the sky was bluer, and the air fresher. "When I drove here the first day it was like I was finally coming home. Does that answer how badly I want this to work?" She tipped her head back and looked up at Sean. "This is my life. I have nothing else." Tears threatened to spill down her cheeks and she blinked to avoid another waterfall.

"Then you have to not let your pride get in the way. Let me help, for old times' sake?" He smiled at her, his eyes soft and filled with concern. "I have some ideas that might help, starting with a visit to my cousin and her husband as soon as I can finish up at the clinic tomorrow." He reached out and put his fingers under her chin. "What do you say?"

Maggie reluctantly nodded. Sean had a point; she was letting her pride stop her from doing whatever she had to do to make sure that she didn't lose her grandparents' farm. "Thanks, Sean." She wrapped her arms around him, hugging him tightly. "I appreciate you offering to help me."

He helped her up and took her hand, pulling her close to him and they stood there, by the creek, with the night sounds creating a peaceful melody around them while they just held each other. She smiled at the familiar hoot of the owl, the low grumblings of the frogs by the creek, and the gurgling of the water as it spilled across the rocks in the creek bed. The air was getting cool and Maggie shivered.

"Come on, you're getting cold out here." Sean rubbed his hands along her arms. "You've got goose bumps; let's get you up to the house." He released her from the circle of his arms and took her hand, leading her back up the path toward the house.

Once they reached the house, Sean led Maggie over to the porch swing and pulled her down beside him. He grabbed the afghan that was tossed over the back of the swing and wrapped it around her shoulders. "There, that should help you warm up." He pulled her closer to him. "It sure got chilly tonight, considering that it was almost ninety degrees today. Must be a front coming in over the mountains."

Maggie closed her eyes and laid her head against Sean. Bittersweet memories filled her mind of a time, several years ago, when they sat together on the swing. Just the thought of those days brought feelings to the surface that she thought were long buried and a lump formed in her throat. Nothing had changed, her heart still jumped with excitement every time she saw him. The sound of his voice still had the capacity to turn her inside out. She took a deep breath of the air, fragrant with freshly cut grass. "I just love the peace and quiet out here."

"I'm sure it is a welcome respite for you, after living up in the city all those years." She nodded her head.

"Yes, it certainly is. I don't ever want to have to live in a city again." She sighed, her head filling with all the things that could prevent her from being able to stay here. "Even if I can't keep this farm, maybe I could find a job here somewhere and rent a little cabin close by."

She felt Sean's arm tighten around her. "Shhhh...don't worry about that. I'll help you figure out a way to keep the farm." His hand started stroking her hair, sending tingles up her back. "Let's just enjoy sitting here this evening. We'll worry tomorrow."

The rocking of the swing lulled Maggie to the point of drowsiness. The crying she had done all day since she received the papers from Philip's attorney had drained her energy. She felt Sean shift next to her and she curled her body closer to his.

"Maggie, why don't you go on in to bed? I'll have Ellie call and reschedule all my appointments so we can leave in the morning."

"Mmmm...I'm not tired." She murmured against his chest. The truth of the matter was that she didn't want him to go yet. It was comforting for her to have his arms around her, to smell the clean, masculine scent that was familiar to her. Sean chuckled and lifted her from the swing.

"Come on, sleepyhead. I'll take you in and put you to bed."

CHAPTER SEVENTEEN

The day dawned with only a bit of a haze over the mountains. The summer sun peeked above the horizon in a slash of red, orange and yellow and the fragrance of flowers from the beds in front of the house drifted through her open window as Maggie pushed the sheets from her slender form. Sean had called a short time earlier and said that he was going to be there a lot earlier than originally planned because he got Ellie to reschedule his appointments.

She had rested well, talking with Sean last night and agreeing to allow him to help her provided a long-needed relief from the worries that she carried on her small shoulders. On top of that, she felt as though the two of them had taken enormous steps to regaining the friendship she thought was lost many years ago. She was satisfied with having such a friend, even if the romantic side of her secretly wished that things between them could be the same as they were when they were much younger.

Hurrying through her bath routine, she packed a small overnight bag. Sean said that they would be spending the entire weekend at his cousins' horse farm in Lexington. When she had questioned his ability to leave the veterinary clinic for a whole weekend, he informed her that he had it covered. When she mentioned there would be nobody to make sure that

Mama was properly fed and watered all weekend, he informed her that had been taken care of as well. Then he had teasingly accused her that she was just making up excuses not to go with him.

She went downstairs and out on the porch to wait, her overnight bag beside her. She had selected a comfortable tee shirt style dress in a bright pink pattern to wear for the trip and had slipped on a pair of tennis shoes in the same bright pink. Her bare legs were tanned from all the time she spent outside working in the yard and garden, and her hair hung loosely around her face. She closed her eyes and lifted her face to the sun and sighed as the warmth radiated on her.

Maggie heard the approach of Sean's truck down the lane and got up to meet him as he braked to a stop in front of her. "Good morning. Isn't it a great day?" She practically surprised herself with the cheerfulness in her voice. It wasn't the best of circumstances for her, but she was bound and determined to believe there was something Sean's cousin could do to help her out of this ridiculous game her ex-husband decided to play with her.

He swung down from the vehicle and walked across the lawn to pick up her bag from the porch. She admired his body, from the long legs in a pair of well-fitting and faded jeans to the flatness of his abdomen under a dark blue tee shirt. His usual boots had been replaced with a pair of new looking sneakers and a baseball cap was atop his auburn hair. His blue eyes were hidden by a pair of sunglasses but she knew from the brightness of his smile, they were twinkling with life.

"Good morning, yourself. Aren't you in good spirits?" He opened the back door of the truck and tossed her bag on the back seat next to his. "Must have been all the sleep you got last night. Have you had breakfast?"

She shook her head. "No, I was afraid if I fixed something that I wouldn't be ready when you got here." Truth was she just didn't feel like eating after her day yesterday. Despite her optimism, she had a knot the size of a boulder in her stomach.

He nodded. "That's alright. I know of this kick ass truck stop on the way up there. Can you hold out for about forty minutes?" He opened the passenger door and helped her up; letting his hand linger on her waist just long enough to make him want to touch a lot more.

Sean hadn't been kidding about the food at the truck stop. In front of Maggie was a plate of biscuits and gravy with eggs and potatoes so large she couldn't even think of eating it all. On top of that, the waitress had put a plate of pancakes and sausage on the table between them. She eyed the food and lifted her fork, her stomach was growling despite the knot in it.

"Maggie, you can help me eat these pancakes and sausage can't you?" Sean grinned, his fork already digging into the mound of potatoes in front of him.

Her brown eyes widened and she laid her fork down. "I don't even know where to start on my own plate and you want me to eat some of that, too?"

Sean just chuckled and poked a forkful of food in his mouth and mumbled something to the waitress when she asked if he wanted a refill on his drink. Apparently, to Maggie's amazement, the waitress understood his response because she returned with another glass of chocolate milk. She surprised herself as she devoured the food on her plate and managed to eat a pancake and sausage patty off the plate between them.

She put a hand on her stomach and leaned back in the booth, groaning. "For heaven's sake, I am so stuffed I'm practically miserable."" She brushed her hair back from her forehead and pushed the plate away.

"I thought you couldn't eat that much." Sean laughed as he finished up the last of his food and reached for his drink. "I remember you used to eat like a horse."

She knew he was referring to the breakfasts that her grandmother used to make before her grandfather and Sean would go out to work in the barn or fields. Platters filled with pancakes, eggs, bacon and sausage, toast, fried potatoes and sliced tomatoes. It had been a daily morning ritual for her to help her grandmother prepare breakfast, something she always missed when she returned home to Chicago. Her mother was never even awake before lunch if she could help it. Breakfast at home had consisted of toast and grapefruit or a bowl of cereal.

Maggie pushed thoughts of her mother out of her head. "Yeah, I might have eaten a lot back then but you had me beat." She picked up the cup of coffee and took a drink. "But then again, you and grandpa always disappeared and never showed up again until dinnertime."

"Are you about ready to hit the road again?" Sean drained his third glass of milk and reached for his billfold, signaling the waitress to bring their check. Then they were back in the truck and on the road again.

The drive to Lexington was a scenic one. Sean avoided the interstate most of the way and took country roads that led past expanses of rolling pasture with thoroughbred horses prancing behind white fences. He pulled the truck off the road a couple of times to admire things along the way. There was a covered bridge that ran parallel to the road where they stopped and walked along the overgrown path to reach the bridge. They walked across the bridge to the other side where a dirt road led to an old, abandoned shack. Then there was the creek that fed a small pool by the side of the road where they stopped and dangled their bare feet in the water, surrounded by wildflowers and dragonflies.

Later, he pulled the truck over to a roadside vendor that was selling honey and fresh vegetables from an old wooden wagon. "Let's stop here; Sally just loves it when I bring her honey from this farmer."

"Sally is your cousin?" Maggie inquired as they approached the wagon.

"Yep, she's Rick and Emma's daughter." He grinned as he picked up a bottle of honey from the wagon. "She's five years old and full of spunk. You'll just love her. She reminds me of Ellie when she was little." His voice was full of pride as he spoke of his family and Maggie felt a tugging at her gut. She could have been part of his family if things had been different. Maybe they would have had a little boy or girl by now. She pushed the thought out of her head and reminded herself that she and Sean were going to be friends as adults, nothing more.

ꕥꕥꕥꕥꕥꕥꕥꕥꕥꕥꕥꕥ

Maggie dozed off at some point in the trip, and now her head was lying on the seat next to Sean. He watched her sleep as he drove the last miles to his cousin's farm, and noticed that she was more relaxed than he'd seen her since she got back to Tennessee. He resisted the urge to caress her hair, or run a finger down the smoothness of her skin and instead focused his attention on the road.

As he drove, he wondered how the two of them could have let her mother drive such a wedge between them all those years ago. Had they both been so naïve and uncertain of their feelings for each other that they hadn't even questioned? Or had their love been merely a summer fling between two young people who had nothing better to do with their evenings than to spend them together?

He had been bitter for a long time after that fateful day. His sister had just been diagnosed with cancer and given a short time to live and he finds the girl he was in love with wasn't in love with him. From her mother. He jumped into his studies to try to finish up school in record time so that he could keep his promise to his sister that he would take care of Ellie. He quit being bitter and became resigned that a relationship and marriage with Maggie was just not in the cards. Since that day, he vowed not to get emotionally involved until he was absolutely sure that both parties were equally committed. It was necessary for both he and Ellie, not wanting his niece to get attached to a woman only to have her walk away from them both.

Maggie stirred on the seat and he reached out to touch her shoulder. "Hey, we have about five more minutes until we are there." His hand lingered a bit longer than necessary, enjoying the feel of her slender frame under his fingertips. When she finally sat up, he let his hand join the other one on the steering wheel as he made the final turn on a narrow, but paved, road leading to his cousin's farm.

CHAPTER EIGHTEEN

A little girl ran up to Sean's side of the truck and climbed up on the running board while a tall woman with blonde braids trailed behind, wiping her hands on her cut off shorts. "Cousin Sean! We got new kitties in the barn! Hurry! Come see!" The little girl said in an excited voice with a distinct southern accent. The woman reached out and pulled the squirming little girl off the truck.

"Climb down Munchkin and let Sean get out of the truck. He can't go see the kittens if he can't even get out." She stepped back and the little girl jumped down. "Sorry, Sean. She's been waiting all morning to show you the kittens."

Sean swung the door of the truck open and looked over his shoulder at Maggie. "Come on, I'll introduce you to everyone." His smile was reassuring and he stopped long enough to reach out and put a hand on her arm in encouragement.

The little girl realized that Sean had a passenger and she ran around to the other side and waited for Maggie to climb down before she started talking again. "I have kitties in the barn. You come see them too." She reached out and pulled at Maggie's hand. "Are you Cousin Sean's lady friend? Mama said that Cousin Sean was bringing a lady friend to visit with him."

Maggie bent down and squeezed the little girl's hand. "Hi there, I'm Maggie. What's your name?" She couldn't help but smile at the little girl's upturned face with a sprinkling of freckles across her nose and cheeks. There was a smudge of dirt on her forehead and she wanted to reach out and rub it away but stopped herself.

"I'm Sally Grafton. My mama's name is Emma Grafton and my daddy's name is Rick Grafton. He's out in the barn cleaning out the horse stalls and cussin' like a sailor, that's what my mama says anyhow." Her red-gold curls bounced as she skipped back and forth in the grass beside the driveway. Emma met them halfway around the truck and held out a slender hand that was smudged with oil.

"Hi there, Maggie, I'm Emma Grafton as you've already been told. Please excuse my little one here, she can't be quiet for a minute and she's never met a stranger. Worries me to death to take her anywhere for fear of someone walking off with her. But then again, my husband is probably right when he says they'd turn her loose real darn quick because she'd drive 'em nuts with the incessant chattering."

Maggie smiled as she took Emma's hand. She felt immediately at ease with this woman, Sean's cousin. "It's nice to meet you. You have a beautiful farm here." The farm was set on rolling land, and there were horses grazing in the green pastures behind white fencing and off in the distance, Maggie could see sheep behind another enclosure. There were two barns and a long stable to house the horses. The house was a long, low ranch with a porch running all the way across the front. Hanging baskets filled with ferns and bright colored petunias adding a welcoming touch.

"Thank you. It's a lot of work, though. Rick does what he can but most of it falls on me and our hired hand. My husband is a lawyer up in Lexington and he's all the time working late. Or so he says. Probably avoiding all the work out here." She smiled good-naturedly, and Maggie realized that she was just teasing. "That's why he got stall cleaning duty today." She turned toward Sean and grinned. "And he's out there cussin' like a sailor just like Sally said he is." She laughed in a musical, carefree sound that was befitting the woman.

Sally started dancing around Sean, tugging at his jeans. "Come on! Y'all gotta go down to the barn and see the kitties." She grinned at Maggie. "Daddy won't cuss in front of company."

The three adults followed Sally down the graveled path that led to the larger of the two barns. As they approached, Maggie could hear a man swearing over the sounds of country music that was coming from a radio somewhere inside. Sally stopped abruptly and turned to look at the adults. "Wait here, I'll tell daddy that we have company so he won't say bad words." She ran inside and Maggie could hear her yelling at her father, telling him that they had company and he should quit his 'damn' cussing before her mother got on his case. Maggie stifled a giggle as Emma rolled her eyes and shrugged her shoulders.

"She sometimes slips and blurts out some of the words she hears her father say. I'm hoping that by the time school starts in the fall, she will be passed that. God only knows, I don't want to have to get called to school every other day because Rick doesn't watch his mouth."

The little girl returned with a bulky man without a shirt. Straw stuck to his dark hair and the knees of his jeans were damp and muddy. "Lookie here, Daddy. I told you Cousin Sean was here with his lady friend. Her name is Maggie." She stopped in front of him and he nearly tripped over her.

Smiling sheepishly, he reached out and shook Sean's hand. "Good to see you, Sean. Been too long since you've been up our way." He released Sean's hand and reached out to Maggie. "Pleased to meet you, Maggie. Sean said that he was bringing company with him. We were all starting to worry that he didn't like women." He was rewarded with a poke in the ribs from his wife.

"Don't start in trying to embarrass Sean. It's no wonder he never brings a woman around any of us." She pushed away as Rick tried to put an arm around her. "Get your sweaty hands off me. You smell like a pile of horse manure." Rick swatted his wife on the bottom and reached for an old tee shirt that was lying over a rail on top of a saddle. "Okay, okay. I wouldn't smell like horse manure if you hadn't saved the worst of the chores for me this weekend."

Sally interrupted them. "Come on you guys. Let me show you the kitties. They're back here behind the feed sacks." She jumped up and down until she knew that the adults were going to follow her, and then led the way to where she said the kittens were. Maggie and Sean bent down to admire the kittens who were nursing off a big gray tiger cat. There were five of them in varied shades of gray, black and white and they fought among themselves for a place to nurse. The mother opened a yellow eye, let out a meow, and promptly went back to her nap. The kittens could have only been a few days old because their eyes were still closed.

Satisfied that the newcomers had spent enough time admiring the kittens, Sally jumped up and turned to her mother. "Okay, Mama. You said we'd start cookin' on the barbecue grill when Cousin Sean got here." She tugged at Emma's hand. "Remember? You said that we'd have strawberry pie for dessert? I want my dessert before I have a burger." She turned to Sean. "Cousin Sean, is your lady friend Maggie gonna sleep in the guest room with you?"

Emma reached down and covered her daughter's mouth with her hand. "Shhhh. You aren't supposed to ask those kinds of questions. You run up to the house and make sure your toys are picked up off the kitchen floor so we don't trip on them." She gave Sally a slight nudge before releasing her hand then watched as the little girl ran out of the barn. She turned toward Maggie. "I'm sorry, she shouldn't have said that. She must have heard me and Rick talking this morning about whether I should fix up two rooms or one." Her face was flushed with embarrassment.

Maggie stood up and put a hand on the other woman's arm. "Don't worry about it. No harm done." She grinned at Sean who stood to the side, his face as red as his cousin's. "Sean and I are just friends." He looked down at the floor of the barn and tucked his hands in his jeans pockets.

"Don't go to any trouble. Just give Maggie the guest room and I'll sleep on the sofa in the family room."

"Nonsense, Sean McDonald. We have five bedrooms in this house and you can sleep in a bed just like the rest of us." She stomped her foot and shook her head. "Besides, Buster is liable to climb up on the sofa with you. That's where he generally sleeps in the summer because the leather is cooler for his thick fur." She led the way up to the house as they walked into the garage, the back door burst open and a big, black Newfoundland ran out and jumped up on Sean. The massive dog about knocked him over and Maggie stepped back to avoid him stepping on her toes.

"Down, Buster." Sean commanded. "Damn dog, you need to learn how to be polite when greeting guests." He was rewarded with a loud bark.

Emma reached over and grabbed the dog by his collar. "Come on, you big lug. You're going to your bed for now." She pulled the dog up the steps to the back door and inside as Sean and Maggie followed.

The room off the garage was a huge kitchen. Copper pots hung from a rack above an island with a black granite countertop where a bowl of strawberries sat next to two empty pie shells. The floor was gray slate and had several hand-woven rugs scattered around. A crock on the counter by the refrigerator held an arrangement of wild flowers and the dog was lounging on a cushion in the corner, his tongue lolling out of his mouth as his big eyes watched the visitors come in the door.

"Stay there, Buster." Emma ordered to the dog as she motioned Sean and Maggie inside. "He just loves people. We got him to be a watchdog but if thieves broke in the only thing he'd do is lick 'em to death while they cleaned us out." Buster laid his head on the cushion and his big tail thumped against the floor.

Sean turned to look at Maggie, who was standing right behind him. "Don't look at him, that's all it takes to get him started again." He chuckled as he commented. "Seems like with all the money the big-time attorney makes y'all could afford some obedience classes."

Emma laughed. "Obedience classes would take the personality right out of him. His personality is what makes him so lovable." She gave the dog a sharp look as he started to get up from the cushion. "Don't you dare!" The dog groaned and let out a snort as he laid his head back down on his bed, his eyes focused on the newcomers.

"I'll go grab our overnight bags out of the truck." Sean chuckled as Sally ran into the room and insisted on helping him. He took her hand and the two of them went back out the door, the little girl chattering about one of her playmates while Sean nodded and took in every word she said, leaving Emma and Maggie standing in the kitchen watching them.

"Come on, Maggie. I'll show you where your room is." Emma led her through a dining room with a massive oak table and chairs that could seat a dozen people easily. A copper pot of cut flowers sat in the middle of the table atop a lacy table cloth. A leafy fern was on a wicker stand in between the two windows that looked out over the front of the property. The floor was covered with a patterned rug in shades of green and violet. Adjoining the dining room was a sitting room with floral patterned sofas facing each other with a coffee table between them. A grand piano sat in one corner of the room and two wing chairs with a library table between them sat in the opposite corner. The floor was carpeted in a thick, ivory plush and a couple of framed watercolor floral prints graced the walls of the room. They entered a foyer that split off into two halls. Emma pointed to the shorter one. "The family room is back there and the deck and pool is beyond that. We'll cook on the grill out there later." She motioned for Maggie to follow her down the longer hall and opened the second door on the left. "Here you go; I just put fresh linens on the bed and towels in the bathroom this morning." She stood just inside the room. "The bathroom adjoins with one of the other guest rooms. I will probably put Sean in there so just remember to lock the door on his side if you want privacy." She studied Maggie for a moment, her curiosity evident.

Maggie walked in the room that was carpeted with the same ivory carpet as the hall and living room. The bed was a four-poster covered with a pink chenille spread and floral patterned throw pillows. On the dresser was a bowl filled with rose scented potpourri, the scent gave the room a feminine touch. Pink, lacy curtains covered a set of French doors and

Emma walked over to open them.

"My flower garden is out these doors. All the rooms on this side have doors out to the garden. It's always nice to walk out there in the early morning or the evening. In the daytime, the bees are too bad." Maggie followed her and looked out the doors to admire the array of flowers that bloomed there. The area had privacy fencing closing it off from the rest of the lawn and she could see several birdhouses and bird feeders scattered throughout the gardens.

"This is beautiful. Did you plant it all yourself?"

Emma nodded. "Yep, it's one of the many things that keep me busy out here in the middle of nowhere." She sat down on the bed. "I grew up in Atlanta. In an apartment. My dad is Sean's mom's brother and he was a corporate accountant before he and mom retired to Florida a couple of years ago. I always envied Sean and his sisters living out in the country with cows and horses and pigs." She brushed at an imaginary piece of lint on the bed. "When I met Rick he was in law school and I was working as a paralegal for the office where he did his internship. After we hooked up he told me he wanted to live in a big farmhouse with lots of horses. So here we are." She grinned and stood up as Sean came in the room carrying Maggie's bag. Sally was right behind him with her purse.

"I brung you your purse. It was laying on the seat of Cousin Sean's truck. Daddy always gets on Mommy when she leaves her purse sitting in the car. Says that one of these days someone's gonna up and snatch it from her." She laid the purse on the floor next to the bag. "Ain't nobody gonna snatch it out here but Daddy says it's a bad habit to leave it in the car."

Maggie ruffled the girl's hair. "Thank you for bringing it to me." She put on a mock look of seriousness. "Your Daddy is right; it's a bad habit to leave a purse in the car."

Emma walked over to the door, taking her daughter's hand as they went. "Come on, Sean. Let's leave Maggie to freshen up while I get a room ready for you."

CHAPTER NINETEEN

After Maggie unpacked her small, overnight bag she went into the bathroom to wash her face. The tiled floor was adorned with grey throw rugs that matched the marble tiles and a glassed-in shower stood in one corner. Satisfied that she had freshened up adequately, she ventured into the hallway and was met by Sally.

"Hiya there, Maggie!" The little girl couldn't stand still for a moment. "Do ya wanna come see my toys?" She tugged at the hem of Maggie's dress while she danced around on her little, bare feet.

Maggie grinned and squatted down to the little girl's level. "Sure, I'd love to see your toys. Is your room down this way?" She looked down the hall to a couple of doors that were closed to the hallway. The head full of the red-gold curls bobbed up and down. "Yep. I got a room across from the one Cousin Sean is stayin' in." She pointed to a door that had a pink sign with white letters that said 'Sally's Room'. "See, my door even has my name on it. Cousin Ellie gave it to me for Christmas at Granny's last year."

Maggie stood up and took the little girl by the hand. "Well, come on and let's see what kind of toys you have in there." She had never been around a child as exuberant and outgoing as Sally. Her ex-sister-in-law, Donna, had twin boys about the same age but they were always solemn and quiet when the family got together for their stuffy dinner parties. She much preferred the constant chatter of Sally over the snobby little boys that were prone to temper tantrums when they didn't get their own way.

Sally's room had a window seat that overlooked the pond out front and it was filled with cushions of pastel colors and several stuffed animals. The bed was a canopy covered with a pastel plaid quilt and was piled high with more stuffed animals and dolls. A toy box in the corner was overflowing with more dolls and a variety of other toys. The little girl plopped down on a braided rug in the middle of the floor and patted a spot beside her. "Come on, sit down and we can play like we are having a tea party."

Maggie crossed over and sat down on the floor next to Sally. "A tea party? That sounds like fun." She examined the little tea set that was strewn all over the floor, white plastic pieces with bright blue flowers painted on them. The little girl's nose wrinkled up and she shook her head.

"Naw. Tea parties are dumb but Alexis says that we are girls and we are supposed to have tea parties." She picked up a little plastic tea cup and sat it in front of Maggie. "Alexis lives down the road and her mommy is 'vorced and her daddy lives in the city. She's real prissy and don't ever wanna play outside in the barn with the animals. Daddy said she's a brat."

Maggie laughed at Sally's candor. "Well, I don't think that just because you are a girl that you have to have tea parties. I'm a girl and I'd rather be outside than having tea parties inside." She took the cup that the little girl offered and pretended to take a drink.

Sally jumped up and took the cup from Maggie. "Come on, then. Let's go out and play in the barn." She jumped around the room excitedly as she waited for Maggie to get up off the floor. "We can climb up in the hayloft and play in the hay. That's what Alexis said her mommy wanted to do with Cousin Sean last year when they came to our Halloween party." Her nose wrinkled up again. "Maggie, why would a grown up want to play in the hay while everyone else is sitting by the bonfire?"

Maggie swallowed as she felt her stomach do a flip flop at the thought of Sean and this

Alexis' mother being up in the hayloft together. She silently chastised herself for worrying about it. After all, Sean was a grown man and she was sure he didn't spend all his nights alone.

"Sally! You need to stop telling everything Alexis says." Emma walked into the room and shot an apologetic look toward Maggie. "Sorry, Maggie. Some people just don't understand that they can't say anything in front of a five-year-old and expect them not to repeat it."

Under the woman's watchful eyes, Maggie recovered from the unexpected burst of jealousy and smiled at Emma. "No harm done. Sean and I are just friends, so what he does is his own business." She stood up and smoothed the fabric of her dress and tried for casual and unconcerned.

"Am I in trouble, Mommy?" Sally went to stand in front of Emmy, a solemn look on her face. "I don't want to have to go without strawberry pie because I got in trouble."

Emma bent down and picked up her daughter. "Of course not, silly. You just have to quit repeating everything that Alexis says about her mom." She rolled her eyes over the top of Sally's head in a look of frustration. "For the record, Sean didn't go play in the hay with Corinna at our Halloween party last year."

Sally turned her head and looked at Maggie. "Cousin Sean told Daddy that she was a real witch. I don't know why he said that though 'cuz Alexis's mommy is real pretty and witches are real ugly. And she wasn't even wearing a witch's costume either."

Emma put Sally down on the floor and gave her a hug. "Why don't you go see if Daddy and Sean have the barbecue grill started?" She patted the little girl on the backside as she ran out the door, then turned to Maggie and sighed. "One of these days that little girl of mine is really going to hurt someone's feelings or get Rick in trouble for some of the stuff she overhears him say." She shrugged her shoulders and shook her head. "Would you like to go sit on the deck with the men while I finish up in the kitchen?"

Maggie smiled. "I'd much rather come help you in the kitchen if you still have things to do." She didn't want to just sit around and think about Sean and some unseen woman making out in a hayloft or anywhere else.

"I'd love the company. How are you at shucking corn?" Emma led the way back to the kitchen shooed Sally out the back door. “Go outside and play while you can, we are going to eat soon and then it will be getting close to your bedtime. Stay out of trouble and stay out of the pond.”

Maggie sat on a high stool at the kitchen counter and cleaned corn while Emma cut up strawberries and mixed them with strawberry gel for the pies. She learned Emma worked at home, providing Rick's law firm with paralegal services from a desk in their library. She lamented on the advantages in working in her pajamas or blue jeans. Occasionally, she would have to go into the city when their law library at home or the internet couldn't provide her with what she needed. Usually, Sally would stay with Alexis' grandmother at a farm down the road from theirs on those rare occasions.

"I hear that you are refurbishing your grandparents' farm house and turning it into a bed and breakfast inn." Emma emptied the scraps from the cleaned strawberries into the garbage and walked over to the refrigerator. "Do you want a glass of lemonade?" She inquired over her shoulder as she filled two glasses with ice.

"Lemonade would be great. Where do you want these ears of corn?" Maggie stood up and walked over to get the icy glass of lemonade. She could see out the window, and Sally was romping in the yard with Buster, throwing a rawhide toy and watching him chase it.

Emma put the corn into a stainless-steel kettle on the stove. "When do you think that you will be ready to start taking guests?"

Maggie shrugged. "I don't know if I will be able to. My ex-husband is trying to sue me for half of the property's value." She sat back down at the counter. "Sean said that maybe your husband might be able to tell me if he really can do that or not."

The other woman sat down across from Maggie. "We looked at the papers last night after Sean faxed them to us." She reached across and laid her hand on top of Maggie's. "If anything can be done to stop your ex-husband, Rick will be able to do it. Don't you worry.

Sean did the right thing by calling us. In the meantime, you just enjoy your weekend here. Sean said you've been working real hard and needed the break."

Rick came in the kitchen and Maggie noticed he had showered and changed into a pair of khaki shorts and clean tee shirt. "Darlin' you got them burgers and brats ready for the grill?" He bent to kiss the top of his wife's head then looked over at Maggie. "Em's right, don't you worry 'bout a thing this weekend. Next week, I'm gonna look into this ex-husband of yours." He walked over to the refrigerator and pulled out a platter of hamburger patties and bratwurst.

"I really appreciate it. It's so nice of the two of you to help me, with me being a stranger and all." Maggie observed the easy affection between Emma and Rick and recalled that her marriage to Philip had never been easy or affectionate. She found herself wishing that things between her and Sean had been different because she was sure he would be the same with whomever he chose to spend his life with.

"Any friend of Sean's is like family to us." Rick grinned and kissed Emma as he went back outside again, balancing the platter of meat in one hand and holding a couple of cold beers in the other hand.

Maggie saw the affection on Emma's face as her husband disappeared out the back door. "It's good to see Sean with a woman. I mean, I know that he's dated a bunch of women over the years but apparently, none of them were important enough to bring around his family." Emma laid two, enormous tomatoes in front of Maggie and handed her a knife. "Will you slice these if I slice the onions?" She started peeling a red onion while Maggie started slicing the tomatoes onto the platter on the counter. "Anyhow, I'm glad to see he got past that girl who broke his heart while he was in college. I can't imagine what kind of girl could be so uncaring about another person to dump them at Christmas while they are trying to deal with their sister's terminal illness. She must have been a real piece of work."

Maggie cringed inwardly as she listened to the disgusted tone in Emma's voice. She felt her eyes tearing up and she blinked to try to avoid them spilling down her cheeks. Sean's family must have such animosity toward her for something that had been beyond either of their control. Silently, she cursed her mother for her interference.

"Here's a tissue, Maggie." Maggie looked up at Emma who was holding out a tissue for her. "Guess them onions were a lot stronger than I thought they were." She wiped a tear from her own cheek and grinned at Maggie. "If the guys come in and see us both cryin' over them onions they'll tease us to no end. Wipe your eyes, I just heard someone come in through the patio doors."

They ate a dinner of hamburgers, bratwurst, potato salad, corn on the cob, baked beans, chips and strawberry pie under the big umbrella that sheltered the table from the evening sun on the deck. Sally entertained them with childish stories about imaginary friends and talking farm animals. After dinner, Maggie helped Emma clear and put away everything while Sally went to put on her swimsuit.

"Did you bring a swimsuit?" Emma asked as they finished loading the dishwasher. "If not, I have one of my sister's in the laundry room that will fit you."

Maggie hadn't brought a swimsuit and she thanked Emma when she handed her the sporty, black suit. She slipped into the guest room to change into the suit and pulled a long tee shirt that she had brought to sleep in on top of the suit. She met Emma and Sally in the hall and they went back out to the deck. The men were nowhere to be found.

"They probably went out to the barn to put the horses up." Emma commented as they sat at the edge of the pool and dangled their feet in the warm water while Sally splashed around on a blow-up sea serpent. "That's fine by me because they'd just want to rough house and play water basketball when I'd rather just float around in peace."

Sally paddled over to them and grinned up at the two women. "Alexis's granny called on Daddy's cell phone while you were in the house. Said that Alexis's mommy's car broke down up the road a piece and they took Cousin Sean's truck to pull it home." She splashed her arms in the water. "Daddy said her dumb ass prolly ran out of gas." Her eyes widened and she put her hand over her mouth as she realized she said a word she wasn't supposed to say.

Emma rolled her eyes and sighed. "Sally, you know better than to repeat bad words that your daddy says. What am I going to do with you?" She splashed some water at her daughter and shook her head.

"I'm sorry, Mommy. It just slipped out. I can't help it sometimes." She paddled out of reach of Emma. "Please don't make me go in the house yet."

"I'll let it slide this time Little Missy, but the next time you say a bad word I'm going to take away your television for a week." Emma slid into the cool water and swam over to where her daughter had floated on the sea serpent.

"What are you gonna do when Daddy says a bad word again? Will you wash his mouth out with a dishrag like you said you were going to do yesterday?" Sally giggled as Emma splashed her and stole the serpent for herself.

It was after dark when the men returned, Rick was muttering under his breath and Sean was grinning from ear-to-ear. They found that Rick's initial comment about running out of gas was indeed what happened to the car.

Both Emma and Maggie had changed into shorts and shirts and were sitting on the chaise loungers by the pool and Sally was asleep in her mother's lap. Rick leaned down and picked up his daughter. "I'll go put this little busy body to bed. Sean, can I get you something to drink while I'm in the house?"

Sean nodded and looked over at Maggie, whose eyelids were starting to droop. "Looks like someone else is getting sleepy."

Emma glanced over at Maggie and touched her on the arm. "Honey, why don't you go ahead and go to bed if you're tired. It won't hurt my feelings. In fact, I'm thinking of going in and taking a nice bubble bath and climb into bed myself. Unlike Rick, I was up with the chickens this morning."

??????????

After Maggie had gone in the house to go to bed and Rick returned with two bottles of beer for him and Sean, Emma glanced over at her cousin and smiled. "So, what gives between you and Maggie? You've never brought a woman around any of us before."

"Maggie's a nice woman. I've known her for a long time." Sean took a drink from the bottle of beer and sat it on the table. He looked off to the horizon where the last light from the sun was vanishing. He wasn't sure how much information to share with his cousins, he wasn't sure about how he felt right now himself.

"You didn't answer my question. What's going on between the two of you? Is she someone you are dating or is it true that you are just friends like she said? You sure did turn red when Sally asked if you were going to sleep in the same room." Emma chuckled softly as she reminded him of the scene earlier.

"Darlin', why don't you leave poor Sean alone?" Rick put his hand on his wife's arm then grinned at Sean. "Okay buddy, are you gettin' any action with this one?"

Emma reached out and swatted her husband. "Richard Elliott Grafton! That remark was uncalled for!" She sighed and looked over at Sean. "Sorry, Sean. I guess we all have been worried that the thing with that horrible girl that dumped you when Kate was sick left you with a bad taste in your mouth for relationships."

Sean cleared his throat and met his cousin's gaze. "Emma, that horrible girl just happens to be Maggie and it's not the way I thought it was all those years ago." He went on to explain what Maggie's mother had done that Christmas Eve when he visited Chicago, then the story about how she showed up at his cabin just a few weeks before. When he finished, he noticed the pinched look on Emma's face. "What's the matter, Emma?"

"I feel so terrible. I said some really nasty things earlier about the girl who hurt you. How must Maggie have felt? I should go in and apologize to her." She started to rise from her seat and was stopped by her husband.

"Don't worry about it, darlin'. I'm sure she realized that you didn't know it was her that you were referring to." He grinned at his wife. "Now we know where our daughter gets her big mouth from, huh?"

CHAPTER TWENTY

It was sometime between midnight and dawn when Maggie awoke in the unfamiliar room. The house was quiet, the only sound coming from the central air conditioning as it kicked on and blew cool air through the vent in the floor. She pushed aside the sheets and turned so that her feet hit the cushioned softness of the ivory carpet. Sitting on the side of the bed, she found herself wide awake. Her gaze ventured to the French doors that led to Emma's flower garden and she was compelled to go outside.

Barefoot and clad in just a cotton shirt that brushed her thighs, she stepped outside on the brick path that was lit by a full moon in a clear, midnight blue sky. Stopping to inhale the fragrant blend of roses intermingled with other unidentified floral scents, she felt a slight breeze brush across her face. Quietly, she walked along the path away from the house until she found a wooden bench tucked in a corner across from a bird feeder that had purple and white clematis climbing up its pole. She sat down and imagined that this corner was a pretty active area when the birds came to feed during the day. Curling up on the bench, she looked up at just the right time and saw a shooting star cascade across the night sky.

Closing her eyes, she recited the old rhyme her grandmother taught her years ago. "Shooting star, shining so bright. Wish I may, wish I might, have this wish I wish tonight." In her mind, she wished she could go back to the Christmas Eve that her mother had turned Sean away. What she wouldn't give to turn back time and start a life with Sean. To erase the years she had wasted in a loveless marriage. Where would she be right now? Would she and Sean be sharing a family of their own right now, or would they still have gone their separate ways?

Sighing, she opened her eyes and there he was, standing in the shadows. How long had he been there in the dark watching her since she slipped out the French doors? She averted her eyes and stared down at her toenails polished in a bright pink color. Self-conscious, she knew the cotton night shirt left little room for imagination and she crossed her arms protectively across her chest. Even though he had been her first all those years ago, it made her uncomfortable having him gaze at her with that hooded look.

She felt her face flush as she remembered how her body had responded to his kisses and caresses. He stepped out of the darkness just enough so that the moonlight illuminated part of his face. He smiled. "Did you wish for something good?" The deep voice was spoken softly in the quiet garden.

Maggie straightened on the bench and drew her arms tighter around her torso. "I woke up and couldn't go back to sleep." She felt like a child who got caught with their hand in the cookie jar even though her hostess had invited her to enjoy the garden whenever she wanted.

"Emma's garden is certainly a good place to spend a restless night." He stepped closer. "Do you mind if I sit with you for a while?"

She moved over to make room on the bench for him. "No, I don't mind. I just hope Emma doesn't mind that I made myself at home out here." The breeze blew a wisp of hair into her face and she tucked it behind her ear.

~~~~~~~~~~~~

As Sean sat down on the bench, he caught a whiff of the subtle fragrance that he had
~~~~~~~~~~~~

always associated with Maggie. Something like fresh air and sunshine, that was the only way he could describe it. He remembered in those first months after her mother turned him away that fragrance would assault his senses in various public places and he would find himself looking for her. Just wanting to find her one time so that he could confront her with his hurt and disappointment. In hindsight, and knowing what had really happened that Christmas Eve, he counted his blessings that he had not had the opportunity to take his anger out on her.

He was suddenly hit with an overwhelming desire to touch her. He needed to know whether her hair still felt like satin under his fingertips or if her skin was still as soft as a summer breeze. He reached out and caught a lock of the dark hair and let it slide through his fingertips. As he released it, she turned to look at him, her dark eyes soft and uncertain. Reaching out again, he ran his fingertips down her cheek, stopping to cup her chin and pull her toward him. He saw her tongue dart out and wet her pink lips and the gesture was so sensual to him, he felt a rush of heat shoot through him like an electric shock. He captured her mouth with his and her tongue met his in a slow, sensuous dance that left him wanting more when she pulled away.

He felt her tremble and he pulled her close to him, wanting to protect her from the world. Sean stroked her hair and her back before moving away just enough to cup her face with both hands, his thumbs stroking her cheekbones. Her lips parted in invitation and she whispered his name. It didn't matter who made the first move, because the next movement they each made brought them together simultaneously.

Their lips joined as their arms went around each other. Her fingers dug into the muscles of Sean's back through the barrier of his tee shirt as his hands tangled in the silky softness of her hair. Sean groaned as he felt her nipples harden against his chest and he moved to cup her buttocks as he pulled her onto his lap. In the distance, an owl hooted and something scuttled through the garden, causing the rustle of leaves. Another breeze stirred the air; cool against the heat of their bodies. Breathing became a struggle as one of his hands roamed under the hem of her night shirt and Maggie's head tipped back wantonly as his fingers caressed her thighs, then those same fingers slipped under the lacy leg of her panties. He heard her gasp as his fingers dipped into the moistness between her legs and he stopped for a moment, partly to tease and partly to give her the opportunity to catch her breath. He dipped his head down and claimed her mouth again, his tongue tracing the outline of her lips. He moved his hand again, his fingers stroking her until he felt her muscles tense. He caught her cry of release with his mouth. When he lifted her chin to urge her to look at him, a single tear rolled down her cheek and she pressed her face against the hardness of his chest. Suddenly, she sobbed and buried her face in his chest.

"Sshhh..." He murmured against the fragrant softness of her hair. "We'll figure this out, everything will be all right." He could feel her shoulders heaving lightly and he waited until the sobs calmed before he set her away from him. Once again, like he had earlier, he cupped her face in his hands. "Go in and go back to bed." He had to compose himself before he took her right here in his cousin's garden. "We're far from finished, but this isn't the time or place."

CHAPTER TWENTY-ONE

It was dark when Sean pulled the truck into Maggie's driveway on Sunday night. The back of the truck was loaded down with various pieces of furniture that Emma insisted Maggie take home with her. A roll top desk that was missing a couple of drawer pulls, a brass bed frame that only needed a good polishing, a wing chair and ottoman that would look nice in the corner of the one bedroom that still needed furnishing. Emma swore that the furniture was leftovers from a garage sale earlier in the summer that was just collecting dust in a corner of the barn. He knew his cousin all too well and he was grateful for the smile the odds and ends of furniture had put on Maggie's face.

Sean put the truck in park but left it running. He turned to look at Maggie who had been quiet for the trip home except to comment on some of the scenery. He was sure that she had a lot on her mind after their interlude in the garden the first morning at his cousins', so he didn't try to push her for conversation. There was much weighing on his mind as well. "I'll come back tomorrow evening to unload this furniture. Will Tom be around to help me?"

She shook her head. "No, I told Tom and his buddies not to come until I know more about what is going to happen with the property. No use in spending the last of my money to repair something if I'm going to have to pay off Philip."

He reached across the truck seat and squeezed her hand reassuringly. "Don't worry too much, Rick thought that he could get your ex-husband's attorney to advise him against pursuing this asinine case." He brushed his lips across her forehead. "Go in and go to bed. I'll have Ellie bring Mama home in the morning." He waited while she walked up and unlocked the door to the house. When the porch light went off and the light in the foyer went on, he put the truck into gear. He grinned as he thought of her surprise tomorrow. Ellie was going to come out and insist that she go with her to pick up supplies for the clinic tomorrow. While Ellie had her away from the house, he had arranged for Tom and his buddies to get the barn and stalls in order and her first horse boarding customers would start arriving the following day. The income from boarding the horses would help her add to her diminishing bank account and he hoped the chore of taking care of them would keep her occupied enough to keep her mind off the legal battle that Rick was taking on as a favor to him.

Sean wasn't sure where things were going to go between them, but he was determined to make sure she had reason to stay here in Possum Creek. He had seen the plans she had sketched out for Tom and his buddies and he could tell she had put a lot of thought into this dream of hers. He wanted to make sure it came true.

From some of the conversations they had, he knew her marriage had been a farce. And she had been too naïve to realize it until her husband's indiscretions had slapped her square in the face. He felt a little guilty, but he had called her friend Dixie and talked with her at length about the years between the worst Christmas of his life and where she was today. He was sure Dixie hadn"t shared everything with him, but he got enough from the conversation to know the other woman was very protective of her friend. He grinned as he remembered her blunt warning that she was going to kick his ass if he hurt Maggie.

ꕥꕥꕥꕥꕥꕥꕥꕥꕥꕥꕥꕥ

Inside the house, Maggie watched his tail lights until they disappeared down the lane. Resigned to the fact that he wasn't going to change his mind and come back, she wandered into the living room and curled up on the end of the sofa. Glancing over at the end table, she saw the message light flickering on the telephone. Choosing to ignore it, she pulled the afghan from the back of the sofa and covered up with it. Pushing back the lacy curtains, she looked outside at the stars in the sky. In the quiet of the deserted house, she could vaguely hear the crickets outside chirping. Above, on the roof, the tiny feet of the raccoon family pattered like they did each night. She knew that the owl would start hooting from his perch in the barn soon and if she were outside, she would hear the rustle of bat wings as they searched for flying bugs to pluck out of the air for dinner. This was home to her and it pained her to think that she might have to give it up.

A sudden burst of fury came over her and she jumped up from the sofa. "Sorry Philip, you aren't going to win without a fight." She stated to the empty living room. Full of energy, she went out to the back porch and grabbed a bucket of paint. With one more room to finish and the upstairs hallway to paint, she decided to put her anger to good use and she headed upstairs.

Char was sitting on her front porch next to the bed and breakfast. With the Fourth of July holiday coming up, the restaurant was extremely busy and she needed to unwind after serving family after family tonight. She chose to leave the porch light off to avoid attracting bugs, and she propped her feet up on the rail taking a big drink of her soda. Her ears picked up voices in the lawn at the bed and breakfast. A man and a woman arguing. Probably a couple of tourists disagreeing about the choice of vacation destination. However, what she heard next caused her to move closer to the rail so that she could hear the conversation and was surprised who she saw arguing in the lawn.

"Philip, you promised me over a year ago that you would make sure your wife sold me that piece of land." Julia Evans' features were distorted by unchecked anger. "Now I'm being pressured by the investors and I don't have the land that I promised them that I would."

Philip shuffled his feet restlessly in the grass. "Julia, I didn't think she would up and divorce me when I told you I'd get the land for you." He shook his head with disbelief. "I never dreamed she would stand up to me. Margo's mother swore she had never stood up to anyone.""'

"If you had kept your indiscretions more secretive instead of deciding to screw your secretary right in your damn office, maybe she wouldn't have found out what a slime ball you are." She poked a finger in his chest. "I helped you dig out of the mess you got yourself in and now I want what I have coming to me."

"Damn it, Julia. I need more time." He reached out and put his hands on the woman's shoulders. "I've tried everything. I got her mother involved and had little success there. Now I've gone the legal route and I'm hoping that your friend the vet doesn't jump in to help her out with this last move I've made." He cleared his throat and smirked at the blonde woman. "Can't you keep the good doctor occupied enough to keep him away from my ex-wife? You seemed pretty talented when you were in Chicago last winter."

Julia's hand shot out and she slapped Philip in the face. "You are a total ass! How dare you insinuate that I used sex to make a business deal happen for you?" She picked up the bag that was sitting on the sidewalk next to her. "You have one week to get little miss perfect to sell that damn piece of property or I'm going to spill the beans on our little business deal to your company's CEO!" She turned away from him and the heels of her shoes clicked up the sidewalk to the bed and breakfast inn.

On the other side of the bushes, Char sat for a moment on her porch. After she heard the door of the bed and breakfast open and close, she waited while the man walked across the street to a black sedan. As soon as she heard the car start up and pull away from the curb, she got up and went into the house and picked up the phone on the hall table.

CHAPTER TWENTY-TWO

When Sean arrived at the clinic on Monday morning, the waiting area was already full and Ellie was behind the counter setting out files for each of his four-legged patients. He greeted the many familiar faces seated around the room and bent to pet a very pregnant Irish Setter who looked up at him with her soulful eyes. He counted a dozen animals and their owners and realized that it was going to be one of those days.

Ellie glanced up as he walked in the office and gave him a thankful smile. "Uncle Sean am I glad to see you!" She bounced around the corner in a pair of cut off shorts and weathered tee shirt. A stack of pink message slips filled her hand and she shoved them at him. "Char's message is on top; she called late last night and said she needed to talk to you as soon as you got in." She paused for a moment before continuing. "She sounded kind of upset and excited at the same time. Did she get a pet or something recently?"

He shook his head. "Not that I know of. She's always said that she was too busy to have a pet with all the hours she works." He shuffled through the stack, trying to prioritize the calls he would need to make between patients, then grabbed a lab coat off the back of the door and started toward his private office.

He could tell from the aroma in the hall outside the office that there was fresh coffee in there. Thoughts of Maggie invaded his mind after he got home from dropping her off which kept him from getting right to sleep, it had been well after three before he finally nodded off so now he didn't feel as awake and alert as he should. "Do I smell fresh coffee in my office?" He reached for the handle of the door.

Ellie grabbed his arm before he could open the door and she shook her head in warning. "You might want to wait before you go in there." She gritted her and gave him an angry look. "That real estate developer woman is in there and I think she's in heat." She snickered and watched his face turned several shades of red.

"Ellie..." He started to admonish her for the comment then heard the door squeak as it opened. Both he and Ellie turned around in time to see Julia Evans poke her head out the door. The strong scent of her perfume permeated the air and Sean found his nose burning from the overwhelming fragrance. She glided the few steps across the hall and came to stand in front of him, her blouse unbuttoned and revealing a generous amount of cleavage.

"Sean, darling. I have tried to reach you all weekend to claim my rain check from a few weeks ago." She reached out and put a hand on his chest and gathered her lips into a pout. "Your niece said that you were out of town and she didn't know how to get hold of you." Her other hand reached up and she slid a manicured nail down his arm in an intimate gesture.

He silently thanked Ellie for helping him evade Julia. She had carried his cell phone for the office and he carried the pager in case she needed to get hold of him. "Julia, I've got an office full of patients. If you don't mind..." He started to move around her in the hallway but she anticipated his move and stepped in front of him.

"How about if I come by later this evening and bring a nice dinner for two and a pair of candles? Perhaps send your niece to a movie in Knoxville, my treat?" She sidled up to him and ran her manicured hand down his arm again, pushing her body against his in yet another intimate move.

"I have a lot of catching up to do this evening." The truth was, he wanted to see the work that the guys had done on Maggie's barn and stables before his clients brought their horses out to board. He also had a truck load of furniture to unload then he hoped that he could sit on the front porch with her and watch the sun go down over the mountains. But if he didn't get to work now, it would be a very late day at the office. He took her hand off his arm and tried to gently move her aside.

She stuck out her bottom lip and tried another tactic. "Independence Day is coming up at the end of the week. How about you and I go into Gatlinburg and watch the fireworks and rent a nice, secluded cabin for two where we can make some of our own fireworks. I can guarantee you they will be hotter than the ones that light up the sky."

Sean had been chased and seduced by other women, but never had he met up with someone as bold and determined as Julia Evans. A few weeks ago he might have succumbed to her overt efforts to get him into bed. Not now that he knew the truth about what Maggie's mother had done to both of them. As he tried to think of a tactful way to put the woman off, Ellie skidded around the corner and he gave a sigh of relief.

"Uncle Sean, Doc is here to help you out so I'm going to go ahead and head out to pick up Maggie." She picked up her keys from the counter and bent to retrieve her purse from the floor by the reception desk. "Doc has the cat with the BB gun shot in the shoulder in exam room A. He said you could take the puking puppy in B." She grinned at him then turned to Julia. "Ma'am, I think that's your sports car blocking my truck at the side. Can I get you to move it?" She rushed toward the side door and turned back to them. "Thanks!"

Julia reached in her purse and pulled out a set of keys. "I'll make that reservation for us for Friday night and pick you up at six-thirty." She didn't give Sean a chance to respond, but blew him a kiss as she opened the door to the waiting area.

He cringed as he saw some of his clients watch the entire exchange, including the kiss she blew him and felt his face grow hot with embarrassment that she had acted that way in front of people. Letting out a breath, Sean told himself that he would have to try to talk with Julia sometime before Friday to let her know that he wasn't interested in an evening or a weekend or even a quick roll in the sheets with her anymore. He grabbed the chart from the rack on the side of the door of the exam room and stepped inside to deal with the vomiting puppy.

Julia got in her car and put the key in the ignition. After the engine purred to life she put the car in gear and backed out of her parking spot at the side of the building. She pulled onto the street and reached for her cell phone. How convenient that Philip's ex-wife was going to be gone for the day. Perhaps she could go out there and nose around, maybe find some building violations. Better yet, perhaps there were some combustible materials lying around that might just catch on fire before the day was over. After all, if there wasn't a house there, the woman couldn't start a bed and breakfast, could she?

Philip answered her call on the second ring. "Julia, I asked you to give me a few more days on this. My attorney called and said that some attorney in Lexington wants to talk about a deal."

"I'm not waiting to see if you get some sort of deal out of your ex-wife. I'm going to go out there today and see what I might find laying around." She paused and reapplied her lipstick using her rear-view mirror. "In the meantime, I want you to try to keep her busy on Friday. Maybe play nice and ask her to dinner to try to make amends for your past indiscretions."

She smirked as she thought of having the opportunity to get the sexy doctor in her bed. Even though she was angered at Philip's suggestion last night, it wouldn't be a hardship to have hot, steamy sex with the local veterinarian. She was tired of being bored in this little town and she needed some distraction that she was sure the doctor could provide.

"All right, Julia. I will try my best." He paused for a moment. "I think we can get this whole deal resolved by the weekend."

"It better be, Philip. Or I will be flying to Chicago Sunday and meeting with your CEO on Monday morning bright and early." She pushed the button on her phone to end the call and maneuvered the car onto the back road that would eventually take her to the coveted piece of property out in the middle of nowhere.

CHAPTER TWENTY-THREE

Julia sat in her car in the parking lot of the little convenience store and watched the road that led to the prime property that her clients wanted to purchase to develop into a resort of timeshares. She impatiently tapped a polished fingernail on the steering wheel as she wondered what was taking Sean's impertinent niece so long to pick up Margaret Stanford. The girl had been horrid to her on Saturday when she drove up in front of Sean's cabin to invite him for a drive to Knoxville. She started with not even letting her up on the porch, choosing instead to block the steps then refused to give Julia the number where Sean could be reached. When she arrived at the animal clinic this morning, the girl ignored her when she rang the bell at the counter. Finally, the older woman who generally manned the front desk came and escorted Julia into Sean's private office to wait for him. Julia seethed as she recalled the comment she overheard the girl say about her being 'in heat' as if she were some sort of pathetic animal.

Finally, she caught a glimpse of the battered truck turning onto the highway that led to the interstate. She could see two heads in the cab, so she was certain the property would be deserted now. Putting the car into gear, she steered out of the parking lot and headed toward the road that would take her to the prime property with the view of the mountains.

The only vehicle parked in front of the old farmhouse was an old pick-up truck. Julia remembered seeing Margaret driving the old truck in town; she must have gotten rid of the Lincoln. As she parked behind the truck, she saw a big dog lumber out of the barn and start toward the car. She hesitated for a moment, then reached in the bag beside her and pulled out a stick of beef jerky. "Here dog, come get this nice piece of meat." She held out the unwrapped stick and waited while the dog sniffed it then took it out of her hand. Patting the dog on the head, she spoke softly. "Good dog. I won't hurt you. I just want to walk around and look at things." The dog wagged its tail and licked her hand, which she quickly wiped on her shorts.

Glancing around the yard, she noticed that a lot of work had been completed since she was out here last. The flower beds were overflowing with bright colored blooms and the front porch held a swing at one end and wicker furniture at the other. She stepped up on the porch and peered in the window. A dining room table sat in the middle of the room with a massive flower arrangement in the center and the built-in china cabinets were filled with dishes and glassware. She walked over to the door and tried the knob, the door was locked. Stepping off the porch, she walked around to the back of the house and found a sun porch where several buckets of paint sat. The porch door was unlocked and she twisted the knob and stepped inside. She crossed the cement floor and tried the door that went to the house. It was locked as well. She paused for a moment, surveying the cans of paint and the pile of newspaper next to them. Could be useful.

She ventured back into the lawn and crossed the driveway to the barn. Stepping inside, her nose immediately twitched from the odor of old straw and dust. Several horse stalls lined one side of the barn and she walked down the center to another door which led out to a fenced pasture. At the end stall, she opened the gate and looked inside. Several bags of old clothes sat in the corner and the straw on the floor was dry and brittle. Maybe this was an even better scenario than the paint and paper on the back porch. A couple kids were using the barn to make out one night, one of them smoking and don't get the cigarette stubbed out. The straw catches on fire and ignites the bags of clothes. *Yes, this could work really well.*

"Hey, lady. What are you doing in here?" A male voice demanded from the open stall door. Julia jumped and her mind struggled to come up with a response. "Umm, I was just looking around. I heard that Mrs. Stanford had made a lot of progress out here and I wanted to see for myself." She smiled at the young man and stepped out of the stall.

Tom frowned and gave her a skeptical look. "Well, all the work she's done is to the house. Why are you out here lookin' around?" He stepped back and waited for her to walk past him.

"Oh, I thought I heard something out here and just came out to investigate." She walked out of the barn and stood outside, waiting for him to join her. "Guess I must have been hearing things." She put on a smile for the young man. "I thought I might see if she would let me board a horse out here, I am thinking about buying one."

"Well, if you would like to see the inside of the house, you might want to come back when Maggie gets here. Right now, me and my buddies have work to do." He motioned toward the three other young men that were sitting on the back of a big truck filled with supplies.

She smiled at all the young men. "I'll have to do that. Perhaps she will be home later this evening?" She stretched her arms and thrust her bosom forward to entice the boys and take their minds off why she was even out here to begin with. She watched as one of the boy's eyes widened and looked at her appreciatively.

Tom nodded. "Yeah, Doc McDonald is supposed to meet her out here later with some furniture. You can come back then." He stood to the side and motioned for her to leave.

ꕥꕥꕥꕥꕥꕥꕥꕥꕥꕥ

From her place in the driver's seat, Ellie grinned at Maggie. "Alright, what kept you up so late last night? Uncle Sean was tossing and turning all night too. I heard him get up a couple of times."

Maggie scratched a spot of paint off her kneecap that she missed when she showered this morning. "Oh, I was just trying to finish up painting the last guest room last night. Your cousin gave me this

awesome brass bed to go in there and I wanted to make sure the room was painted and dried before Sean brings the stuff in this evening." Silently, she wondered if Sean's reason for being sleepless were because he was thinking about her.

"How was Rick, Emma and Sally? Isn't their house just fantastic?" She steered the truck up the ramp to the interstate. "I just love Emma's garden." She glanced over at her companion and lifted an eyebrow curiously.

At the mention of the garden, Maggie thought of the intimate moment she and Sean spent there in the hours just before dawn. Those thoughts caused her heart to do a flip and she felt a tightening in her stomach as she recalled how Sean had touched her, how he had so easily pushed her over the edge right there in the predawn moments. Taking a deep breath to calm her thoughts, she answered Ellie. "Your cousins seem like such nice people, and their little girl is just adorable."

Ellie burst out laughing. "Sarah is the most precocious child I have ever been around! God, I remember at Christmas we took her to see Santa Claus and she told him that her mama wanted some time alone with her daddy so they could make her a baby brother." Her eyes filled with tears from her laughter. "Then she told Santa that they might need some clay to make a baby with."

Maggie joined in laughing with her. "She doesn't miss a beat, does she?" The little girl had tiptoed in her bedroom the previous morning and climbed up on the bed and woke her up by prying her eyelids open with her tiny fingers. She whispered that it was time to get up because her mama was 'fixin' to make pancakes and ham for breakfast and couldn't start until everyone was up. "Sean said that she acts like you used to act when you were little."

"Uncle Sean always has to point out that I was a handful." She smiled wistfully. "I don't know how he did it, stepping in and taking care of me when my mom died. He put his own life on hold for all these years just so he could make sure that I got through school and sent off to college." She glanced over at Maggie before continuing. "It's time for him to start his own family and be happy. I don't know what happened between you and Uncle Sean in the past, but whatever it was, I hope that the two of you can put it behind you and go on from here."

Maggie was speechless. She didn't even know how to respond to Ellie. All the dreams that she had of marrying Sean and having his babies were shattered when he quit contacting her. Now, knowing the truth, she couldn't understand why Sean hadn't tried to see her anyway despite what her mother told him. She felt like he hadn't trusted her enough or believed in her enough or he surely would have tried to contact her. Despite that, her heart ached with wanting to be with him the way they planned when they were younger.

"I'm sorry, Maggie. I didn't mean to upset you. It's just that I see how Uncle Sean looks at you when he thinks nobody is looking." She reached across the seat and patted Maggie's hand. "I hope that the two of you end up together. Then you could be my aunt *and* my friend."

Through the threat of tears, Maggie smiled. "That is a really nice thing for you to say." Her heart fluttered, the younger girl couldn't have said anything nicer to her at that moment.

CHAPTER TWENTY-FOUR

Sean's day was extremely busy. Halfway through the day, he got called out on an emergency where a horse got bumped by a car on one of the narrow back roads that led to Gatlinburg. It always frustrated him when tourists didn't watch their speed on the back roads, there was always the chance that an animal of some sort could run out of one of the wooded areas. He remembered the first year after he set up practice with the old veterinarian that everyone referred to as "“Doc". It had been the weekend before the Fourth of July and a group of young tourists went around a sharp curve too fast, not expecting the mother bear that was in the middle of the road. Even though they swerved, they caught the mother bear with the back bumper of their car and knocked her into the ravine. Sean accompanied the game warden and sheriff to the scene but the best they could do was shoot the bear to put her out of her misery. The two cubs were tranquilized and taken to a wildlife refuge where they could be cared for until they were old enough to be reintroduced to the wild. That incident stuck with Sean to this day and when he drove out to tend to the horse this afternoon, he was less than patient with the driver of the car who struck the horse.

It was nearing five when he finally sat down in his private office and put his feet up on the desk. Running his hand through his hair, he closed his eyes for a moment to try to rid him of the beginning of a stress headache. The office was quiet except for his attendant cleaning up in the last treatment room and he could hear her humming while she worked. He sat up and started going through the stack of messages that appeared to have grown since this morning and discovered the one from Char. It was marked "urgent", but he couldn't for the life of him figure out what might be so important unless it was about the boys working out at Maggie's.

He hoped that they were able to accomplish the list of things he gave them to do when he hired them on Friday night. He picked up the phone and dialed Char's number, only to be greeted by the answering machine. Not leaving a message, he hung up the phone and tackled the other calls that needed immediate attention and sat the other messages aside for later.

His assistant, Alice, stuck her grey head in the doorway. "Hey, Dr. Sean, I've finished cleaning up. You want me to lock the door behind me when I leave?"

Generally, he would have told her to leave it alone since he was going to be heading out himself shortly. However, remembering Julia Evans' visit, he didn't want to chance that she might show up and delay him from getting out to Maggie's before too late. "Yes, please." He paused for a moment before he finished. "Alice, thanks for your patience today. I appreciate it."

Alice Malone smiled at her employer. "Think nothin' of it, Dr. Sean. Been one heck of a day around here and it looks like you could use a good meal and a bit of sleep." A lifetime resident of the town, she also had little patience for the carelessness of the tourists. "Heard you gave that tourist hell. I'm sure he got what was comin' to him, driving like a maniac on Lower Valley Road." With a wave of her plump hand, she shut the office door and he heard her let herself out the side door.

Before he left, he picked up the phone and called the owner of the horse to check on it. Just a good-sized gash on its foreleg and a nasty strain, the horse would be fine after the proper care and rest. The bumper on the Mercedes convertible was another story, and in the shock of being hit, the horse had managed to defecate all over the front of car. Sean grinned as he remembered the look of disgust on the face of the female passenger as she sat in the car fanning herself with a map.

Sean didn't take the time to shower and change clothes before he drove the truck full of furniture out to Maggie's. He knew he smelled like animal flesh, sweat and disinfectant but it was already getting late and he wanted to be out at Maggie's when she and Ellie returned from Knoxville. The drive went relatively quickly, even though the winding roads were such that he couldn't drive as fast as he'd like to be driving.

He pulled the truck into the driveway and saw Char sitting on the porch steps with Tom and his friends. She stood up and put her hands on her hips as he stopped the truck in front of the house and waited while he shut off the ignition and climbed down from the cab. "Thank goodness you're here. I need to talk to you before Maggie gets home." Her hands moved frantically as she continued. "I overheard that vile woman talking to Maggie's ex-husband in the lawn last night. They didn't know I was there." She tugged at his arm and pulled him toward the porch swing. "Sit down while I tell you the whole damn thing."

As Sean sat and listened, Char related the whole conversation that she overheard the previous night. When she was finished, Tom stepped up on the porch and Char looked up at him. "Tell him the rest, Tom."

"Well, when we got out here today, that Julia lady was here snooping around in the barn." He put his hands in his jeans pockets and kicked at a twig on the porch. "She said she was thinkin' about boardin' a horse out here but I don't think that woman would want to be within three feet of a horse, let alone bein' on top of one." One of his friends snickered a little bit and he grinned. "Eddie here thinks that the only thing she'd be good at ridin'..."

"Tom! Don't you dare repeat what Eddie said! I raised you better than that, boy!" Char gave her son a warning look before she turned back to Sean. "Sorry, Sean. These boys tend to have dirty minds these days." Sean's face turned red as he thought of Julia's propositions to him and of Ellie's earlier remark. He couldn't resist shocking Char. "That's okay. Ellie said the woman was in heat this morning." This earned a chorus of laughter from the young men standing around the porch. Sean winked at the boys. "You guys think you can unload this furniture into the house while I call my cousin?"

When Maggie and Ellie returned to the farm, Sean was wandering around the barn making sure the stables were in condition to take the boarders that would arrive the next day. He heard the women chatting as they approached. He was going to save Char's information for later, much later. Rick's advice was that they call a meeting with Philip and his attorney and invite Char to join them. The thought was that Sean would also ask Julia to accompany him to the meeting under the premise that he was taking her to dinner after a business meeting. Sean's concern was how he would unload Julia after the meeting, so they decided to get Julia on speaker phone during the meeting.

"What are you doing, Sean?" Maggie inquired as she took a sweeping glance around the clean barn with new feed bins constructed and the stalls full of fresh straw. Her suspicious gaze came back to Sean's face.

"Well, I had this idea that until you were able to make money boarding guests, you could make money boarding horses." He grinned from ear-to-ear at his idea. "Your first guests will start arriving tomorrow. Old Alex had more horses boarded this summer than he had room for so he encouraged the owners to bring 'em out here. There will be five boarders in all." He quoted her the amount she would receive in advance for boarding the horses for the remainder of the year.

Her face went from bewildered to pure excitement and it did his heart good to see the bright smile on her face. The income would help her finance the remainder of the work that needed done before she could open the bed and breakfast. Now all she had to do was resolve the legal issue with Philip. "I don't know what to say!"

"It will be a little extra work for you to take care of the horses, but Ellie and I will come out and help you with them as much as we can." He walked over and put his arms around both women. "Right now, though, I'm starved to death. Can I interest you ladies in dinner in town?"

ꟸꟸꟸꟸꟸꟸꟸꟸꟸꟸꟸ

Philip watched as the threesome walked into the greasy spoon diner on Main Street. Margo was dressed in a pair of ratty jeans and had a ball cap on top of her dark hair. He shook his head in bewilderment as to why his ex-wife would dress like she was and go out in public. It must be because she wasn't as polished as her mother and stepfather led him to believe. She was just a country bumpkin underneath. It's no wonder she couldn't appreciate the finer things that he offered her during their marriage. Had she appreciated those things, she might have been more inclined to overlook his little affairs instead of hitting him with a divorce suit.

Most of the women in the circle he traveled would have been more than happy to overlook the little bit of fun he allowed himself in return for the expensive clothes, jewelry and cars. He felt his family was misled by her mother when she encouraged the meeting of the two. His current lover, Melanie, would be more than happy to take him for what he had to offer in material things. And she wasn't too bad in the sack, either. At least she showed an interest in doing some of the things he liked to do in bed whereas, Margo never had the slightest interest in experimenting with other couples and such.

Unfortunately, Melanie wasn't as bright as Margo. Even though she pressed lately for a commitment, he would never take her as a wife. She would be a detriment to his career if she was left to entertain his business associates. The only conversation she could carry on was about the latest Hollywood gossip. That was the polar opposite of Margo who was an intelligent woman able to discuss politics and business with a high level of knowledge. Or so he thought. Before she made the decision to try to start some silly bed and breakfast down here in the middle of Podunkville. What a waste of intelligence for her to live down here among a bunch of inbred idiots.

He watched through the window of the diner as she and the veterinarian and his niece laughed at something the dumb, blonde waitress was saying to them as she poised with an order pad by their table. Steeling himself for what he needed to do to satisfy Julia for right now, he opened the car door and started across the street.

CHAPTER TWENTY-FIVE

They were in the middle of eating dinner when Philip approached their table with an apologetic smile pasted on his face. "I'm sorry to disturb your meal, but could I speak with Margo alone for a moment?" His question was directed at Sean who was sitting stiffly in the booth with a murderous look on his face.

"You might try asking me that question, rather than my friends." Maggie spoke up to break the silence that fell over the table when Philip approached. She glared at him and fingers tightened on the fork she was holding to the point her knuckles turned white.

"Well, I wanted to do the polite thing and make sure your companions didn't mind." The sheepish look on his face was obviously fake.

"Go ahead, Philip. What is it that you wanted to talk to me about?" She laid her fork on the table and looked at him expectantly. "Whatever it is, you can say it in front of my friends."

Philip shook his head, annoyance flaring briefly in his eyes. "Really, I need to talk to you in private. Could you step outside with me for a moment?" He stepped to the side and motioned for her to go ahead of him.

"I hardly see that anything you would have to say couldn't be said in front of my friends.

I'm in the middle of eating dinner right now." She picked up her fork and stabbed a piece of meat in a dismissive gesture.

"Margo, please. I need to talk to you." He did his best to sound calm while his body language belied what was obviously becoming anger.

"I think the lady has already told you that she wasn't interested in speaking with you alone." Sean straightened up in the booth in a protective action. "If you don't mind, we are eating dinner and you are interrupting it." His blue eyes darkened as he stared at the man standing by their booth.

Philip held up a hand. "Sorry to disturb you." He backed away from the table. "Margo, I will catch up with you later." He nodded at the threesome. "Have a nice dinner."

Ellie was the first one to speak after Philip left the table. "Imagine the nerve of that jack..." She was abruptly cut off by Sean's severe look. "Elizabeth Marie, just drop it for now." He warned his niece as he kept an eye on Philip, who was walking across the street to an expensive, black sedan. "Sometimes it's best not to speak what is on your mind."

Ellie blushed at her uncle's reprimand. "Sorry, Uncle Sean. It's just that he is a real jerk to think he can walk up here and demand that Maggie go outside with him. Couldn't he see we were eating dinner?" She flipped her pony tail indignantly.

Maggie reached across the table and patted Ellie's hand. "Don't worry about it. That's just how Philip is. He thinks everyone should jump at his beck and call." She nudged Sean with her leg under the table and shot him a warning glance about chastising Ellie too much.

Sean dragged his eyes away from the window to see the plea in Maggie's dark eyes. He glanced across the table at Ellie. "Sorry kid. I've just had a rough day and I'm taking it out on everyone. Maybe I ought to just go home and go to bed." He looked out the window again.

Maggie could see Char watching them from the door of the kitchen and she thought she caught Sean and Char exchange a look. She wondered what that was about. It was already rough enough having their peaceful dinner interrupted by the man who was threatening to ruin her carefully thought out plans. Her dreams. Now there was something the two were hiding from her. Silently, she chided herself for imagining things.

Sean reached across the table and touched her hand. "Do you have plans for the Fourth?"

She shook her head. Maggie hadn't even thought of the upcoming holiday. "No, why?"

"I was thinking maybe we could go over to Gatlinburg and check out the fireworks. Maybe grab dinner while we are over there?"

"That sounds nice." She looked over at Ellie who was beaming like a lantern.

As they walked outside, the scent of fresh rain coming over the mountains intermingled with the scent of mountain laurel. He took Maggie's hand as they started down the sidewalk toward the truck and gave it a squeeze. "Do you want to go home or do you feel like taking a drive?"

They reached the truck and Maggie turned to Sean. She could see the weariness around his eyes and smiled as he tried to swallow a yawn. She covered their entwined hands with her free hand. "As much as I would enjoy going for a drive, I'm really worn out. Besides, it's going to rain before long and I'd rather be curled up at home in my bed with a good book before it starts." She tugged at his hand. "Come on; take me home so that you can get a good night's rest before you have to work tomorrow. We can go for a drive another time when we are both up to it."

After Sean and Ellie dropped her off at home, she waited on the porch till both pair of tail lights faded down the lane. In the distance, she could hear the first rumblings of thunder and the leaves on the trees rustled with the stirring winds. She leaned over the rail and inhaled deeply. The air here was so refreshing, with the scent of freshly cut grass, flowers, and rain mingling together with the already unique smell of mountain air. Closing her eyes, she smiled and let the wind blow across her face until the first drops of rain splashed against her skin. She turned and went into the house where Mama was waiting patiently on the run in the hall and the cat was perched on the newel post of the stairs.

ᨐᨐᨐᨐᨐᨐᨐᨐᨐᨐᨐ

Philip steered the car down the lane to Margo's house. The wipers squeaked across the windshield as the last drops from the passing shower fell. He could see her porch light was on but the only vehicle in the drive was the old truck that she had traded his prized Lincoln for. He cursed at the thought, but trailed off as he realized the end of Margo's little escapade was near. She wouldn't have any choice but to give up the old farmhouse and all the land surrounding it. Perhaps, she would even beg him to let her move back into the condo. He smirked at the thought of having her come crawling back to him. Right now, though, he needed to try to get her to go to dinner with him on Friday evening so that Julia could work on the veterinarian.

He didn't care much for the woman or her brassy ways, but he would do this little thing for her if he could help her drive a wedge between Margo and her new boyfriend. Knowing the history of their relationship, he doubted that either of them had much trust for each other. His plan was to make sure that when they went out for dinner on Friday, they just happened to run into Julia with the vet. He knew that Julia planned on taking the vet to Gatlinburg for dinner and to watch the fireworks, then she was going to use one of her company's time shares to seduce him afterward. He figured if Margo and the vet were to run into each other with someone else, they might each be willing to give the person they were with some revenge sex.

Parking the car, he could see that there was a light glowing in one of the rooms upstairs. He straightened the collar of his shirt and checked his hair in the rear view mirror before getting out of the car. Whistling to himself, he started up the porch steps and lifted his hand to knock on the door. He listened as he heard the sound of footsteps and pasted on his best smile as he waited for the door to open.

Her face was expectantly bright, then it faded and he watched as she made sure the lock on the screen was latched and peered out. "What are you doing here, Philip?" She sighed resignedly.

"Come on, Margo. Just let me in for a minute." He smiled at her through the screen. "I just wanted to talk to you and tell you how sorry I was for everything."

"Okay, you've told me. Now go get in your car and go back to where you came from." She started to turn away from the door but he spoke again.

"Margo, I know I did a lot wrong in our marriage. I know that I shouldn't have tried to sue you for part of this property. Can I make amends for it?" He cleared his throat and reached for the door handle. "Come on, let me in and I promise you that I will drop the lawsuit."

"How about you drop the lawsuit then come back and try to make amends? You've done a lot of despicable things in the time that I've known you but this one has to beat all! You knew damn well that I had this property and what it was worth because you are the one that took the liberty of having an appraisal done when I inherited it." Her words were clipped.

"Margo, I was just trying to help you divest yourself of a piece of property that you had no use for." He raised his voice and drew his hand impatiently through his hair. "You had everything you needed in Chicago, this piece of land..." He motioned around him before continuing. "This piece of land is just a ball and chain that will tie you here whether you want to stay or not."

Her eyes blazed at him furiously and her cheeks flushed. "Philip, this is my home. Repeat it to yourself until it sinks in that thick skull of yours! This is the only home that I've really had and this is where I'm going to stay." Her voice continued to rise and the damned dog got up from the rug in the hall and growled. "Now, get off my porch and off my property or I'm going to call the sheriff and have you arrested for trespassing. Won't that look good on your impeccable background?"

He took a deep breath and stepped back from the door. "I suppose that joining me for dinner on Friday is out of the question?"

She let out a frustrated sound and slammed the door in his face. He heard her throw the dead bolt and he realized that the situation was hopeless. There was no convincing her to sell this property and come home with him. Not that he wanted her back but to keep himself out of trouble at work, he'd do just about anything. He stood on the porch for a moment and found himself in darkness as she switched the porch light off. Well, there was still the lawsuit. That would tie her up in legal fees and hopefully break her to the point she would have no choice but to sell the property to Julia.

CHAPTER TWENTY-SIX

Friday morning dawned bright and sunny with not a cloud in the bright blue sky over the mountains. Sean took this as a good sign that the meeting that Rick managed to set with Philip and his attorney in Lexington would go well. He glanced at his watch as he waited on Char's front porch for her to come out. With the drive up and the drive back, and allowing about an hour for the meeting, he should be able to make it back to town by late afternoon. That would leave plenty of time for him to take Maggie out for dinner and then to drive into Gatlinburg for the fireworks show tonight.

Char came out, her usual jeans and shirt replaced with a sharp, business-like suit in navy blue. She had a polka dot shirt on underneath the jacket and her feet were clad in a pair of sensible pumps instead of sneakers or sandals.

"Wow, Doc! You sure do clean up nice." She pinched the fabric of his suit jacket between her fingers. Sean grinned at the older woman and offered her his arm. "You look really nice, too. Big change from blue jeans and sneakers." She took his arm and they walked out to the truck. "This is my battle suit. Last time I wore it was when I went to court against Tommy's parents when he got killed in that accident down in South Carolina." She referred to her late husband, Tommy Grimes, who was a stock car driver that was killed in an accident on the track when another driver lost control and forced him into the wall. His parents fought her tooth and nail for the proceeds from the insurance settlement but Char had won, and used the money to purchase her little house and the diner. She worked herself hard from dawn to dusk to make the bar and grill a success, and to take her mind off the man that she and her son had idolized.

Sean patted the hand that was tucked into the crook of his arm as he opened the truck door for her. "Let's get this show on the road, Char."

Char chatted amicably, as she usually did, as he made the drive to Lexington. It made the time go a lot quicker and for that he was grateful. She was pleased with herself that she had overheard the conversation between Phillip and Julia and hoped that it would help Maggie. "I sure do like that little gal a whole lot." She poked him from the passenger seat. "And I think that you do too. So what's going on between the two of you? Do ya think y'all are going to be able to work things out?""'

He shrugged. "I think you are making too much out of this."

"Oh really? Come on, Doc. You were her first love and I'd bet my bottom dollar that she was yours. How awesome is it that you both end up back where it all started?" She chuckled. """I've heard all the stories about you two back then. You were quite an item."

"I think that you listen to too much gossip." He couldn't help but grin. The residents of Possum Creek were a tight knit bunch and everyone knew what everyone else was doing. Sometimes that was good and sometimes it wasn't.

"I think she's sweet on you too." Char shrugged her shoulders. "I"ll shut up about the two of you. Did your cousin think what I found out is going to help our Maggie?"

He sure hoped so. During their last conversation, Rick had mentioned he had called in a favor from one of the private investigators he used and the guy had managed to dig up quite a bit of dirt on Phillip. Dirt that could get him indicted for fraud if they were to press the issue. He didn't much care either way if the little bastard went away and left her alone.

Rick was waiting for them in the lobby of the office building in downtown Lexington when they arrived. He grinned at them. "The pompous ass and his attorney are already upstairs. I have Emma serving them coffee and bagels while they wait on us to join them." He stuck out a hand to Char. "I'm Rick Grafton, Sean's cousin."

Char smiled at the self-confident, young attorney. "Pleased to meet ya. I'm Charlotte Grimes." Her eyes twinkled. "Let's go up and burst this little jerk's balloon."

Rick and Sean laughed as they headed for the elevators. "Mr. Stanford thinks that his ex-wife is going to be joining us." He turned to look at Sean. "Does Maggie know what's going on today?"

Sean shook his head. "No, I didn't want her to know until it was all over and done with." He hesitated for a moment. "Just in case this doesn't work and she ends up having to go to court to keep the property."

"Well, I seriously doubt if it is going to go that far." Rick explained. "Emma did some research and found that Stanford had an appraisal of the land done long before Maggie filed for divorce. We have a copy of the appraisal as well as a signed statement from the appraiser that he personally delivered the document to Stanford's office three weeks before the divorce was filed. He's barking up the wrong tree here. And to top that off, my investigator found some other business dealings that are tied to Stanford that were less than above board."

Rick escorted them to an office adjacent to the conference room where Philip and his attorney, Melvin Dancer were ensconced. Sean could hear Emma's musical voice asking them if they would like more coffee and Philip's response that he would prefer to get this meeting over with. Sean grinned as Rick gave him and Char the thumbs up and went into the conference room, leaving them to wait for a moment in the office.

Char snickered as she heard Philip raise his voice when he found that Maggie wouldn't be joining them. His face reddened and a vein in his neck started throbbing as he gripped the pen in his hand a little more tightly. "What do you mean that Margaret won't be here for this meeting?" Philip turned an agitated face toward his attorney. "Mel, you told me that there wouldn't be any glitches. Did you lie?" He stood up and faced Rick Grafton. "Or is this some scheme to get me to agree to let this drop? My ex-wife lied about the value of the property she owns in Tennessee during the divorce proceedings and I have suffered financial injury due to her lie."

Rick looked at Melvin Dancer. "Mr. Dancer, would you please ask your client to calm down?" He walked over to the door leading to the adjoining office and pulled it open. "I believe you both will want to listen to what we have to say."

Philip sat down in the chair before his attorney could say anything to him. "What do you mean? Who are we?" He crushed the paper cup that was sitting in front of him. "I thought that my ex-wife wasn't here."

"Oh, Ms. Stanford isn't here. However, there are a couple of persons who you will definitely want to meet." He opened the door and motioned Sean and Char in the room. Sean watched the look on Philip's face grow even angrier as the two newcomers sat down at the conference table across from him.

"What are they doing here? I don't want to talk to my ex-wife's lover or some waitress in a greasy spoon out in the middle of nowhere." Philip looked at his attorney for guidance.

"Mr. Grafton, perhaps you should give a quick and concise explanation to us before we go any further with this meeting." Mr. Dancer opened flipped open his briefcase and pulled out a legal pad to take notes.

"Certainly." Rick pulled out his notes and started speaking. "Mr. Stanford, do you recall a meeting with a certain Julia Evans on Sunday night of this week in the lawn of Main Street Bed and Breakfast in Possum Creek? Or perhaps you would like to take a look at what is in this file?" He pushed a manilla folder across the table and waited.

Three pairs of eyes watched Philip's reaction to the information contained in the file. His face paled beneath his tan as he looked to his attorney for direction.

Prodding him, Rick spoke again. "Perhaps we could get Ms. Evans on the speaker phone here with us to jog your memory?" He turned to Sean. "Do you have Ms. Evans' cell phone number?" He took the business card Sean handed to him and picked up the phone in the middle of the conference table.

"Stop. I need to talk with my attorney privately." He looked around the room, his gaze coming to stop on Char's face. "You do know eavesdropping on a private conversation is rude don't you? Of course, what would one expect of a backwoods..."

"Philip, don't add insult to injury here." His attorney looked up at Rick. "Might I have a private word with my client?"

They all got up and left Phillip and his attorney alone. Sean kept glancing at his watch as he paced back and forth in front of the windows while Char sat on one of the chairs and tapped her foot impatiently. "What are they doing in there?"

Rick smiled and sat down on the edge of his desk. "I'm sure they are going through all the documents I supplied. Enough information to ruin the guy if not put him in prison. Just give it time. This is going exactly like I believed it would."" He looked over at the closed door. "If his attorney's got any sense at all, he will convince his client to let this go."

Finally, the door opened and Mr. Dancer motioned them in the conference room. Phillip's head was bowed and he didn't even look up as everyone filed into the room. Once they were all seated again, Mr. Dancer inclined his head toward his client. ""Mr. Stanford has agreed to drop the suit against his former spouse. But there are conditions."

The conditions were that Rick would relinquish the information he obtained on Phillip. Char and Sean would have to sign an agreement they would not share their knowledge of the matter with the authorities. Rick pushed for a no-trespass order for Phillip to refrain from contacting Maggie, which he grudgingly agreed would be appropriate under the circumstances. After everything was signed, Rick stood and held out a hand to Mr. Dancer. "Thank you for meeting us today. I hope your client understands the circumstances he narrowly escaped today."

"He does." He nodded toward Phillip. "Tell them the concerns you shared with me."

Without looking anyone in the eyes, he related the conversation where Julia insinuated that if there were no house there, there would be no reason for Maggie to not sell the property. He felt that she meant to do something destructive to the property because apparently, Julia had made a deal with some investors the year before where they deposited a large sum of money to arrange for the purchase of the property. She stood to lose a great deal if the sale didn't go through.

Char looked at Rick questioningly. "Do you think that someone should call the sheriff and alert him that this Julia woman might do something to harm Maggie?" Rick nodded his head and looked over at Sean. "I've already contacted the Tennessee State Police." He glanced at his watch. "I have a friend who is a commander of the unit that is responsible for your sector of the state and he is going to pay this Evans woman a visit any time now."

"Are you going to call Maggie and tell her? She will be so relieved." Emma asked Sean as she entered the conference room once Phillip and his attorney had departed. "Now she won't have to worry about anyone trying to take over her grandparents' property."

Sean grinned and shook his head. "No, I think I'll wait to tell Maggie. I have plans for tonight and I'll tell her then." He was glad that this was one obstacle they wouldn't have to face. He couldn't wait to get back town and pick Maggie up to take her to the fireworks show. He remembered a Fourth of July many summers ago where he watched as her eyes danced with delight when the fireworks went off above them in the night sky. He hoped that tonight would be the same, and he would see the excitement in her eyes like he had that night.

"Let's go grab a bite to eat. I've got court this afternoon and Emma has to file these documents before the courthouse closes. There's a little place across the street that has some great sandwiches."

Later, Char and Sean bid their good byes to Rick and Emma as they stood on the curb in front of the restaurant. Emma stood on tiptoe and hugged Sean. "Good luck, cousin. I hope that all your dreams come true. Maggie is a wonderful person and you both deserve the happiness that was stolen from you a long time ago."

Sean called Maggie from his cell phone when they were about an hour away from town.

She was out of breath when she answered and he chuckled. "Sounds like you were busy."

"I was mucking out the stalls. What are you doing?" He could imagine her with straw stuck to her hair.

"I had some business out of town and wanted to call and remind you about our plans for tonight." He glanced over at Char who was sleeping on the passenger side of the truck.

"No, I haven't forgotten. I asked Ellie to join us but she said she was busy."

Sean could hear the disappointment in her voice and grinned. Ellie had managed to do her part and make an excuse if Maggie asked her to go along tonight. It had cost him twenty bucks, but it was well worth it. "When I get back to town, I have to run a couple of errands but I will come get you right after. Say, around six?"

"That would be fine. I've got plenty to do around here until then."

"I'll call you when I get ready to head out your way." He grinned again as he thought of his plans for them that night.

CHAPTER TWENTY-SEVEN

Maggie stood under the shower in the new bathroom in her master suite that Tom and his crew finished up for her this week. The hot water spraying out of the shower head was heavenly relief to her aching muscles. Mucking out the stalls in the barn and caring for the five horses that she was boarding was a lot more work than she remembered.

Thankfully, Tom and his friends moved all her bedroom furniture from the brick smoke house into the completed master suite while she was working in the barn. Then Ellie showed up and put fresh linens on the bed, hung the curtains, and connected the computer at her desk. They had all been sitting on the porch with secretive smiles on their faces when she dragged in from the barn and practically shoved her into the bedroom to show her the completed project. She was surprised but worried because now the property would be worth more to Phillip and she hated thinking she may have to sell it all.

She stepped out of the shower and reached for one of the thick, new towels that were on a stand outside the walk-in shower and wrapped it around her. The tiles were cool under her feet which were still feeling hot and blistered from the heavy boots she wore out in the barn while she was working.

Standing in the bath, she admired the textured, cream colored walls with the contrasting brick colored tiles. Two sepia prints of some old cabins tucked away in the surrounding mountains hung on the walls and were framed with barn wood that still had some red paint stuck to it. Tom had also fashioned the stand by the shower that held the red and blue towels as well as a planter in the corner out of the same lumber.

Maggie turned and walked out into her bedroom and sitting area. One of her grandmother's quilts covered the high, four poster bed and several embroidered pillows were tossed fashionably against the bed pillows. In one corner of the room was Emma's roll top desk holding her computer and a brand-new office chair and in the opposite corner was a love seat facing the armoire which held her television. On the bureau, Ellie had arranged several different sizes of candles on a pewter platter and a picture of her grandfather and grandmother was on the night stand by the bed. Lacy curtains hung at the windows which overlooked the wooded area to the back of the house and there was thick, navy blue carpet underfoot.

The room smelled like the vanilla and cinnamon candles she lit before she stepped into the shower. Although she was tempted to lie down on the inviting bed for a moment to rest her screaming muscles, she glanced at the clock on the desk and realized that she only had about thirty minutes to finish getting ready. Sean called her from his house and told her he would be leaving his house on time to get there by six.

Maggie picked up the denim skirt and white camisole from the bed and let the towel fall to the carpet. She slid into her undergarments and then pulled on the skirt and camisole before going back into the bathroom to dry her hair and put on some makeup. Fussing a little longer than normal, she added some fullness and wave to her hair with a curling iron then applied just a touch more make-up than she normally wore. Just as she sprayed on some perfume, she heard the door-bell ring.

Grabbing her sandals, she dashed down the hall to find Sean waiting on the porch. "Hi there." She smiled as she opened the door to let him into the foyer. "Did you get your business taken care of today?"

He smiled, nodded and bent to brush his lips across her forehead. "Yes, actually it was a very productive meeting. Are you ready to go?"

"Let me grab my purse and slip on my sandals and I will be ready. Are we going to eat in town? I heard Char was making blueberry and cherry cobbler as a special for the Fourth."

He put an arm around her shoulders as they stepped outside and onto the porch. "I thought we would go into Gatlinburg and eat before the fireworks. Do you mind?"

"Not at all." She let him help her up in the cab of the truck. "It's nice that the fireworks for Gatlinburg are on a different night than in Possum Creek. I promised Char I would help her out because she is short a waitress."

"Yeah, I think that Pigeon Forge and Knoxville are doing theirs tomorrow too. We could go right after you get finished helping Char."

"I think I would like to see what the park has to offer. If I get finished helping Char early enough." She settled in the passenger seat and fastened her belt as she waited him to walk around the truck and climb behind the wheel.

She was glad Sean chose the most scenic route through the foothills to get to Gatlinburg so it took a while to get there. When he pulled the truck onto the main highway, they noticed that a lot of the parking lots were filling up. He glanced over at Maggie. "Do you want to park outside of town and take the trolley? It might make it easier to get back out later."

She nodded, taking the trolley in Gatlinburg was one of her favorite things to do because it gave her an opportunity to watch the people milling about on the streets of the little mountain town that was one of the two tourist hubs of all the smaller towns in the area. She loved the quaint little shops they passed and there were vendors selling flags on several street corners. When the trolley stopped at their destination in the middle of town across from the aquarium, she stopped and handed one of the vendors her money and stuck the pole of the little flag into her purse.

Sean took her hand as they crossed the street and started walking up the hill toward the restaurant he decided they would eat. He had called and made reservations for a table outside so that they could sit and watch the tourists walk by. Reaching the entrance of the restaurant, Sean gave his name to the hostess who seated them outside on a balcony that overlooked the street. The street was jammed full of families visiting the area for the holiday weekend. A line of teens stood in line outside the amusement park ride simulator that boasted the '3-D Experience' while another group of teens made their way noisily toward a tower where there were arcade games.

Sean reached across the table and put his hand on Maggie's after the waitress came and took their drink order. "Do you want to watch the fireworks from down here on the street or take the tram up the mountain?"

Maggie lifted her eyes from the menu and smiled across the table. "Are you serious? Do you really think we will be able to get a tram ride as busy as it is here tonight?" For effect, she used her hand to motion at the masses of people jostling each other on the crowded sidewalks.

Sean grinned, his blue eyes twinkling. "I have connections." He laughed at her doubtful expression. "The tram it is."

ꟷ

Sean debated throughout their steak dinners when he should tell Maggie the good news about what transpired in Rick's office earlier that day. He held the copy of the court document that dismissed Philip's suit against Maggie for the property in the pocket of his jeans. It was waiting on the fax machine in his office when he returned from Lexington late in the afternoon compliments of Rick.

His thoughts were interrupted by a nudge from Maggie's foot under the table and he shifted his attention back to the woman across from him. "You sure drifted off there a moment." She spoke softly as she touched his hand. "I asked you about your day. You never said a whole lot about your meeting." She stopped and frowned. "Unless I'm prying."

Sean shook his head and squeezed her hand. "No, not at all." The waitress approached and he waited while she removed their plates and handed her his credit card. When the young woman walked out of earshot, he continued. "In fact, I was just getting ready to tell you all about it." He reached into his back pocket and pulled out the folded document and passed it across the table to her.

Puzzlement creased her forehead as she held the paper in her hand for a moment. "What's this?"

Sean grinned and motioned at the paper. "Go on, open it." He urged as the waitress returned his credit card and receipt to sign. When he looked up from signing the bill, Maggie's eyes glistened with tears.

"I don't understand." She read the paper again and looked back up at Sean. "How did Rick get him to drop the suit so quickly?" She sat quietly in her seat and listened as Sean told her the whole story of how Char had overheard Philip and Julia in the lawn and how they confronted him in front of his attorney. He told her how Emma had been able to find where Philip ordered and paid for an independent appraisal long before Maggie filed for divorce. He watched as her expression went from amazement to sadness to anger in a matter of moments.

"I don't understand how someone who claimed to have loved me could do something so despicable!" She hissed between her teeth while fury sparked from her dark eyes. Standing up from the table she looked across at Sean. "If you don't mind, can we go for a walk?"

They walked down the sidewalk not speaking. Sean could see the stiffness in her gait as she maneuvered through the crowds of people as if they didn't exist. He followed her until she reached a quiet spot on a stone bridge that crossed a bubbling creek and stopped. He watched her from behind as her shoulders slumped and when he noticed her trembling, he reached out and pulled her against him.

She turned and buried her face in his chest and he held her while she sobbed. He could smell the fragrance of her shampoo in the silky strands of her hair as he bent down and kissed the top of her head. Vanilla and flowers. "Shhh...don't cry, baby. Everything will be all right now." Her silent sobs tapered off and she shook her head. When she looked up at him, her brown eyes were troubled.

"You don't understand. It's not going to be all right. Everyone who has claimed to love me has betrayed me in some way. My mother...Philip...how can I ever trust anyone who says they love me again?"

Sean gazed down at her tear stained face and seeing her hurt like this tore at his heart. Was she referring to him as well? He probably deserved her feeling that way because he should have insisted on talking to Maggie in person that day in Chicago. But he had been so preoccupied with Kate's illness and trying to help take care of Ellie, he just accepted what her mother told him and walked away.

How could he ever make up for walking away that day and never looking back? How would he ever be able to make her believe that he loved her?

She wiped her eyes with the back of her hand and smiled up at him. "Let's go watch the fireworks and try to enjoy our evening." Sean reached for her hand and they started back up the sidewalk to the tram as the sun started falling below the mountains, illuminating the lush greenness of the trees that stood high on the mountaintop. Lights started coming on throughout the town and in the houses that were nestled in the side of the mountains as the sky exploded in shades of orange, purple and blue in one of the most magnificent sunsets that one could find. By the time they reached the boarding station for the tram, Maggie's tears were gone and he prayed she could once again believe that this part of the country would be her home.

CHAPTER TWENTY-EIGHT

As the tram rose on its cables, the first explosions sounded from below them. "Test ignitions." Sean chuckled as the first explosion startled Maggie, causing her to jump in the seat next to him. He patted her thigh as she blushed from her reaction.

"It's been so long since I've seen fireworks. I guess I forgot about how loud they could be." She smiled and tentatively grasped the hand that was on her thigh. Her eyes sparkled as she turned her face toward the sky.

Sean enjoyed watching her, her face animated with excitement as they reached the top of the mountain. She reminded him of a child discovering Christmas presents under the tree on Christmas morning, and they joined the line of people climbing off the tram. Despite the luxury she must have experienced with her mother and then her ex-husband, she still appeared to get excited over the simplest things.

Sean felt warmth in his chest as he realized that through the years, her innate values had not changed. He took her hand and led her off to an observation area that was already beginning to fill with families waiting for the fireworks show to begin. They found a relatively private corner that still afforded them the opportunity to get a good view of the fireworks. When the first cascade of golden light spread across the dark sky, the crowd cheered and Sean pulled Maggie close to his side.

A huge burst of multi-colored showers spiraled down toward the rooftops in the town below them and Maggie tugged at Sean's arm. "Oh, look! Isn't that the most awesome one we've seen so far?" Her eyes danced as she looked up at him.

His blue eyes met her brown ones and he reached out to touch her face. The only light was from the fireworks that were lighting up the sky in a grand finale of red, white and blue. Cautiously, he leaned down and brushed his lips across hers, then waited to see if she would continue the kiss. Her breath was warm against his face and her eyes opened for a moment, searching his before she brought their lips back together again.

As the final flickers died out in the sky, another type of fireworks were beginning to ignite between Sean and Maggie as his mouth urged her lips apart and his tongue slipped inside. Their tongues met and danced together in the wetness of her mouth. His fingers entwined in the strands of her hair as he pulled her closer to him and her hands fisted in the cotton of his shirt. For a long moment, it was just Sean and Maggie standing atop the mountain with the evening breeze swirling around them.

Sean pulled away first, his eyes searching her face. While his hands still cupped her head, he allowed his thumbs to stroke the softness of her cheeks. "Can I come home with you tonight?" His blue eyes darkened as he waited for her to respond.

She leaned her forehead against his chest and he heard her sigh. He wanted to hold her close to him. Feel her warmth and her touch on his body. "Maggie, if you aren't ready for that..." Sean spoke gently, his lips against her hair as he felt her nod her head.

"I want to make love with you, Sean." She lifted her head and smiled at him. "Let's get on the tram and go home."

She was quietly thoughtful on the drive home and he hoped she wouldn't change her mind. Her profile was illuminated by the moon overhead and the dashboard lights and he marveled at how peaceful she appeared. Maybe this would be the beginning of something lasting for them. But he didn't want to get ahead of himself here. It was just tonight and that's all he could hope for. Well, he hoped for more but wasn't quite sure what that something would be. As soon as Sean pulled the truck into the yard in front of Maggie's house, he shut off the ignition and reached for her. He lifted her chin with his finger and searched her eyes for any sign of doubt. "Are you sure about this?"

In response, she leaned toward him and kissed his face. Her lips brushed softly across his face and then down his neck causing him to shiver. Taking control of the situation, Sean pulled her against him and claimed her lips with his own in a kiss that left them both gasping for air when they finally pulled apart. Not ready to stop the kiss, he bent his head again and his tongue traced the outline of her lips until they parted and he slipped his tongue inside.

Her hands dug into his muscled shoulders and by the time the kiss ended, he found her settled across his lap. Sean opened the door of the truck walked around to the passenger side to lift her out of the cab. Setting her down gently until her feet were on the grass, he took her hand and led her toward the porch. Taking her keys, he unlocked the door and pulled her inside the darkened foyer. Once the door was shut firmly behind them, Sean tossed the keys on a side table and pulled her against him. "Can you feel how badly I want you right now?"

His arousal throbbed against the softness of her stomach and he heard her gasp as he ran his tongue around the outside of her ear. When she pulled away from him for a moment, he feared she was having second thoughts. But then she reached for his hand and led him through the house toward her bedroom.

Inside her bedroom, watched as she lit the grouping of candles on her bureau, filling the room with a soft, warm glow. When she turned toward Sean, they approached each other across the soft carpet and she reached for the buttons on his shirt. He was going to come undone before they ever made it to the bed.

He took her hand and they walked together to the bed where he sat and pulled her gently on his lap. When their lips met this time, it was her tongue probing inside of his mouth and her hands exploring the solid warmth of his chest. When she wriggled against him, he groaned and fell back on the softness of the mattress and pulled her with him.

Her mouth left his and she traced a wet trail from his mouth down the smoothness of his chest to the line of hair that extended above the waistband of his jeans as her fingers deftly unfastened the opening. He reached down and pulled her up the length of his body then rolled her over onto her back. "My God, woman! You are driving me mad!" He growled as he raised the bottom of her camisole to reveal the skin beneath it.

His teeth bit through the fabric of her bra as he nipped at one nipple while his fingers caressed the other one. He chuckled as her hips rose off the mattress and he reached underneath her to cup her buttocks with his free hand. When the air hit her bare skin as he removed her camisole then her bra, her nipples puckered in invitation and he dipped his head to encircle one of the taut buds with his mouth.

He alternated between sucking and licking while his fingers caressed the smooth skin of her stomach, and then reached below the waistband of her skirt. He stood long enough to remove his jeans then bent to remove the rest of her clothes. He ached with need for her. A need to bury himself in her warmth and take her over the edge of pleasure.

Taking a moment to gather his composure, he lowered his head again until his mouth grazed the soft skin of her stomach. Sean parted her legs with one hand, his mouth traveled lower until his tongue licked at the moistness in the area that her panties had covered. As her breath started coming in gasps, he moved his tongue against her delicate bud in quick movements and her back arched as she gripped the quilt covering the bed before she cried out in release.

Reaching in the pocket of his jeans, he removed and unwrapped the condom before positioning himself between her legs that were hanging over the side of the bed and pressed his hardness against her opening then slipped inside. Slowly, he moved until she was able to join him in the slow, sensuous rhythm of his lovemaking. Her legs wrapped around his waist as his mouth found hers and their movements became more urgent. Sean moaned her name against her mouth as her body tightened around him in her second orgasm. She gasped as he plunged into her harder and faster until both of them fell off the cliff together.

Sean rolled over and cradled her against him as she wrapped herself around his body. His hand smoothed over her hair as she nestled her head against his chest. "I could stay like this all night."

Maggie tightened her arms around him. "What's stopping you?" She smiled against his chest. Sean managed to pull the covers over them while they lay wrapped around each other until they dozed off, only to awaken a short time later to make love again.

CHAPTER TWENTY-NINE

Sean was stumped. The woman was a mystery to him. He busied himself putting away supplies in the clinic as he thought back over the last couple weeks. Maggie had been fine when he picked her up at Char's Place right before the fireworks in the park on Independence Day. He hadn't thought much of it when she gave him a swift kiss at the door that night. After all, their lovemaking the night before had been exhausting and it was well after midnight before the festivities at the park ended.

Hell, he didn't mind going home and going to bed himself that night. He'd have rather spent it holding Maggie against him in that soft bed in her house, but he didn't complain or think anything of it when he ended up sleeping in his own bed in the loft of his cabin. He'd gone home and slept like a baby. That night.

Now, it was three weeks later and he was still sleeping in his own bed. Only, he wasn't sleeping like a baby. Instead, he tossed and turned every night while thoughts of Maggie's silky skin and soft lips found their way into his thoughts and dreams. He paced the floor, he read books, and he even resorted to a cold shower last night when a particularly vivid memory intruded into his dreams.

It wasn't that she had totally ignored him. They'd had dinner several times and attended a

Saturday night concert in the park by a local blue grass group. But she had insisted on meeting him there instead of letting him pick her up. When he tried to use helping her with the horses as an excuse to stop out at the farm, she had thanked him and said he was a lifesaver.

She made excuses to avoid being alone with him at either of their homes. Stupid excuses. Like she needed to run into Knoxville to pick up some supplies to finish up the last of the renovations on the house. She'd gone to the outlet malls with Ellie to shop for things to return to college in Indiana. "So why the hell don't she have time to spend a whole weekend with me?" He kicked at a five-gallon bucket of disinfectant and ended up missing it altogether. That resulted in landing square on his backside on the concrete floor of the kennel. "Son of a bitch!" He took off his ball cap and slapped it on the floor.

That's where old Doc found him. The old man looked at the younger one sprawled on the floor and scratched his head in bewilderment. "You okay in here, son?" He walked over and held out a hand. "Need some help up?"

Sean shook his head. "Naw, I think I'll stay down here for a while and see if I can figure out what the hell happened."

Doc pulled up a chair and sat his lanky frame. "Well, it looks like to me you done fell and busted your ass." His blue eyes twinkled under the bushy, white eyebrows. "Question is, what was ya doin' that caused you to end up there? Ya never struck me as being a clumsy one." The old man chuckled and sat down on the bucket, surveying his successor with interest.

The old man had caught him talking to himself several times the last few times he'd stopped in to offer a hand. And much like he was doing now, he just scratched his head in bewilderment and gone about his business. But today was different.

“In my eighty years of livin’ the only time I’ve seen men in such a state was when there was a woman involved.” He chuckled and reached for a stick of gum from his pocket. “Seems to me that you've done gone and got yourself all wrapped up in that purty little Coulter gal."

Sean scowled up at the old doctor. "And what makes you say that?" He thought to himself that wrapped up in Maggie was where he wanted to be and that was the whole damn problem.

The old man howled with laughter. "Don't take much to see it, even though my eyes are dimmer than most these days. I saw ya'all at the diner the other night and you didn't take them eyes off that little gal's backside when she went over to talk to Char."

Sean felt his face grow hot from the old man's comment. Maggie had been wearing a tight pair of jeans that hugged her bottom in a way that he wished he were. Then she'd leaned against the bar to talk to Char and made that part of her even more obvious to him. Did she not realize what the hell she was doing to him?

The old doctor took a wheezing breath in an attempt to recover from his fit of laughter. "Son, take some advice from someone who's been there. Put a ring on her finger and make her yours. From the looks of you right now, you ain't gonna get her out of your system very soon." He stood up and pushed the bucket out of the way before he turned back to Sean, who was still sprawled on the floor. "I remember how the two of you were when you were kids. Ain't nothin' changed 'cept ya all ain't wet behind your ears no more. Now get up off your ass and do something."

Sean sat on the floor and watched the old man's bent back as it retreated through the door of the kennel before he made a move to get up off the floor. Just as he started to pull himself up, the door burst open and Ellie ran in. She stopped in her tracks and frowned at her uncle.

"What in the world are you doing on the floor of the kennel? Don't you know it's dirty down there?" Her face was flushed and the cover of freckles across her nose and cheeks had darkened over the summer. Sean shot her a warning glance. "Don't say another word. I was down here looking for something." He pushed himself up and stood to his full height. "What are you in such a hurry for?"

Ellie grinned and pointed toward the door. "Mamaw and Papaw are here! They just pulled up out front of the cabin and I told them I'd come get you."

Sean put his cap back on his head and sighed. "I'll be right there. Can you get my room ready for them? I'll sleep on the sofa while they are here." Just what he needed, his mother seeing him in the state he was in. She'd play twenty questions with him until she figured out what was wrong then insist that he invite Maggie over to have dinner where she'd play twenty questions with her.

Daniel and Mary McDonald were waiting in the waiting room of the clinic when he emerged from the back. His father's red hair had faded to white but his complexion was still ruddy and reminiscent of times past when he'd spent days on the tractor. These days, the redness came from days spent in the sun with his cronies in the mountain retirement community where he and Sean's mother had retired.

Mary McDonald was still trim, her dark hair cut in a short, elegant cut that revealed the simple gold studs in her ear lobes. Her slender figure was clad in a pair of Bermuda shorts and floral print blouse. Her blue eyes lit up as she saw her youngest son come into the waiting area. "Sean!" She walked over and wrapped her arms around his waist, the top of her head barely reaching his chest. She pushed away and surveyed him with a once over. "It's so good to see you! Have you met that special young lady yet?"

"Mary! Don't start on the boy already!" His father's voice boomed from the corner where he stood. "For cryin' out loud, woman! We just got here and you're already naggin' at him." His bark was worse than his bite and he smiled affectionately at his wife before turning to Sean. "Don't you go rushin' into gettin' all involved with a woman; they'll nag the life out of ya."

"Hey Dad. Hey Mom. It's good to see both of you." He picked his mom up and gave her a hug and kiss on the tip of her nose before setting her down and walking over to hug the big bear of his father. "What brings you up this way and how long are you going to get to stay?"

"Well, we decided to take a trip up to see your cousin in Lexington then head up to

Indiana to get Ellie settled in at college." His dad grinned and patted Ellie on the head. "Thought we'd stay here about a week and then up at Rick and Emma's about the same time. Ellie here can drive up to Lexington and we'll follow her up the rest of the way."

Sean cringed inwardly. There was no way he would be able to fool his mother that long. Maybe if he could get Ellie aside and ask her not to mention Maggie. He wasn't too worried about Maggie popping in unexpectedly; hell, he couldn't get her to even come over for dinner. This could actually work.

Mary smiled up at her son. "So, do we get to meet this little lady that has my son's heart in her hand while we're here? Ellie told us what a wonderful woman she is and I just can't wait to meet her."

CHAPTER THIRTY

The truck was loaded with bags of feed for the horses and Maggie backed it up to the barn so all she had to do was slide the heavy bags off the back of the truck. She hoped that Sean would swing out this way and empty them into the feed bin for her. Not that she would be around when he did, or if she was, she'd manage to find something in town to do.

It wasn't that she didn't want to be around him. Quite the contrary. She had experienced many a sleepless night over the past few weeks wishing that she could just give in and let him stay the night. When she thought about the way his hands and lips had felt on her skin the night they had made love, her body vibrated with desire and her heart ached with need. It was taking every bit of resolve to keep them away from situations where she would be tempted to give in to her desire to wrap herself around his naked body and feel the way she had that night.

But she couldn't give in to this. She didn't want people in town to think bad of her for having a wild, illicit affair with their well-respected veterinarian. And that's all it could be. Their days of loving each other had passed with their youth twelve years before. She winced as she thought of the sadness in his eyes when he had walked her to her car after the bluegrass concert in the park a few nights earlier. There was a certain plea there when he dipped his head to brush his lips across hers. And oh, how she had wanted to make that kiss last. How she had wanted to wrap her arms around him and deepen that kiss until they were both spinning out of control and rushing for the closest bed they could find.

She tugged too hard on the bag of feed she was sliding off the back of the truck causing it to strike her in the middle of her chest, knocking her to the ground. She lay back and looked up at the birds nesting in the eaves of the barn while Mama came over and licked her face. She closed her eyes and cursed out loud.

"Looks like you're in a hell of a predicament there."

She opened her eyes and saw Sean grinning down at her. Just what she needed. And how did he get here without her knowing it? "Well, don't just stand there grinning at me like some idiot. Help me get this damn bag of feed off."

"I don't know. I kind like seeing that you're all helpless." His smile flashed in the light of the sun that was beating down on her. "What are you gonna do now, little woman? I think I have you where I want you."

She squirmed under the heavy sack of feed as he squatted down next to her and she could see the twinkle of mischief in his deep, blue eyes. She took a deep breath and prepared for his assault as his face got closer and he wet his lips with his tongue. "Sean..."

He brushed a light kiss across her forehead and flipped the bag off her in one move. When he stood up and grinned down at her, she sat up and brushed a lock of hair from her face. "Do you want me to help you with the rest of these?" He nodded toward the few bags that were left in the bed of the truck.

She sat on the ground and just gaped at him. She couldn't believe he had let her off so easy. But Sean had never been one to put pressure on her, not back when they were younger and certainly less now. He was watching her expectantly as he bent to ruffle Mama's coat. She finally stood up and brushed the dirt off the seat of her jeans. "If you wouldn't mind, I would really appreciate it."

He grinned and stuffed his keys in his pocket and walked over to the bed of the truck.

"It's gonna cost you." He winked as he pulled the first bag of feed off the truck with ease and hefted it over his shoulder to carry it into the barn.

ꕥꕥꕥꕥꕥꕥꕥꕥꕥꕥꕥꕥ

She was sitting on the steps of the porch when he finished with the feed. Walking over, he stood and looked down at her. "I just wanted to let you know that I brought a colt out and put him inside the fence. His name is Diamond in the Rough and he's not broken yet."

"Who does he belong to?" She plucked a couple of blades of hay off her jeans and looked up at him.

"He's mine. If you stop by the house later, I'll write you a check." He thought of his mother waiting back at the house to meet his "lady friend" and grinned. Maggie didn't know what she was in for when his mom started her twenty questions on her. He'd already suffered the questions since his parents arrived the prior day and the way he looked at it, it was someone else's turn to get grilled. He secretly thought it would serve her right for the way she'd been putting him off.

"Thanks for taking care of the feed for me. Don't worry about writing me a check; you don't need to pay me for boarding your horse after everything you've done to help me out." She stood up and called to the dog.

There she went, looking for reasons not to come to his house. "Don't be so damned stubborn." He had to figure out a way to get her to the house; his mother would do the rest. "Stop by around six, I should be done at the clinic by then and maybe we could go grab a bite at Char's." The truth was, his mother was fixing enough fried chicken for an army and would insist that Maggie join them.

She sighed and glanced at her watch. "I guess that would work. I need to see Char anyway about doing the arrangements for my opening weekend. I've got some bookkeeping to do this afternoon and should be able to finish up by then."

He tipped the bill of his cap and grinned. "I'll see you in a little bit, then." He resisted the urge to skip across the lawn as he thought about turning his mother loose on Maggie. He and his dad could sit out on the porch and leave the women to their chat. He chuckled as he reached the truck. It was going to be an interesting evening.

CHAPTER THIRTY-ONE

Maggie spent the afternoon working on paperwork at the desk in her room. Thanks to Dixie, the entire month of September was already booked and the room deposit checks already in the bank. The web designer emailed a link to the template he had put together for her review and approval and the printer in Gatlinburg sent her some samples of brochures with pricing to review. The highlight of her day was drawing up ideas for floral designs that she would give to Char when she and Sean went to the diner for dinner.

She had decided to use hollowed out pumpkins for containers to hold the fall arrangements that would sit on the tables in the dining room and kitchen. She planned on finding the material to make a scarecrow for the front porch and surround him with mums, gourds and pumpkins. Next year, she had plans to grow her own pumpkins and gourds but this year, she had been promised all she needed by one of the farms up the road in return for allowing them to sell their overflow in the brick smoke house next to the barn.

She had taken time for a quick shower and to put on clean clothes before she locked up the farmhouse and climbed into the old truck. Now, she drove the truck around the familiar curves toward Possum Creek and let the late summer wind blow through her hair while she listened to a CD of her favorite country music songs on the radio. The evening was perfect and she smiled to herself as she remembered that this was her home now. No more traffic jams and the smell of diesel fuel on the toll road. No more of the pristine, carefully planned lawns around the lakefront. Instead, she inhaled the fresh air filling the cab of the truck and enjoyed the wild, haphazard landscape of the foothills. Here was a place that one could call home. Where all the people knew each other. She silently thanked God for all the new friends she'd made since she arrived. People who genuinely cared for each other and helped each other out when they needed help. This was a place of content and satisfaction. A simple life that one would be able to look back upon years later and realize that all the material things in the world couldn't hold a candle to the richness of life here.

As she took the final curve, she remembered the night that she was stranded in the rain and Sean came to her rescue. She thought of his blue eyes dancing with laughter as he found her lying flat on her back with a bag of feed on top of her. She heard his soothing words as he held her the night that she sat by the creek crying because she thought that she was going to lose her grandparents' legacy. Sighing, she remembered the way his hands had touched her in Emma's garden, the way his lips had touched every inch of her skin the night they spent making love in her bed, the way his blue eyes darkened right before he took them both over the edge.

She pulled the truck over and stopped along the side of the road. Sitting there, she thought of how special their relationship was. All the things that they shared during their time together years ago. Picnics by the creek, walking through the midway at the county fair, laughing in the hayloft while they spied on her grandfather and his cronies. Drinking cheap wine out of paper cups on a blanket under the stars then making love for the first time while the crickets chirped and the owls hooted and her grandmother and grandfather slept soundly in the house.

Since coming home to Possum Creek, even though they started off on the wrong foot, they had discovered her mother's deception. He laughed with her, talked to her, helped her plan and even caught her tears when they fell. So what if he wasn't madly in love with her, why should she give up a minute of the time they could be spending together? They could be spending days being friends and nights as lovers. Nobody had to know, they could be discreet and then when the time came to end the physical part of the relationship, they would still have their friendship.

Putting the truck into gear, she was a woman with a plan. Instead of going to the diner for dinner, she was going to walk up on the porch of his cabin and when he answered the door, take hold of him and plant the most seductive kiss she could on his very inviting mouth. The man was smart and he'd know where she was coming from. They wouldn"t need dinner until later, much later.

Maggie's heart took a plunge as she pulled down the road that led to the clinic and cabin. He already had company from the looks of the newer Trailblazer parked between Ellie and Sean's vehicles. She would have driven on past if Ellie hadn"t glanced up from unloading a carton of soda and a bag of groceries from her truck and waved Maggie in next to her. She left the carton of soda on the ground next to the truck as she came over to Maggie's open window.

"Hi there! I'm glad you were able to come join us for dinner."

Maggie frowned at the younger woman. "Sean told me to stop by and pick up a check for the horse he's boarding out at the farm." What the hell was going on? Why would Ellie think she was joining them for dinner? And who was us?

Ellie jerked the door open and tugged at Maggie's arm. "Come on; help me carry this stuff in. Mamaw is making fried chicken for dinner tonight and my mouth is already watering."

Fried chicken? Mamaw? *I thought that Sean and I were going to the diner for dinner this evening. Isn't that what he said? Am I losing my mind?* She followed Ellie around to where the back of the truck held several bags of groceries and took the two that were handed to her. Then she followed Ellie up the sidewalk to the porch where a tiny, dark-haired woman flew out the front door wiping her hands on an apron.

"Great! You are finally back, and you've brought a friend." The woman's face crinkled in a grin. "Are you going to introduce me?"

Ellie laughed and kissed the woman on top of the head. "Mamaw, the list you gave me was a mile long. I hurried as quickly as I could." She turned and rolled her eyes at Maggie who was standing dumbfounded on the steps behind her. """Mamaw, this is Maggie Coulter. She owns the new bed and breakfast that's up the road a piece."

Sharp, perceptive eyes gave her the once over before the woman stepped forward and held out her hand. "Ahhh…you must be Sean's friend."" Maggie got the impression that she was sunk as the woman took her hand and led her inside. "Come on in the kitchen, you and I can talk while I make dinner." She turned to Ellie and shooed her away. """Why don't you go and make sure your grandpa and uncle don't get all wrapped up talking business and shooting the bull with the rest of the men up at the diner? Tell them I expect them back here in an hour.""

Yes, I'm definitely sunk. Sean knew what he was doing when he invited me over here tonight. Well, if he thinks he's going to get off that easy, he's dead wrong!

Mary McDonald alternated darting around the kitchen preparing food with sitting at the table shooting questions at Maggie like a seasoned police detective. Maggie marveled at the woman's level of energy as she deftly cut up and breaded pieces of chicken without hardly glancing at what she was doing. """So Maggie, you own a bed and breakfast inn?" She peered over the half-moon glasses perched on her nose while she rolled out dough for homemade biscuits.

"Yes, ma'am. I'm not scheduled to open until Labor Day weekend, though." Maggie found a colander of potatoes in front of her and was handed a paring knife.

"Would you mind peeling those taters while I cut out these biscuits?" Mary picked up a glass that she had floured to cut the dough into biscuits. "What made you decide to open your own business?"

Maggie picked up the paring knife and started peeling the first potato.

"The property belonged to my grandparents. They left it to me and the only way that I could keep it up and support myself was to turn it into a bed and breakfast."

"Oh, single career woman, huh?" She continued to cut biscuits. "No man to help you out so that you wouldn't have to worry about doing it all on your own?"

Maggie dropped a potato on the floor and bent to retrieve it. Anything to avoid answering Mary's question. She walked over to the sink and rinsed the potato off. "I went to college for business and actually I'm looking forward to opening up my own place."

Mary walked over and patted her on the back. "I'm sorry. I shouldn't have asked that question. I helped Sean's dad out with his farm and contracting business for years. I enjoyed having something to do when the kids were in school."

Maggie turned and smiled up at the older woman. "Don't worry about it. I've really enjoyed refurbishing the house. Ellie has been a great help to me this summer.""

Mary opened up the refrigerator and hauled out a tub of margarine. "These two kids, not a stick of real butter in the house. How about Sean, has he been some help to you?"

Maggie took a long drink from the glass of lemonade sitting beside her. "Sean lined up some customers to board their horses, which really helps a lot with some income until I actually have my opening in a few weeks."

Sean's mother started cutting corn off the ear into an iron skillet filled with melted margarine. "But dear, who did all of the heavy repair work for you? Did you have to hire it out?" She paused and watched Maggie finish peeling the potatoes. "Even though my Sean is a veterinarian, he actually helped his daddy when he was growing up. Shame if the boy didn't lend a hand to a neighbor in his spare time. I guess I need to talk to him."" Not missing a beat, she went over to the sink and rinsed the dishes before putting them in the dishwasher.

"Oh, no, Mrs. McDonald. Sean has been a great help to me. There's no need to talk to him. He's carried furniture and bags of feed and mucked stalls."" Not to mention fixing her breakfast the morning after he spent the night. No need for Sean's mother to know about that.

Mary sat down at the table across from Maggie and patted her hand. "Please, call me Mary." She took off her glasses and laid them down. "Maggie, dear, I''ve known about you for years. You were the little gal who broke my boy's heart years ago when our dear Katie was so ill."

Maggie's eyes widened before she dropped her head. "Mrs. McDonald, Mary, I don't know…"

"Sshhh…I know the whole story. My little Ellie doesn't need much prying to tell me everything she knows about everyone else."" She squeezed Maggie's hand. "Ellie and I had lunch down at the diner today while Sean and his father went to pick up the horse that got delivered out to your place. She told me everything that happened then. Sounds like your mama needs to learn the value of something other than money and material things." She smiled across the table. "Don't be too hard on her, dear. One of these days, when you are a mother, you will understand that we sometimes do the wrong things for the right reasons." Winking, she got up from the table and took the colander of peeled potatoes from Maggie. "It's almost time for Ellie to bring those two scoundrels home. What do you say to helping me set the table for a good sit down dinner?"

Daniel entertained them over dinner with risqué jokes that had Ellie in stitches and Mary chastising her husband for his "inappropriate dinner etiquette". The fried chicken was the best that Maggie had ever eaten and even though she was stuffed from the meal, when Mary brought out two warm apple pies fresh out of the oven, her mouth watered.

Sean kept shooting her discreet glances across the table during dinner and she occasionally felt his feet nudge against hers as he stretched his long legs under the table. Maggie had the distinct feeling that the nudges were purposeful, even though he apologized on the occasions that it happened. After dinner, Mary insisted that the men clean up after their dinner while the three women retired to the front porch for another glass of lemonade.

As they sat in the rocking chairs, a breeze blew through with a slight fragrance of pine from the trees surrounding the cabin. Mary closed her eyes and leaned back in her chair. "Is it as peaceful at your place as it is here?"

"Yes ma'am. I'm at the end of a lane with nothing but rolling hills, woods and pasture ground around me." Maggie thought of her little piece of paradise in the middle of the foothills and felt a sense of pride swell in her chest.

"Would you mind if I came out to see your place tomorrow? Ellie could bring me." She rocked with her eyes closed. "I have friends that I could refer your way."" She stifled a yawn behind her hand.

With a promise to show Sean's mother the farm the next day, Maggie got up from her rocking chair and told the other two women good bye. None of them had seen the men since they were relegated to kitchen duty. She walked down the sidewalk to her truck and had just reached for the door handle when a voice came from behind her.

"Hey, where are you going without giving me a kiss goodbye?" The question was accompanied by a low chuckle. She turned to see Sean approaching from between two pine trees at the back of the clinic. Off in the distance she could hear the rustle of some animal in the brush.

"Sean, I need to go." She glanced nervously toward the porch to see if Sean's mother had stirred from her spot in the rocker before finding herself pulled against the hard column of Sean's warm chest. "Sean…" She hissed between her teeth and tried to pull away.

Laughing quietly, Sean reached down and tipped her face up while his lips descended on hers. Urging her lips apart, his tongue probed the inside of her mouth while one of his hands twined through her hair and the other one held her tightly against him. Even as she wriggled to try to free herself from his grasp, her body responded to his touch, to his kiss and she felt his hardness press against her stomach.

Just as quickly as he launched his assault, he pulled away. "Maggie, we have unfinished business…" He murmured against the top of her head as his hands gently stroked her shoulders. "You aren't going to keep slipping away from me so easily. Just wait until my parents leave…"

They both heard the gravel crunch at the same time and pulled apart just as Mary McDonald came around the side of the truck. "Oh…there you are, Sean." She glanced from one of them to the other with a knowing smile. "Maggie, don't forget that I'm going to come out tomorrow to see your place. Would eight be a good time? I'm an early riser so after I help Sean open up the clinic, I'll have Ellie drive me out there."

"That would be fine, Mary. I will see you in the morning." She glanced over at Sean who was grinning like a Cheshire cat. "Good night, Sean."

CHAPTER THIRTY-TWO

Sean breathed a sigh of relief as he watched his mother exit the clinic with Ellie. For as much as he loved her, he was ready for all the energy the little whirlwind created as she bustled all around the clinic to go bestow that energy on Maggie. He grinned as he thought about the day Maggie was going to have with his mother chasing at her heels out at the farm. Turning around and heading toward his office, he chuckled as he saw his father stick his head in the side door.

"Is she gone yet?" Daniel McDonald raised an eyebrow as he looked at his son.

Sean grinned, his father did a good job of dodging his wife after all the years they were married. "Where have you been hiding this morning? She's already moved furniture and cleaned the tops of every surface in the clinic." Sean crossed over and patted his father's shoulder. "You sure know how to make yourself scarce don't you?"

His father let out a loud bellow of laughter and came in the clinic. "I love your mom with all my heart, but for the life of me, I just can't keep up with her first thing in the morning. I didn't retire to work on everything she gives me to work on." He walked over to the coffee pot and poured a cup before turning back to look at his son. "So, while your little gal and Ellie keep her busy, what do you say the two of us head over to Cherokee and do some gambling at the casino?""'

Sean glanced at his watch then at the appointment book by the reception area. He had a pretty light day and could probably be finished up by lunchtime if no emergencies came up. An afternoon gambling at the casino with his father would give him some time to talk about an important decision he made the night before. "Sure, that sounds like a great idea. I think we could probably leave here around noon. Think you can hold off that long?"

His father nodded. "Yep, that works for me. I think I'm going to haul myself back to your living room and have me a nice nap on your sofa." He lifted a hand as he started out the door, then turned back. "You see your mother heading back that way before we leave, you better give me fair warning." He tapped his pocket where his cell phone poked out the top. "Call my cell phone. I don't want to hear her go on if she catches me napping."

Sean laughed. "I've got your back, Dad. If I see her coming I will sure let you know. But I'm hoping she pesters the hell out of Maggie all damned day.""'

"Sounds like you got a bone to pick with the gal. Wishing your mother on her like that."

"Believe me, she has it coming. Now you go take your nap while I try to get finished up here then we'll slip off to Cherokee without anyone being the wiser."

ꕥꕥꕥꕥꕥꕥꕥꕥꕥꕥꕥꕥ

Mary McDonald walked through each room of the old farmhouse, commenting on the décor and gushing over the job that was almost complete. "So, you are planning on sticking around and making a go of this endeavor?" Her blue eyes fixed pointedly on Maggie.

They were standing in one of the upstairs guest rooms and Maggie glanced over at Ellie who was having a hard time holding back a chuckle. Obviously, this was Mary's way of making sure that Maggie wasn't going to bolt and leave Sean with a broken heart to mend. "Yes, I always loved being here in the summers with my grandparents and the only way that I can really keep the property and stay here is for the whole plan to work out."

Mary picked up one of the pillows that Dixie had brought and examined it carefully, its delicate embroidered flowers matching the colors in the quilt on the bed perfectly. "Did you make this, Maggie?" She fingered the little blossoms before laying the pillow back on the bed.

"No, my grandmother taught me how to embroider and knit and just about anything else crafty you can think of, but this one isn't mine. I haven't had the time to do those things since I was growing up." Honestly, Philip would have scoffed at anything handmade so she just hadn't even bothered. She secretly hoped that once the farm was open for guests she may have some time to do things like that, as it had been a relaxing past time for her once upon a time.

Mary headed back toward the top of the stairs, admiring the freshly stained and polished bannister and commenting on the quilted wall hanging on the wall above the steps. "This is a nice piece as well, where did you find it?" The quilt was actually one of her grandmother's that Maggie had salvaged from a trunk in the attic and trimmed down the frayed edges, turning them and hemming them before soaking the quilt in a detergent solution that had removed most of the yellowing brought about by aging. She told Mary as much, who then reached out and squeezed Maggie's hand.

Back in the dining room, Mary walked over to the window and peered out at the flower beds that were vibrant with rioting late summer colors. There were the deep golden yellows of the Blackeyed Susans, the soft thistle color of the Echinacea, various shades of pinks, purples and blues intermingled with the green leaves surrounding them all. Maggie was proud of how well the flower beds had thrived once she cleaned and weeded and mulched during those early, hot summer days. Mary nodded thoughtfully and turned, about tripping over the dog that had joined them. She reached down and absently stroked the animal's fur. "This sure is a homey place, nice place to have a family."

Maggie heard the question in her voice and smiled. "Well, I haven't really given much thought to having a family at this point, I've been so busy just getting this place ready and trying to rebuild my own life." She walked over and ran a hand along the top of a dining room chair. "I like children and I hope that someday I get the opportunity to have some of my own. I guess it will all depend upon what the good Lord has in store for me."

In her mind she could picture a little boy running around with a mop of red hair and his father's eyes. Sean's eyes. But that would require Sean to want to marry her and commit to a lifetime with her. She never wanted to go through another divorce, even though the first one was her own doing and very much necessary. She stopped her train of thought, Maggie was getting ahead of herself but it wasn't a bad dream. Maybe someday.

Mary started to say something, and then clamped her mouth shut. Straightening, she turned to Ellie. "What do you say we girls all go do some shopping? I'm thinking that I would like to go to the outlet malls in Pigeon Forge." She let out an exaggerated sigh. "God knows I haven't been able to talk Daniel into doing much of anything this trip but hanging out at the café or bothering Sean at the clinic."

She walked over and plucked her purse up from the dining room table then looked at Maggie and Ellie who were sharing a discreet smile. Both knew that Daniel and Sean were enjoying a day's peace without Mary fussing over both of them. Without another word, she briskly walked to the front door, turning only long enough to prod the other two women to hurry and join her.

And shop they did. Maggie and Ellie were breathless trying to keep up with Mary as they shopped at practically every outlet store in the mall. The truck was loaded with packages by the time they were finished and Mary insisted that they still weren't done. She wanted to go hit all the little shops in the arts and crafts loop by Gatlinburg as well.

Ellie finally talked her into taking a lunch break sometime in the middle of the afternoon and they sat outside on the porch of a little café that was tucked into the wooded foothills in the midst of the little arts and crafts shops. Ellie's face was flushed and her hair was coming loose from the braids that she had carefully wound this morning. Maggie"s hair was damp and limp from the humidity and exertion and her feet ached inside of her sneakers. Mary sat perched on a chair sipping an iced coffee and looking about as unruffled and groomed as she had when she left that morning. Maggie marveled at how much energy the woman had. "How in the world can you sit there looking so cool and collected and put together after all this shopping?" She glanced over at Ellie who looked like she was ready to drop.

Mary raised an eyebrow and shrugged. "Do I? Look cool and collected, that is?" She pushed aside her salad plate as the waitress brought her entrée of grilled chicken and vegetables, sitting it in front of her. Ellie groaned and leaned forward to take a French fry off her plate and dunk it in the cup of catsup. "For God's sake, Mamaw, you run circles around Maggie and me. Where were you when we were doing all the work at Maggie's house?"

The older woman's eyes twinkled and she laughed. "If I had been here, that house would have been done in time to have had guests for the Independence Day weekend."

Ellie rolled her eyes and put an arm around Maggie's shoulders. "If only you knew how much work we have put into that house, you would understand. The place was a mess from neglect when Maggie first got here and I think we did a damned good job of getting it in order.

Maggie nodded her agreement. "Ellie, without you, Dixie and the guys I could never have gotten it ready in time. I had no idea before I got here just how much the house had fallen into disrepair." She wearily stabbed at a bite of her tuna salad piled on top of the nest of lettuce on her plate.

Mary smiled and reached over to touch Maggie's hand. "My dear, I am so inspired by your motivation to restore your family's home place to where it is today. Most young folk would have turned up their nose and had the place bulldozed and let some contractor build a new one in its place."

Daniel looked over at his son as they pulled up in front of the jewelry store. He anticipated what Sean was going to say to him next and he couldn't have been more proud to know that his son was finally going to settle down and start a family. That would sure get his wife off his case about how their son needed to find a woman to marry. He liked Maggie and he was sure his wife did as well, especially since she commented on how she was going to convince Sean to ask the girl to marry him just last night as they were sitting on the porch before bed.

Sean gripped the steering wheel and took a deep breath. "Dad, could you do me a favor and help me pick out an engagement ring? I think I am going to ask Maggie to marry me as soon as I can get a moment alone with her." He cocked his head and watched for his father's reaction.

Daniel burst out in hearty laughter. "Thank God! Now your mother can stop annoying me about how you aren't married yet." He reached over and smacked his son on the shoulder. "Maggie seems like a good choice and your mother likes her." Turning, he opened the door and looked over his shoulder. "Come on, let's go find that ring and I will make sure that your mother leaves the two of you alone tonight."

The elderly woman behind the counter greeted them with a bright smile and listened as Sean described what he was looking for. Reaching into the glass display case, she pulled out some diamond solitaires and put them on the counter in front of them.

Sean looked at them, most were very large and although, price was not a problem for him, none of them seemed to suit the Maggie he had fallen in love with. He shook his head. "The woman that I am buying this for isn't about the big, shiny things. She is more down to earth and petite and full of life. These rings are more suited for someone who is looking for a status symbol rather than a token of what the ring means." He felt his face flush as he realized he was sharing a private side of himself.

Daniel grinned and pointed at a sign by the cash register that said that they had estate jewelry. "I think his girl would probably like something old and more like an heirloom. Maybe you have something in your estate jewelry collection that might be more suitable."

The elderly woman nodded and put the tray of rings back in the case. "I think I may have just the thing for you. Hold on, I will be right back." Her heels played a staccato on the wood floor as she walked to a door at the back of the shop and disappeared, only to return a couple of minutes later with a small, red velvet box. She held it out and flipped the lid open, revealing an antique filigree ring with a square, princess cut diamond in the center. It was simple, yet timeless and as Sean turned the box in his hands, he nodded. It was perfect.

CHAPTER THIRTY-THREE

When Ellie and Mary dropped Maggie off at the farm, it was dark and the sky was full of stars. They sparkled against the indigo sky and the moon left a glow over the lawn as she walked toward the door. She was tired and lugged the two bags that Mary pushed at her as she got out of the truck up the porch steps and set them down on the mat as she fished for her keys. The door opened with just a push and she admonished herself for being in such a rush that she must have forgotten to lock and pull it closed when they left that morning.

She picked up the bags and carried them inside, setting them on the dining room table and kicking her shoes off, leaving them lay on the floor where they landed. She would worry about going through the bags to see what treasures Mary had bestowed on her in the morning. As she walked toward her living quarters, she heard music playing softly and she shook her head. She must have left the radio on this morning too. What a long day it had been.

Maggie opened the door to her living area and stopped in her tracks at the sight in front of her. Rose petals covered the bed, candles burned in every corner of the room, and Sean was sitting quietly in one of the chairs. "Hi. What are you doing here?" She tipped her head curiously. "What is this all about?"

He smiled held out a hand. "Come here. I've been missing you."

She looked around the room then back at him. She had missed him too. A lot more than she was willing to admit. Not that they hadn't seen each other but she had missed the feel of his arms around her. His touch. How it had felt sleeping next to his warm body the night they spent together just a few short weeks ago. Their first night in a bed. Their first night as two adults sharing their bodies. Years had passed but the feelings had not and in this moment, they overwhelmed her. Her eyes misted up with tears. "Sean…"

"Come here, Maggie. Please." He stood and held out his hand again and waited for her to take the few steps to breach the space between them.

When their hands met, he pulled her to him and wrapped his arms around her weary body. It was comfortable and she lay her cheek against his chest where his heart beat steadily. His hands stroked her hair and he rested his chin on her head. "Sean. Your mother and father will be waiting for you."

He chuckled and tightened his hold on her. "No they won't. Dad said he would keep Mom occupied tonight. I wanted to see you." He set her away from him and kissed her forehead.

"How in the world did you pull this off?" She spread her arms to the room. It was nice. Romantic. What was she doing? She shouldn't be questioning him. She should be appreciating his thoughtfulness. The effort he had made to make her homecoming something special. "Never mind." She put her arms back around him and inhaled the masculine scent of his aftershave.

"Did you have a good day?" He whispered against her ear. "I know Mom can be a little overwhelming."

Maggie nodded. "Actually, I did. Your mother is like an energizer bunny."

"Can I stay with you tonight?"

Her breath caught in her chest and her heart fluttered. Where was this going? Rose petals. Candles. They were alone. There was nothing more she wanted in this moment. To curl up and lay her head on his shoulder. To feel his touch. To kiss his lips. Maggie sighed. "Yes. I'd like that very much."

Their lips met and he gently stroked her back, causing her heart to melt. It felt so right, being here with him. His hands slipped up the back of her shirt and sent a shiver through her entire body. She reached up and ran her fingers through his hair and tipped her head to the side to allow their kiss to deepen. And it went on until she was breathless.

Sean stepped away and took her hand and led her to the bed. He sat down and pulled her on his lap where he claimed her lips again. They both laid back on the bed and touched. Stroked. Kissed. She didn't know when it happened, but they were soon naked. Skin to skin. Warmth turned into heat and when they joined, there was nothing but the two of them. They moved together fluidly together as the candles flickered on their naked bodies. And when they both came to the edge he took them both over. Spinning into the whirlpool of warm satisfaction.

As they lay there, he pulled her close to him. "I could do this every night for the rest of my life." He murmured against her head, which was tucked against his shoulder.

Maggie felt her heart skip a beat as she heard his words. Had he really said that he wanted to do this every night for the rest of his life? She pulled back and looked up at his face. His eyes were penetrating as he put a hand under her chin and brought his lips to hers. When he pulled away, she again found herself in his dark blue gaze and she frowned.

"Why the serious look? Is there something wrong?" She reached up and took hold of the hand that was resting on her hip. "Tell me."

He didn't answer, instead pulling her toward him again and taking her mouth with his own. This time the kiss was gentle, sweet and short but still enough to make her heart jump a beat and her whole body tingle. When he ended the kiss this time, he set her aside and got up to retrieve his jeans on the floor. When he turned around, he came to sit on the side of the bed and took her hands in his.

"Maggie. I know we have been through a lot and I am so blessed to have found you again. To find the truth that we both needed to find." He held out his hand and in it was the most exquisite ring she had ever seen. "I don't ever want to lose you again. I want to spend the rest of my life with you. I want to grow old with you and have children with you. Marry me?" He held the ring out to her. "Please? Will you be my wife?"

Maggie took a shaky breath as tears welled up in her eyes. She felt goose bumps spring up on her bare arms and her hand trembled as she reached for the ring and nodded. "Yes, I would like to be your wife. Sean, I love you."

He took her trembling hand and placed the ring on her ring finger and pulled her to him. "Oh Maggie, I love you too. I will love you for the rest of my life."

∽∽∽∽∽∽∽∽∽∽

It was nearing midnight when Sean pulled the sheet over Maggie's naked shoulders. He had loved her with a tenderness that he didn't know he was capable of and she had wrapped herself around him until he couldn't hold back. She reached out in her sleep and put her hand on his chest. The antique diamond ring sparkled in the fading candlelight and he laid his hand on top of hers. He looked at the relaxed features on her face, the soft lips parted and swollen from the passionate kisses they had shared. Maggie had come home and brought him with her and now they had their whole lives to spend together. He closed his eyes and silently thanked God for what he had in his arms.

CHAPTER THIRTY-FOUR

The autumn sun shone through the stained-glass windows of the old chapel in the woods. In the small room to the back of the church, Maggie turned to look at Ellie. She got a glimpse of herself in the full-length mirror and took in the simple, sheath style ivory gown with long, lace sleeves. Her hair was adorned with baby's breath and a short, lace veil that fell down the back of her head but did not cover her face. "Where is your grandmother?"

Mary had been visibly missing for the last hour, muttering something about something that she needed to take care of before the wedding and then disappearing in Sean's truck. Ellie shrugged, her own dress being a shorter copy of Maggie's in a deep burgundy, just like the one that Dixie wore. Dixie had also stepped out of the room a short time after Mary had, and she had just returned with a pinched look on her face.

"Dixie, I know that look. Something is going on and I want to know right now what it is." She stamped her foot for emphasis. At that moment, the door to the makeshift dressing room opened and Mary stepped inside. "I need a moment with the bride if I may." She shooed Dixie and Ellie out of the room with her hand and came over to stand in front of Maggie. Her look was serious and she grasped both of Maggie's hands.

"Maggie, dear, you know how much I care for you right?" She glanced toward the closed door and took a deep breath. "I may as well just tell you what I've done." She gripped Maggie's hands harder. "I invited your mother to the wedding and she's right outside."

Maggie pulled her hands loose and stepped away from Mary. "You did what?" She turned and walked over to the small window in the room and opened it, taking a breath of the autumn air in hopes that it would calm her. *Her mother? Here? At my wedding?*

Mary came up behind her and laid a hand on her shoulder. "My dear Maggie, I know that you and your mother parted on poor terms and I know that she did a horrible thing." She urged Maggie to look at her by putting a hand on her shoulder, and as Maggie turned she continued. ""Sometimes, as parents, we do things that we think is the best for our children and not once thinking about what is really the best for them. Your mother and I have been talking these last few weeks. In fact, I spent a weekend in Chicago with her a couple of weeks back. If I can forgive her for hurting my son and future daughter in law, would you please try to do the same?" As if on cue, Brenda slipped in the door and paused to look at her daughter. There were tears glistening in her eyes and she took a tentative step forward.

"Margaret, you look so beautiful. More, you look happy and that makes me happy. Forgive me for what I did?"

Maggie looked from Brenda to Mary and then back at Brenda. "Mother, what you did was wrong. But since it turned out the way it is turning out, I'm not going to ruin my wedding day by asking you to leave."

Her mother was dressed in a copper colored linen suit, diamonds sparkling from her earlobes. Her expensive fragrance filled the air in the small room. Brenda took another step forward and reached for Maggie, who backed away.

"You need to understand one thing. I will forgive you if you promise me never to meddle in my life again. The damage you could have done, the tears that I shed, the miserable life I had to live until I got here were all your doing." She took another deep breath to calm herself before continuing. "I love Sean, and I love living here. I don't put value on material things because they are just that. Things. You might try to do the same someday."

Brenda nodded and wiped a tear from her cheek. "Margaret, I love you. I did what I thought was the right thing to do at the time. Now I see just how wrong I was."

Maggie shook her head and stepped toward her mother who now had tears streaming down her face. Pulling her to her, she hugged her. "Mom, I love you too. Now, stop crying before you get make up all over my dress or make me start crying."

Dixie and Ellie stuck a tentative head in the door. "Can we come back in now? It's almost time and we need to touch up your make-up."

They fussed over the bride until they were satisfied she was ready. The first strains of piano music drifted into the room. Mary and Brenda left the three women alone as they went to take their seats on the aged pews in the chapel.

Ellie smiled softly and reached out to hug Maggie. "I'm so happy for the two of you. My uncle is getting a great wife and I'm getting an aunt. I love you both so much." She stepped aside and Dixie descended.

"Let's get this show on the road. I'm getting hungry and Char has one hell of a spread out at the farm." She grinned and pulled her friend to her in a bear hug. "I love you girl."

Ellie and Dixie led the way as the threesome walked down the aisle of the church. Sean stood at the altar, dressed in a black suit, with Rick and his father standing beside him. His eyes sparkled as she reached the front of the church and he reached for her hand and lifted it to his lips and he smiled as he mouthed the words. *I love you.*

Made in the USA
Columbia, SC
22 May 2021

38241518R00134